Secrets, Lies, and Puppy Dog Eyes

Secrets, Lies and Puppy Dog Eyes

A Bliss Bay Village Mystery – Book Two

Sherri Bryan

Sherri Bryan

CONTENTS
Dedication 4
Prologue 6
Chapter 1 18
Chapter 2 35
Chapter 3 51
Chapter 4 59
Chapter 5 74
Chapter 6 94
Chapter 7 114
Chapter 8 126
Chapter 9 137
Chapter 10 150
Chapter 11 157
Chapter 12 176
Chapter 13 193
Chapter 14 204
Chapter 15 224
Chapter 16 232
Chapter 17 236
Chapter 18 249
Chapter 19 260
Chapter 20 270
Chapter 21 279
Chapter 22 298
Chapter 23 312
Chapter 24 324
Chapter 25 333
Chapter 26 341

Secrets, Lies, and Puppy Dog Eyes

Chapter 27	354
Book Three Preview	369
Join my Readers' Group	383
Acknowledgements	384
A Message from Sherri	385
All Rights Reserved	386

Sherri Bryan

DEDICATION
For my husband.

Secrets, Lies, and Puppy Dog Eyes

Sherri Bryan

PROLOGUE

In the staff room at Bliss Bay School, Dawn Hillier opened another exercise book and sighed at the sight of the illegible handwriting on the page.

Three times a week, she spent an hour every afternoon after school, giving extra tuition to the students who struggled with their reading and writing, but for those who'd gone for years having barely *held* a pen, let alone written with one, she had her work cut out.

She picked up her marking pen and put right the errors, writing encouraging comments in the margins until the white pages were hardly visible for red corrections.

They were only a week into the new school term and Dawn had already had to deal with a detention for a disobedient student, and a visit from anxious parents following their daughter's return home with a black eye after a playground game had turned a little too boisterous.

All she wanted to do was get home and curl up on the couch with her husband, and a big bowl of the stew that was bubbling away in her slow cooker.

The door creaked open and a head poked around it, its auburn hair cut in the popular pageboy style of the day.

"Oh, Sandra. You startled me," said Dawn. "I thought I was here on my own."

Secrets, Lies, and Puppy Dog Eyes

"I had some work to do, but I'm off home now. Will you be long?"

"I'll be leaving for the bus in about an hour, I should think, but I must finish marking these books. I'll see you tomorrow."

"I don't suppose you get to give many of these out, do you?" said Sandra, sidling over and picking up a small bag of gold stars that was on the table.

"Not as many as I'd like to, but some of the students really do try, so I always give one for a good effort."

Sandra nodded and perched on the arm of the chair Dawn was sitting in.
"I suppose you're off home to see that lovely husband of yours? Lucky you to have someone to go home to."

Dawn shifted uncomfortably, but managed a smile. "Yes, I am lucky." For a moment, she almost felt as though she should apologise, she felt so guilty about the awful tragedy Sandra had suffered not so long ago. Instead, she said, "Anyway, I don't mean to be rude, but I must get on with these books, or I'll still be here at midnight."

Sandra smiled, despite the rebuff. "Yes, of course, sorry. I'll be seeing you."

The door closed with a click, leaving Dawn alone in the staff room once more. She pinched the bridge of her nose and blinked hard. Her eyes ached after poring over all those exercise books at the students' scrawl.

Forty minutes later, she finished the last book and closed it with a breath of relief. Checking her watch, she calculated that if she caught the quarter-past seven bus, she'd be home in five minutes. She could walk it, but the wind would be blowing in her face all the way and, besides, she didn't want to risk getting a blister on her heel from her new shoes.

It had been a while since she and Edmund had spent an entire, uninterrupted evening together. Since his promotion from Senior Clerk to Assistant Manager, he'd taken his job at the bank even more seriously than usual. Every day, he worked much later than he needed to make sure everything was shipshape and accounted for before he left for home.

Today, though, was one of the rare occasions he'd promised to leave work on time. Usually, Teresa and Barnaby—Edmund's children from a previous marriage—would be home at this time of the evening but tonight, Teresa was out at the cinema with some friends, and Barnaby was at a Scouts' meeting. Dawn was thrilled that she and Edmund would have the house completely to themselves for a few hours.

Secrets, Lies, and Puppy Dog Eyes

She'd been feeling a little low recently. Sometimes, she couldn't help it. She wanted to forget all her troubles tonight, though, and make the most of the evening.

Belting her new suede coat, and slinging her handbag over her shoulder, Dawn flicked off the staff room light and called out to the caretaker who was doing his rounds, checking that the school was empty before he locked the doors.

"Goodnight, Walter, see you in the morning."

He smiled and touched the tip of his flat cap, his russet curls poking out from underneath it. "G'night, Mrs Hillier. See you then." He stared after her as she walked off down the corridor, her handbag swinging jauntily from her shoulder.

The chunky heels of her purple suede platform shoes clunked against the pavement as she walked briskly to the bus stop. They were a little higher than she usually wore, but when she'd seen them in the shoe shop, she hadn't been able to resist them. She couldn't believe her luck when, a couple of days later, she'd seen a card in the village shop window with a Polaroid photo, advertising a nearly-new suede coat for sale, in almost the same colour. She'd called the number right away and nabbed a real bargain.

Sherri Bryan

She took a tube of peppermints from her pocket as she waited for the bus, popping one into her mouth and pushing it against her cheek where it could dissolve slowly.

As she pulled up the collar of her coat against the stiff breeze, the sound of approaching footsteps made her turn.

"Hello," said Dawn, her smile dimmed by the puzzled furrow at her brow. "What are you doing here?"

Those were the last words Dawn Hillier ever spoke.

A sharp jab on the forehead, followed by another on her shoulder, pushed her off balance and she fell backwards with a scream. Her arms flailed wildly, grabbing at nothing, as she tumbled down the incline beside the road, landing with a sickening thud, and leaving a solitary shoe behind on the pavement.

"Bloody hell, Red! What did you do that for? What's wrong with you?"

"Shut *up*, Curly! I wasn't expecting her to fall down the hill, was I?"

They stumbled down the incline, panting and shuddering at the sight of Dawn's motionless, twisted body, its leg sticking out at a strange angle, and blood seeping from a head wound caused by the impact against a tree trunk.

Secrets, Lies, and Puppy Dog Eyes

"Do you think she's dead?" said Red, in a trembling voice.

"She can't be," said Curly, trying to keep calm. "She only fell a few feet. Why don't you feel for a pulse?"

Red hesitated. "Can't *you* do it?"

"No, I can't." Curly took a step back. "Sorry, but I'm not touching a dead body."

Red took a deep breath and leaned forward, moving Dawn's handbag out of the way and placing two fingers against the inside of her wrist. "There's nothing."

"Well, try the pulse at the side of her neck."

"Nothing there, either." Red stood up and took stock of the situation. "We'd better get out of here. If the bus comes and anyone sees us down here, they'll think we had something to do with it."

Curly's eyes opened wide. "We *did* have something to do with it. Well, *you* did, anyway."

"Yes, but what's going to happen if the police found out I pushed her? They have ways of finding out things like that, you know. I've seen it on TV. And, in any case, you'd be implicated, too, so it wouldn't just be me who'd be in the frame."

Curly gulped. "It doesn't seem right to leave her here and do nothing. She's a nice woman. We should at least tell someone."

"A nice woman?" repeated Red, with scorn. "That might be your opinion, but it certainly isn't mine. Anyway, what's the point in telling anyone? There's nothing they can do for her now, is there? I think we should just get out of here before someone sees us."

Curly's beady eyes surveyed the scene, darting this way and that as the shock began to turn to fear. "You touched her handbag when you felt her pulse, didn't you? You'd better take it and get rid of it somewhere in case you've left any fingerprints on it."

Red tugged the bag from Dawn's lifeless body, struggling against the literal dead weight. "Look, we don't tell anyone about this, okay? Not a word."

"Don't you think we... we should call an ambulance?" Curly's voice faltered.

"I just said there's no point, didn't I?" snapped Red. "She's already dead, so what would they do for her. Anyway, did you hear what I just said about keeping quiet?"

Curly nodded and took great gulps of air. Red was not a good person to get on the wrong side of. "I won't say anything, I promise, but what are we going to do now?"

"Nothing—that's what we're going to do. We're going to get out of here, find somewhere to get rid of this handbag, act normal and keep our mouths shut. Got it?" Red threw Curly a threatening glare. "We won't go back up the

Secrets, Lies, and Puppy Dog Eyes

bank, though, in case the bus comes and someone sees us—we'll go along the low road and no one will ever know we were here."

As they ran from the scene, the sleeve of Red's jumper caught against a branch on a nearby bush, leaving behind a strand of wool, which fluttered, unnoticed, from a twig.

When they had run until they thought their lungs would burst, they stopped to get their breath.

"Oww, I've got a stitch," said Red, bending forward and breathing heavily.

Curly pointed to the snag in the jumper. "You mean you *need* a stitch to fix that hole. You must have done it when you caught your sleeve on that branch."

Red peered closely at the hole. "Damn it! Now I'll have to get rid of the handbag *and* this jumper. We can't risk going back now to check, but if I left any wool on one of those thorns, and someone sees this snag in my sleeve and puts two and two together, I don't want to think what might happen."

"Well, I doubt that's likely," said Curly, "but it'll probably be for the best. You don't want to take any chances, do you? Now, come on, let's find somewhere to dump that bag before someone sees us with it."

ooooooo

Dawn Hillier's body was found later that evening,

Sherri Bryan

When she didn't come home, her husband, Edmund, had driven to the school to find it closed. He'd driven back home again and called all their friends, before driving to the Scouts' hall to collect Barnaby, and the cinema to find Teresa to ask if either of them knew where Dawn might be.

His children hadn't been happy to see him.

Barnaby, because he lived for the time he could be away from his dad and his constant criticism, and Teresa, because she didn't appreciate being embarrassed in front of her friends: even in the gloom of the cinema, her cheeks glowed like beacons.

When they'd seen how troubled their dad was, though, Barnaby had left his Scout meeting and Teresa had left the screening of the film she'd waited so long to see, both promising to help search for their stepmother.

"How was she at school today, Teresa?" said Barnaby who, at almost eighteen, was in a different class to his sister.

"She was fine." Teresa squeezed Edmund's hand. "Don't worry, Dad, she's bound to be somewhere not far away. She's too sensible to have run off, or done anything adventurous. Like I just said, she was fine today at school. You know how she gets sometimes—she's probably gone off somewhere to be on her own for a while."

Edmund acknowledged her with a distracted smile. "I hope so, but she's never been gone so long before, and she's always found a phone box to call from to let me know she's okay. This time feels different. Don't ask me why, but..." They were all thrown forward in their seats as he braked hard, bringing the car to a sudden, sliding stop.

"Flippin heck, Dad! I almost broke my nose on the dashboard," grumbled Barnaby. "What did you do that for?"

Edmund pointed with a shaky finger and opened the car door. "Look."

Teresa and Barnaby's eyes followed his finger, coming to rest on a solitary shoe—purple suede with a platform sole—next to the bus stop at the side of the road.

ooooooo

Dawn's death was eventually ruled as suspicious.

Originally, the police had suspected it was accidental: based on the information given to them by her husband and stepchildren, it appeared that Dawn was unused to her new high heels, and could simply have stumbled and fallen down the incline.

However, when it came to light that her handbag was missing, a bag snatch which had caught her off guard, and pushed her off-balance, was thought to be the reason for the fall.

The case took a turn, though, when the post-mortem revealed a fresh bruise just below her shoulder, indicating she'd received a significant push before she'd fallen, and the police finally changed the status of the case to suspicious.

A small strand of wool on a branch, a gold star which was stuck to Dawn's forehead, her coat and shoes were the only potential items of evidence in the vicinity of her body.

In the absence of any suspects, the evidence was bagged, referenced, and put away in an unsolved case file.

ooooooo

The funeral was well-attended.

Dawn had been a popular member of the community and highly thought of by the majority of her students, along with every teacher in the small Bliss Bay School.

All through the service, Sandra's sniffing and wailing rose above the sermon as she leaned against her brother, Walter, for support. This was a devastating event for them both. So soon after their own family tragedy, Dawn's death was almost too much to bear.

As the coffin was lowered into the ground, Edmund Hillier stood beside the grave, his mouth set in a thin line, and the muscles in his jaw tensed as he fought not to

Secrets, Lies, and Puppy Dog Eyes

break down. Next to him stood his son, Barnaby—his eyes puffy and bloodshot—and his daughter, Teresa, clinging to his arm, her face red and her cheeks wet with tears.

Edmund stepped forward and threw a single white rose into the grave. "I'm sorry, Dawn," he said, before stepping back, turning on his heel and taking his children with him.
ooooooo

Three weeks after Dawn's death, a lone figure lurked by the row of lockers that lined the entire length of the wall outside the school assembly hall.

Looking around to make sure no one was watching, and wearing a pair of gloves, Curly shoved a textbook into the narrow gap behind the lockers and breathed a sigh of relief.

The note inside it was short, but it told the true events of what had happened to Dawn Hillier on the evening of her death.

Curly knew that going to the police with a full confession would have been the proper thing to do, but Red would have found out and gone berserk, and Red wasn't a good person to have as an enemy.

Leaving the note was just a small gesture but it made Curly feel better. At least, this way, the truth may become known at some point in the future, and the identity of Dawn Hillier's killer would finally be revealed.

Chapter 1

Forty years later

Megan Fallon peered out from behind the counter of The Cobbles Café and Flower Shop at the queue of impatient customers, which was growing at an alarming rate.

"I know you said it was going to be busy," she said, tucking a lock of dark hair behind her ear, "but I didn't think it'd be *this* busy. Not at this time of day." She turned to Petal Montgomery, her friend and owner of the café. "It's barely eight o'clock."

Petal gave her a customary eye-roll. "What d'you expect? It's market day. And word's got round about you and your uncle Des helping out today—you know how popular his baking is. I'm expecting to be mobbed from now until closing time."

"Well, that's what you want, isn't it, love?" said Des appearing from the kitchen at the back of the shop with a warm cherry and almond cake in one hand and a tray of apple and sultana scones in the other. "Happy customers means repeat customers."

He filled the display stands with his latest creations before fiddling with his hearing aid to adjust the volume, and craning his neck to see the line of customers outside. He nodded to the door, particularly to his wife, Sylvie, who was peering through a window

Secrets, Lies, and Puppy Dog Eyes

pane between cupped hands. "I reckon there's going to be a riot if you don't let them in soon. I can see Dora Pickles out there; lovely woman, but her elbows are so bony they're like razor blades, so she's bound to be first in."

Petal chuckled. "Right, Megan, I'm opening the door, so stand clear. And don't look so nervous—you'll be fine. It's going to be busy, but you'll probably know most of the customers, so just think of it as like a big party with friends. Okay?" She turned around the 'Sorry, we're closed' sign that hung on the door to, 'Please come in! We're open', and stood to one side just in time to avoid being trampled by the rush.

"Morning, everyone. You're keen today!"

As Des had predicted, Dora Pickles, with her elbows spread wide, was the first through the door to grab a place at a table in the window for her and Sylvie.

"Hello, my lovely," said Sylvie, catching Megan's cheek between a finger and thumb, and jiggling it about. "How're you getting on?"

"Oh, fine, fine," said Megan, taking an apprehensive look around the café at the number of tables that suddenly all needed to be served at once. "Look, I'll speak to you in a bit, Aunty Sylv, but I need to start taking some orders." She took a pad from the pocket of her apron and a pen from behind her ear. "What would you like?"

Dora sniffed the air. "Is that Des's cherry and almond cake I smell? I'll have a slice of that, please, and a pot of tea."

"And I'll have a couple of slices of toast with lemon marmalade, and a mug of coffee, please, love," said Sylvie. "By the way, Sandra and Walter are on their way, so you'd better be on your toes. You know how pernickety she can be."

"Oh, great, that's all I need," said Megan, pulling a face. "I'd better get a move on."

She moved swiftly from table to table, giving orders to Des, and delivering food and drink to waiting customers. As she fumbled with adding spoons and sachets of sugar to saucers, the bell above the café door jangled and Sandra Grayling barged in like a charging bull, followed by her brother, Walter.

The treasurer of the Bliss Bay Women's Association, Sandra wasn't a popular member of the community. She was overly critical, incredibly bossy, full of her own self-importance, and rarely had a good word to say about anyone, or anything.

She looked around the café as though there was a bad smell under her nose, her snow white fringe plastered tightly to her forehead with a hairgrip. Pointing to a table in the corner, she barked an order at Walter to grab it before someone else did. "I'm going to powder my nose," she announced to the entire café and pointed to Megan. "And you, you make sure you're ready to take our order by the time I come out. Walter and I have an appointment, and we can't be late." She stomped off in her sensible shoes, leaving Megan flustered in her wake.

Petal sent a sympathetic look from the flower shop where she was making up an intricate floral anniversary display. "Well, she seems to be in a particularly vile mood this morning, but don't let her rattle you," she whispered. "She always expects special service. She doesn't seem to understand the concept of first-come, first-served, so just give as good as you get. Politely, of course. Oh, and try not to look so frightened, or you'll scare the customers away." She grinned and gave Megan a wink.

Megan smiled gratefully. Even though she and Petal were friends, she wasn't expecting an easy ride. This was a job, albeit only for a day, and she was determined to give it her best shot. She didn't want to give the impression she couldn't deal with an awkward customer, but she wasn't the most confident of people and, if truth be told, she found Sandra Grayling very intimidating.

Sherri Bryan

She delivered a tray filled with cakes, scones, teacakes and pots of tea to six customers and accepted Des's offer of help. She grinned when he produced a shiny penny from behind an elderly woman's ear and thanked her lucky stars that they were working together. You could put Des in a room full of strangers and they'd all end up being the best of friends. He had an easy way with people that Megan certainly didn't.

She made her way over to Walter Grayling's table. He took off his cap and smoothed a hand across his hair, snow white, just like his sister's, but a receding mass of soft curls in contrast to hers, which was poker straight.

"Sorry, you'll have to excuse me if I'm a bit slow," said Megan, with a smile, "but I haven't quite got into the swing of things yet."

Walter smiled back at her. He kept himself to himself, but he was pleasant enough. As Megan hadn't been back in the village for long, this was the first time she'd seen him in years.

"What can I get you?" she asked. "We've got some lovely cherry and almond cake, or Des has made some apple and sultana scones, maple syrup flapjacks, sticky ginger cake, and individual fruit pies. Oh, and there are also some lavender Madeleines, too. They're Des's speciality. Or if you fancy something savoury, there's homity pie, sausage rolls and sandwiches."

"My, my, he's been busy, hasn't he?" said Walter, with the hint of a smile. "I'll have a slice of ginger cake and a mug of tea, and I think Sandra's having a hot chocolate and an Eccles cake. She said she enjoyed the one she had yesterday. You'd better check with her, though."

"Oh, sorry, we don't have Eccles cakes today," said Megan. "Des thought it would be a good idea to vary the selection, so he's made flapjacks for a change."

"Did I hear you say you have no Eccles cakes?" said Sandra, on her return from the ladies' room, her booming voice echoing around the café. "Well, that's simply not good enough. When a customer comes in one day and chooses something from the selection on offer, they don't expect to come in the very next day to find that the *temporary* cook has replaced it with something else. Honestly, how long are Lionel and Amisha going to be away? The whole place is going to rack and ruin without them."

Megan was about to answer, as well as doing her best to stop her aunt Sylvie from launching herself out of her chair and across the café at Sandra's throat (she didn't take kindly to anyone criticising Des), when Petal called across from the flower shop.

Sherri Bryan

"Come on, Sandra, don't be so awkward. You know very well that Lionel's gone to his best friend's wedding today, and Amisha's got the day off. And I told you yesterday that Megan and Des would be helping out today. I probably would have had to close the café altogether if they hadn't agreed to step in, so we're lucky to be open at all. Now, in the absence of any Eccles cakes, I can highly recommend anything else on offer. It's common knowledge that Des bakes like an angel, so anything you choose will be a worthy replacement."

It wasn't often that people took Sandra to task, but when they did, she didn't like it one bit. "Well, it's jolly inconvenient. And who on earth in their right mind gets married on a Tuesday?" She pulled out a chair and sat down in a huff. "I'll have a hot chocolate and one of those fruit pies. It'll probably be awful, but I need to eat something so I can take my arthritis medication."

With a huge effort, Megan fixed her lips in a smile and took the order. "So, that's one slice of ginger cake and a mug of tea, and one fruit pie and a hot chocolate. Coming up."

She went back to the counter and ripped the order off the pad for Des, the smile fixed on her face like a death mask. "That woman is *so* disagreeable," she muttered. "I hope she chokes on her flippin' pie."

Secrets, Lies, and Puppy Dog Eyes

The bell jangled as the door to the café swung open again and Olivia Brennan from the village shop strolled in. Her hair, the colour of terracotta, was pulled up into a ponytail which swung from side to side as she looked around the café, nodding a greeting to every customer. "Morning, Petal, morning, all," she said, pulling out a chair at the table Sylvie and Dora were sitting at.

"Hi, Megan. When you're ready, can I have a black coffee and something to go with it, please? You'll have to decide what, though, because I can never make up my mind when it comes to Des's baking." She swivelled in her chair and called across to Petal. "I was on my way to the market this morning to stock up on fresh fruit and veg for the shop and I bumped into Kevin from The Duck Inn. Just wait till you hear what's happened!" She looked around the café at the customers, all leaning forward expectantly, their ears cocked for gossip.

"Are you going to tell us, then?" said Petal, bunching a handful of lilies together and binding them with florist's twine. "Or are you going to keep us hanging on until you pop in tomorrow with the next instalment?"

Olivia flashed her a sarcastic smile. "Well, when Kevin went out for his run this morning, he went past St. Mildred's and there was an obituary for Annabel Hillier pinned to the notice board. You know, Edmund's wife."

A collective gasp went up.

"Oh no! I can't believe it!" said Megan. "She wasn't that old, was she? Must have only been in her early sixties. And such a nice woman, too."

Olivia raised an eyebrow and nodded. "Uh, yeah. And she still is, 'cos she's still alive."

"Yikes!" said Megan, as she took Sandra and Walter's order to their table. "I bet someone at the church office is going to get an earful when Reverend Beale finds out. Fancy posting an obituary on the church notice board for someone who isn't even dead."

"Apparently, it was pinned next to a notice about a service that's being held at the church this afternoon for Edmund's second wife, Dawn," said Olivia. "Even after all these years, he still arranges one on the anniversary of her death, even though she's been gone for ages."

"He's on his third wife?" said Petal.

Olivia nodded. "The first one died years ago. Car accident, so I heard. And all his wives have been much younger than him."

"Well, I hope him and Annabel don't find out about the obituary," said Sylvie. "I don't expect they'll be too pleased."

Secrets, Lies, and Puppy Dog Eyes

"Too late," said Olivia. "They already know. When Kevin started out on his run, he saw them standing outside the church and Edmund was in a right state, so he ran over to see what the problem was. They were out on a morning walk and they'd come past the church so Edmund could check that the notice about Dawn's service had been posted. You can imagine what a shock it must have been for them to see the obituary for Annabel right next to it. Edmund told Kevin he was going to call Reverend Beale and give him a mouthful."

"What an awful thing to happen," said Des. "Poor Annabel. It must have really spooked her."

"Are you *sure* it's the anniversary of Dawn's death?" said Dora. "I thought she passed away much earlier in the year—I could have sworn she died during the spring."

"No, she didn't," said a shaky voice from the corner of the café. "The anniversary is today."

Everyone turned to Sandra, whose cheeks had turned pale, and whose lips, which were usually pursed tight in disapproval about something or other, had become slack and downturned.

"Olivia's right. Today *is* the anniversary. Walter and I are going to buy some flowers and visit the grave when we leave here. We never miss a year." She blinked several times and pressed her fingers to her eyelids before pushing her chair away from the table, its legs screeching against the floor tiles. "Give me a bunch of those lilies will you, Petal. Come along, Walter. I want to get to the cemetery and then I want to go home and lie down before the service. This is a bad enough day to get through as it is, but this news has made it even worse."

It was so unusual to see Sandra Grayling show any emotion, no one knew quite what to say.

Walter took some money from his wallet and handed it to Megan on the way out. He looked back to the table where the food and drink sat, untouched. "Sorry we didn't get around to actually eating anything, but here's what we owe you, plus a little extra for the inconvenience." He gave her a tired smile and pulled on his cap.

When he and Sandra had left, the café erupted in chatter.

"Why's Sandra so upset about Dawn Hillier's death?" asked Megan.

"Because they were very good friends," said Sylvie.

"I've hardly thought about what happened over the years," said Des, "but it's just all come rushing back like it was yesterday."

Secrets, Lies, and Puppy Dog Eyes

"*What's* all come rushing back?" said Megan. "What happened?"

Des scratched his head and flicked a tea towel over his shoulder. "It was very sad, wasn't it, Sylv? Sandra was all set to marry a local boy, but he died in hospital during an operation to have his appendix removed. He was only in his twenties and he and Sandra had been engaged less than six months."

"Oh no, that's terrible!" said Megan. "I bet she's never got over it. It makes me feel guilty for thinking so badly of her."

"You're not the only one, love," said Sylvie, spreading a slice of thick buttered toast with lemon marmalade. "I mean, none of us would rush to join her fan club now but back then, she wasn't so bad."

"Yes, she's been such an old battleaxe for so long now," said Dora, "it's easy to forget that she used to be quite pleasant once, isn't it?" She picked up the crumbs from her plate with the pad of an index finger. "Of course, it didn't help that not long after she lost her fiancé, Dawn passed away. She took it very badly, didn't she?"

Sylvie nodded. "Well, after Bernard died—he was her intended—Dawn took Sandra under her wing. She was such a kind woman. They worked together at the old Bliss Bay School, you see. Sandra was the secretary and

Dawn was one of the teachers. They became very good friends."

"Didn't Sandra ever get married?" said Megan.

"Never even looked at another man," said Des, "unless it was to give him an earful. She thinks the world of Walter, though. They're very close."

"How did Dawn die?"

Des shrugged. "Well, she fell down the bank by the side of the bus stop and hit her head on a tree stump." He scratched his chin and frowned as he recalled his memories. "Although *why* she fell is still a mystery. I seem to remember that her handbag was missing, so the police thought she might have lost her footing during a struggle. As they never found the handbag, though, or who took it, what *actually* happened was never proved.

"That was in the days before DNA testing and all the fancy stuff they can do now: back then, I think they used to have to rely on fingerprints and blood samples to catch a suspect. Not that the police found any suspects, mind you, let alone who was responsible. Sandra drove us all mad afterwards, do you remember, Sylv? Asking everyone over and over again if they remembered seeing or hearing anything that might help find out what happened, but no one did."

Secrets, Lies, and Puppy Dog Eyes

"Oh, well, I'll try to be a bit more tolerant with her from now on," said Megan. "Just goes to show, you never know what people are carrying around with them, do you? We've all got our troubles, but some keep them hidden more than others."

"Actually, a lot of people thought she became a bit fixated with Edmund after Dawn died," said Dora. "It started with her taking food round for him, and to have a chat, but then she started turning up on his doorstep unannounced, and at the bank during her lunch hour. As I remember, it all got a bit out of hand."

"I don't think it did either of them any good," said Sylvie. "It was far too soon after their losses for either of them to be a comfort to the other. All they did was remind each other of what they'd lost. Although what you say is quite right, Dora—Sandra did become a bit obsessed with Edmund for a while, until he put a stop to it by going off with Annabel."

"You mean Annabel, as in Annabel his current wife?" said Petal. "Did they get together quite soon after Dawn died, then?"

Des raised an eyebrow. "'Soon' isn't the word. Let's just say there were a lot of people who weren't impressed when news got round that Edmund was getting his jollies in the arms of the woman who was helping to arrange

Dawn's funeral. It was so disrespectful of her memory, and it upset Sandra terribly... quite a few of the other villagers, too."

"Annabel worked at the funeral directors?" said Olivia, with an incredulous gawp.

Sylvie nodded. "Until she was given the boot. Her boss wasn't very happy when he found out she'd been giving Edmund a little more sympathy than was considered appropriate, if you know what I mean. They were married within a year."

"Blimey, I had no idea," said Petal. "What did his kids think about it? It must have been a very unsettling time for them."

"Teresa and Barnaby?" Sylvie shrugged. "I think they just got on with it. They'd already lost their own mum when they were very young—I doubt they even remembered her—so I think they were just glad that their dad was still around. *Who* he was married to didn't seem to matter to them. And then their dad and Annabel had Polly, so they had a little step-sister to preoccupy themselves with."

"And they loved her to bits," said Dora. "I remember Annabel telling me that she and Edmund were a little worried about how Teresa and Barnaby would react when they found out another sprog was on the way, seeing as it had just been the two of them for so long, but they needn't have worried—the kids both took to little Polly right away."

"And what happened to Sandra after Edmund and Annabel got together?" asked Megan.

"Well, she was furious. And heartbroken," said Sylvie. "She never said as much, but she was obviously hoping that her friendship with Edmund might develop into something else. That's why she was so upset when he got together with Annabel. After Walter's wife died, though, he sold their place and moved back into the family home to be with Sandra. As she never got married, she stayed there after her parents passed away, and that's where she's lived ever since. I think Walter moving back in was good for them both. It certainly gave Sandra some comfort, that's for sure. She doesn't speak to Edmund any more, though. Nor Annabel. I can understand why she wouldn't want to."

"It's no wonder she throws herself into the Women's' Association with such enthusiasm," said Dora. "I suppose she doesn't have much else to focus on. It's sad, isn't it?"

Sylvie nodded. "I know I should try harder with her but if she wasn't so bloody infuriating, it would be a lot easier." She looked at her watch. "Right, come on, Dora, we'd better get to the market. We won't find anything that takes our fancy sitting here." She kissed Des on the cheek and ruffled his mop of salt and pepper hair. "Apart from this one, of course. See you all later."

Chapter 2

"Now, *that* was what I call a good day," said Petal, counting the café takings before sharing out the tips between Megan and Des. "Perhaps we could come to an arrangement about you doing some baking for us on a regular basis, Des? I don't think I can remember a day when we sold out of absolutely everything on the shelves."

Des puffed out his chest and gave her a bashful grin. "Well, that'd be great, if Lionel doesn't mind. I love baking so much, I'd do it for nothing, but as you insist on paying me, that's a bonus. The only thing is, I can't do it if it takes me away from Sylvie for too long—she wouldn't be very happy about that, and nor would I. I only agreed to help out this week because it was just for one day."

"Oh, no, I don't mean every day," said Petal, shaking her head, her black curls bobbing. "Perhaps just one day a week to start with, and you can see how you feel about it? We could even call it 'Des's Day'! If you're interested, we can talk about it more another time, but have a think about it and talk to Sylvie, and then you can let me know what you've decided. No rush, just something to mull over. Anyway, I must dash. Daisy and I are meeting Blossom from school and taking her to get her ears pierced. She must be the only teenage girl in the whole of Bliss Bay who hasn't had them done. She's always been a bit queasy about it but she's quite keen, all of a sudden. She's forever losing her clip-ons, so she's decided she wants to take the plunge."

"That's nice that you're going with her," said Megan gathering her things. "A group of us all went together for moral support when we had ours pierced. Do you remember? I seem to recall you felt a bit lightheaded yourself."

Petal nodded with a grin. "Yeah, the girls aren't very good in situations like that, either—they must get it from me. When Lionel sliced through his thumb in the kitchen a few months ago, the hospital spent more time making sure I was okay than him. To be honest, I think Blossom would probably have preferred to go with her mates, than her mum and her big sister, but she's worried she might faint, and you know how people video everything these days and before you know it, it's all over the internet. I mean, you'd hope friends wouldn't do that to you but, these days, you never know, and she'd never get over the embarrassment if it happened, which is why Daisy and I are taking her. And then we're going to get a takeaway and go home to eat with Lionel." Petal pulled the scissor gate across the front of the café and clicked the padlock shut before giving them both a hug.

Secrets, Lies, and Puppy Dog Eyes

"Right, I'd better get off. Thanks again for today—you were both brilliant."

As they made their way to her old Mini at the bottom of the road, Megan and Des chatted about the news Olivia had brought to the café earlier.

"It's a bit creepy, isn't it, that obituary for Annabel going up on the noticeboard the same day as the service for Dawn?" said Megan. "What with them both having Edmund in common, I mean. I wonder what Reverend Beale had to say about it?"

"Put it this way," said Des. "I wouldn't have liked to be in his shoes once Edmund got through to him. I bet his ear's been red hot all day. Edmund's got a way with words, if you know what I mean."

"Do you know him well?" asked Megan. "Edmund, I mean, not Reverend Beale."

Des shook his head. "Not that well. I've always found him to be a bit of a stiff, if I'm honest. We know each other to say hello, and we'll stop to pass the time of day, but that's about it. He's around ten years older than me, so that automatically put us in different social circles when we were young, and it's been that way ever since. He was the bank manager for years, though, so he's very well-known in the village. Now, Dawn was a different kettle of fish altogether. She was a lovely woman. Quite a bit younger than Edmund, too. More mine and Sylvie's age, in fact. She always had a smile and a nice word for everyone. Sylvie and your mum knew her better than I did, because she was a member of the WA."

They chatted as Megan drove the short journey to drop Des back home, via the village green, where two women stood on the flagstones outside the ancient St. Mildred's Church, one screeching and wagging her finger at the other.

"Is that Fern and Julie from the church office?" said Des, squinting through the windscreen at a tall woman towering over a shorter woman who was shaking her head, her hands held up defensively in front of her.

"I think so," said Megan, with a shudder. "And it looks like Julie's giving Fern a hard time about something. Not surprising when you consider her background. That woman should have a gold medal in pushing people around."

"Slow down a bit, love," said Des. "You wait here, I won't be a sec." He'd unfastened his seat belt and had one leg out of the car door even before Megan had come to a complete stop.

"Everything alright, Fern?"

Des had known the Rudd family for years, and was particularly fond of Fern, who had been very supportive to both Sylvie and him during his time coming off the booze.

Secrets, Lies, and Puppy Dog Eyes

A reformed alcoholic, Des prided himself on not having touched a drop for years, but there was no doubt in his mind that he wouldn't have succeeded had it not been for the love and support of his family, and the support which had been given so willingly from certain members of the community, the Rudd family in particular.

Julie Cobb, on the other hand, was a vile woman in Des's eyes. She'd been part of a gang of bullies—led by Megan's childhood nemesis, Kelly DeVille—who had terrorised Megan at school. Even though most of what had happened had passed Des by while he'd been in a drunken stupor, he'd been filled in on the circumstances since becoming sober and was often to be heard telling his niece, in his best gangster style, "Anyone who messes with my family, messes with me."

"Yes, everything's fine," said Julie, in the sickly-sweet voice she reserved especially for Reverend Patrick Beale and the parishioners.

"I wasn't asking you," said Des, barely giving her the courtesy of a glance. "Fern, are you okay?"

Gathering her wits, Fern nodded and gave Des a grateful smile. "Thanks, Des. I'm fine. I don't know if you've heard, but there was an obituary for Annabel Hillier pinned on the notice board today, and I got the blame for it. Patrick went absolutely bonkers when he found out."

"And *was* it you who put it there?" asked Des

"No, of course not, but as Julie had a day off yesterday, I was the only one in the office. I put out the announcement for Dawn Hillier's service, but that was all. When I left, that was the only thing on the board, except for a notice about the Harvest Festival events. I would never make a mistake like that but Julie didn't waste any time in telling Patrick it must have been me, but that I was too worried about losing my job to own up." Fern threw a venomous glare in Julie's direction. "We don't usually work together on Tuesdays, but we were both here today because of Dawn's service."

"Well, if you say it wasn't you, I believe you," said Des. "My whole family's quite friendly with old Patrick Beale, so I'll make a point of putting in a good word for you when I see him." He gave Fern a reassuring pat on the shoulder. "In the meantime, don't pay any attention to what anyone else says."

Julie was so indignant, her cheeks puffed out with rage and she forgot that Des— interfering old busybody or not—was also a member of the congregation. "Er, not that anyone really cares what you think, but if you're so convinced it wasn't Fern, then who

Secrets, Lies, and Puppy Dog Eyes

do you suppose it was? There were personal details on the obituary, which only someone who knew the Hilliers would know, which Fern does."

"Oh, come on, Julie," said Des. "I don't think you can blame this on Fern. The whole village knows the Hillier family."

"Yes, but they don't all type obituaries for the church noticeboard, do they?" snapped Julie. "Anyway, *do* enlighten us with your opinion on the subject. I'm dying to hear it." She crossed her arms and tapped a shoe against the flagstones.

Des shrugged a shoulder. "I've no idea who it was, I just know it wasn't Fern. She's the type of woman who'd own up to a mistake if she knew she'd made one, and accept the consequences." He met Julie's glare. "Unlike *some* people I know."

"Also," said Fern, "I did try to explain that the font used on the obituary isn't even the same as the one we use for church notices. It's very similar, but it's not the same. Of course, at a glance, most people wouldn't notice that, but when you look carefully, the difference is obvious."

Des turned to Julie. "Is that true? Is the typeface different?"

"Yes, but that doesn't prove anything," she snapped. "Fern could have changed the font easily."

Fern heaved a huge sigh, her shoulders rising and falling with her breath. "Yes, I know I *could* have, but why *would* I? I had no reason to. For the last time, Julie, I didn't do it, okay? Why won't you just accept that someone else pinned it to the noticeboard after I left work yesterday, and before Edmund and Annabel saw it this morning?"

"What sort of time frame would that be?" asked Des.

"Between around half-past five yesterday afternoon, and half-past seven this morning," said Fern.

"Hmm." Des crossed his arms and drummed his fingers against the sleeve of his sweatshirt. "And why do you think someone would have put it there?"

Fern shrugged. "I don't know. Someone obviously intended for it to be a very bad joke, or they wanted to spook Edmund and Annabel for some reason. I'd say it was someone who wasn't very keen on them, or held a grudge against them. Or maybe just against Annabel."

"And who would that be?" snapped Julie. "Edmund Hillier's a respected member of the community. When he retired from the bank, Kelly said everyone was in tears, he was so well thought of. You saw how everyone treated him at Dawn's service this afternoon. They think he's the best thing since sliced bread. And Annabel's very popular, too, especially since she's become so involved in raising funds for worthy causes in the village."

"Look, for the last time, I don't know who'd want to put up a fake obituary," said Fern. "All I know is that it wasn't me. Perhaps this will convince Patrick, at long last, that we need a lockable display cabinet for church notices. I don't know why we didn't just get one after he lost the key for *this* cabinet." She glanced at her watch. "And I don't have all evening to stand here arguing about it, either, because Colin's taking me out tonight."

"Colin, eh? That chap who's helping out with the old school renovation?" said Des. "You two are still courting, then? It's been a while now, hasn't it?"

"*Courting*? Do people still do that?" Fern teased. "To answer your question, though, yes, we've been going out for about ten months, and we're going to The Ferry Inn for a bite to eat, and after the day I've had, a few glasses of wine, too. Anyway, I'd better go. Thanks for stopping, Des, and for offering to put in a good word with Patrick." She gave his arm an affectionate squeeze and bent to wave to Megan. "See you around. And I hope you're in a better mood, tomorrow, Julie, or I might be having words with Patrick myself. You know how important he thinks it is to have a happy working environment, and you nagging on at me about something I haven't done isn't really helping to achieve that, is it?" She gave Julie a sarcastic smile before waving to Des and Megan again and going on her way.

"Well, I think that's the end of that, don't you?" said Des. "You're definitely barking up the wrong tree. Whoever it was who pinned up that obituary for Annabel Hillier, it wasn't Fern: you can take my word for it. I've known her since she was a toddler, and she doesn't have a bad bone in her body."

Julie pursed her lips and scowled. Realising this was an argument she wasn't about to win, she turned up the venom. "Well, she can't have been all *that* great when she was a baby, or she wouldn't have been given up for adoption, would she? Her real mum and dad probably couldn't stand the sight of her, and I can't stay I blame them."

Des took a step forward and Julie gasped, clutching her coat around her. "Don't you touch me, or I'll call the police."

"I have no intention of doing anything of the sort," seethed Des. "I've never been violent towards a woman, and I never would be. I just want to be sure you understand that you won't get away with pushing Fern around—or anyone else, for that matter. And you should watch that vicious tongue of yours—if you keep saying disgusting things like you just did, it'll get you into a lot of trouble one day."

Julie swallowed but refusing to back down, she changed her tack.

"I might have guessed *you* wouldn't have the guts to get out of the car, Megan," she called, leaning forward and glaring through the car window. "Nothing changes, does it? Once a wuss, always a wuss. I'll be sure to give your regards to Kelly—I'm on my way to see her now." Her lips curled in a spiteful smile before she turned and stomped off across the village green.

"God only knows how that woman got a job working at the church," said Des, his entire body shaking with rage as he got back into the car. "She's a cold-hearted crone without an ounce of empathy for anyone."

"I heard she was just in the right place at the right time," said Megan. "And it helped that her mum knows Patrick Beale's wife. When the old church secretary retired and they were looking for someone to take her place, Julie had just been laid off from her job at the petrol station and her mum put in a word for her right away.

"She can obviously turn on the charm when she needs to because she pulled the wool right over everyone's eyes. I hear she was offered the job on the spot." Megan shivered. Any encounter, however tenuous, with any member of the gang who had caused her so much distress, caused her anxiety level to shoot up, despite the years that had passed.

Des squeezed her shoulder. "Don't you go fretting about things, now, will you? I know you still get wound up about things that happened long ago, but you've got your friends and family around you now, so you don't need to worry about those women any more. Okay?"

Megan nodded. "I know, I know. I'm thirty-nine years old, so it's ridiculous that they can still give me butterflies, but when I saw Julie yelling at Fern like that, it was a bit too close for comfort."

"One step at a time, love. You're a lot less anxious than you were when you got here in July, said Des, "and that's a real achievement."

"Well, I think that's got a lot to do with keeping well out of Kelly's way," said Megan. "*And* her husband."

Des made a guttural noise that conveyed his disdain. "Now, there's another person who doesn't deserve to be breathing the same air as you. Laurence Ford didn't know how lucky he was to be married to you. Sylvie and I still don't understand why on earth he left you for Kelly. He's obviously got a screw loose. The bloke's a prize pillock."

"I can't disagree with that," said Megan, as she drove off. "Although if we hadn't got together, we wouldn't have Evie." Her mood lifted immediately at the mention of her daughter. "She was definitely the silver lining in my dark cloud of a marriage."

"I'll agree with you there. Evie's the only good thing that waster ever gave you." Des frowned as he fastened his seat belt again and turned to look out of the window, his chin resting in his cupped palm.

"I didn't know Fern was adopted," said Megan.

Des nodded. "I think she was two when she came to live with Emilia and Ken."

"I had no idea," said Megan.

They lapsed back into silence until she turned into Elmwood Road and came to a stop outside number nine.

"Something on your mind, Uncle Des?"

Her uncle turned in his seat, a serious expression clouding his usually jolly face. "If you ask me, there's something very fishy about that obituary for Annabel Hillier. Especially as someone went to all that trouble to make it look like it was an official church notice."

Megan pulled on her handbrake and the old Mini wheezed like a heavy smoker as it sat by the side of the road, its engine ticking over. "Well, I agree that it's a horrible thing for someone to have done, and an even more horrible thing for Edmund and Annabel to have found, but I'm not sure there's anything suspicious about it. Like we said earlier, it's probably just a very bad joke by someone with a very warped sense of humour. Some people are weird, aren't they?"

Des lowered his voice, as if someone outside the car might hear. "Perhaps we should try to find out who put it there? Keeping very low-key and under the radar, of course."

Megan gave him an incredulous stare. "Why? It's nothing to do with us."

"Well, it is sort of," said Des. "It's our community, isn't it? If someone's trying to cause trouble, we shouldn't turn a blind eye— we should try to put a stop to it. If we don't, they could do it again, and if someone with a weak disposition saw something like that about them, or someone they know, the consequences could be very serious."

Megan looked at her uncle, with a smudge of flour on his cheek and his eyes bright and inquisitive, and felt a huge surge of affection for him. She also had a horrible feeling she knew in which direction the conversation was going. She sighed. "Yes, you're quite right. We shouldn't turn a blind eye to things that are going on if they're not for the good of the village, but please don't tell

Secrets, Lies, and Puppy Dog Eyes

me you're going to go all Detective Inspector on me again? I thought you'd got all that sleuthing out of your system after what happened over the summer."

Des shrugged and fiddled with his hearing aid which had started to whistle, causing a passing dog's ears to prick up as it bounded along on a late afternoon walk. "You know me, Megan. I'm not one for a newspaper and a pair of slippers in front of the fire—I like to be doing things and getting involved, not sitting on my backside or peering through the curtains waiting for Neighbourly Watch to do all the dirty work."

Megan nodded. She didn't want to discourage him but, having seen Des in full investigative mode following a recent spate of crime in the village, she didn't want to encourage him to get involved in anything that might put him at risk, either. "Look, why don't you speak to Reverend Beale before you do anything? You never know, Edmund and Annabel might have told him something that'll give a clue to the identity of whoever posted that obituary. You were going to speak to him about Fern, anyway, weren't you?"

"Hmm, I suppose I could do that," said Des, picking at a piece of dried cake mix that was stuck to his trousers.

"I'd feel happier if you did," said Megan, "rather than just rushing off on a wild goose chase as your alter-ego, Chief Inspector Des Harper."

"Alright, that's what I'll do, then," said Des, slapping his palms against his thighs to seal the deal. "What are you up to this evening? Do you want to come and have something to eat with me and Sylv?"

Megan shook her head. "Thanks, but I'm taking Tab to the vet to have his stitches out, thank God. Poor little fella. That cone-shaped collar he's been wearing since he was neutered has been driving him crazy. And keeping him indoors has been a nightmare. He must hate me for putting him through it all."

Des grimaced. "Ouch. Rather him than me. Alright, love, I'll see you soon. Have a good evening."

Secrets, Lies, and Puppy Dog Eyes

CHAPTER 3

Kismet Cottage was Megan's family home. The last in a row of ten cottages, it was situated on the shortest edge of the triangular village green, which played host to a calendar of events throughout the year, including cricket and bowls tournaments, church fêtes, and Women's Association fundraisers.

On the edge of the green to the left of the cottage was a hair salon which catered for the village pensioners, and specialised in blue rinses and shampoo and sets, a boutique which appealed to a similar clientele, and—tucked away in the corner—The Duck Inn, the oldest pub in Bliss Bay village.

The longest edge of the green on the opposite side was home to the village hall and the old stone St. Mildred's church with its adjoining cemetery.

Having lived away from Bliss Bay for seventeen years, Megan had recently returned to the village after a particularly difficult week, during which she'd been made redundant, and her fiancé had left her. To top it all, her daughter, Evie, had left for a gap year at around the same time, leaving Megan feeling incredibly low, without a job, and with an engagement ring she no longer needed.

Having sworn that she would never again live in the village where her cheating ex-husband and his hideous wife lived, she'd been won over by its charm when she'd visited at the start of the summer to organise her parents' wedding vow renewal ceremony. After making the decision to stay, it hadn't taken long to fall back into the easy way of life, and having her family and old friends around was an added bonus.

    She turned her key in the lock and opened the door just a crack, squeezing herself into the house before closing the door firmly behind her to stop the cat from escaping.

    Despite wearing a cone-shaped collar to stop him pulling out his operation stitches, Tabastion—the part-feral cat who'd become a member of the Fallon family in recent months—never failed to make a dash for freedom at every opportunity. He was feisty, but surprisingly loyal for a cat, let alone one that had fended for itself for so long, and he'd found a place in Megan's heart. Feral or not, she adored him.

    As usual, he came rushing to the door, the plastic collar banging into walls as he did, and Megan crouched down to tickle his tummy. "I'm sorry, Tab, but it was for the best. You were getting a reputation for being the neighbourhood stud, and the last thing we need is to add to the number of unwanted kitties that are already out there. I know ten days has been a long time, but I'm taking you to the vet now and then you won't have to wear that thing around your neck any more. I bet you can't wait to get out again, can you?"

He looked up at her with his amber eyes, and blinked slowly before padding off to the kitchen.

Megan picked up the cat box she'd borrowed from a neighbour and steeled herself for the job ahead. She knew it wasn't going to be easy as soon as Tabastion stared at her from inside the cone with a look that said, *Seriously? If you think I'm getting in **that**, you've got another think coming.*

It had been easy to get him to the vet the first time. As he enjoyed trips in the car, all Megan had had to do was open the door and he'd jumped in and curled up on the back seat. Getting him home after the op had been a doddle, too, because the effects of the anaesthetic had made him drowsy and slow to react.

This time, though, Megan knew there was no way she could trust him to walk to the car. At the first sniff of the great outdoors, he'd be off like a bullet. "Come on, Tab. Do it for me. One way or another, you're getting in this box, but it'll be better if you cooperate."

Forty minutes, and multiple scratches later, Tabastion hissed at Megan from inside the box on the back seat of the car.

"Sorry, puss, but the sooner we get you to the vet, the better."

ooooooo

"I think that's it, all done," said Liam, the vet, as he gave Tab a final check.

"It's amazing that he lets you touch him without going for your jugular," said Megan, in awe. "He's not the most amiable of cats when it comes to strangers."

"Well, I'm not a *complete* stranger," said Liam. "I did the op, didn't I?"

"All the more reason for him to want to scratch your eyes out, I'd say," said Megan, with a grin, "but he doesn't seem in the slightest bit bothered about you poking and prodding at him. You obviously have a way with animals, which is probably a bonus in your line of work."

"You could say that," said Liam, as he stroked Tabastion behind the ears. "Give him a day or so and he should be pretty much back to normal. Although it varies from cat to cat, so you're aware, he'll most likely stop marking his territory, become a little less active and a bit more docile."

Megan looked down at the scratches on her arms and raised an eyebrow. "Hmm, somehow, I don't think Tab got that memo."

Liam chuckled. "I'm sure he'll be fine, but if you have any concerns, you know where

Secrets, Lies, and Puppy Dog Eyes

I am. Come on, Tabastion. Let's get you back in the box."

As Megan settled her bill, Liam said, "I don't suppose you know anyone who's looking to adopt a puppy, do you? Someone reliable and trustworthy who could give a dog a happy forever home? It's a big ask, I know, because they're such a commitment, but a guy brought in two Boxer puppies last week that he and his wife thought would be good birthday presents for their two-year old twins." He rolled his eyes.

"Oh dear," said Megan. "I take it that idea didn't work out too well?"

"No, it didn't. Boisterous kids and puppies are not usually a good mix." Liam scratched his head. "Don't get me wrong, I think it's great for kids to grow up around animals, but I would never recommend a puppy as a present for such a young child. Anyway, one of them's been taken by our receptionist for her sister and her husband, but we still have the other one. I'd keep him myself if I could but we've already got four rescue dogs, three rescue cats and an escaped cockatiel at my place. He's staying with us at the moment but if I suggested to my wife that we keep him permanently, I reckon I'd be looking at divorce papers by the end of the week."

Megan shook her head. "I don't know anyone, I'm sorry. My dad's always saying that he wishes he and mum had got a dog years ago—and they've got enough love for a hundred dogs—but I'm not sure they'd want to take on a pup at their time of lives. Like you say, they're a lifelong commitment, aren't they? I could ask them, if you like, although they're on a cruise at the moment and won't be back until late December."

"December?" Liam's face fell as he handed Megan back her credit card. "Oh. I was hoping to have the pup homed long before then. Not that I'm not grateful for you asking them, but if he stays with us much longer, I'll get so attached to him, I won't want to let him go."

"Ah, I see. Is that how you ended up with four dogs, three cats and an escaped cockatiel?" said Megan

Liam nodded. "Yep. Which is why I'd love to see the little fella placed in a good home ASAP. If we can't find a home for him soon, though, perhaps you could ask your parents?"

"Sure. Is there any chance I could see him? Would I be able to pop round to your place when it's convenient?"

"Oh, there's no need for that. I bring him to work with me, so he's in the other room. You might want to leave Tabastion here for a minute, though. Come on, come and meet Boxer."

"Boxer? That's original," said Megan. "Although I'm a fine one to talk. Tab was called Cat until we found out his real name. In fact, we thought—" She followed Liam into another room and stopped mid-sentence.

Lying on a rug, chewing on a rope toy, was a tiny fawn-coloured Boxer puppy with paws that were so enormous, they looked disproportionate to the rest of his body. He looked up at her with big blue eyes and kept chewing.

"Oh, my gosh, Liam! He's absolutely adorable." Megan took a step towards him. "Can I touch him?"

Liam nodded. "Of course. Now do you understand why I can't give him a name? If I do, I'll have to keep him." He gave her a wonky smile.

The puppy stopped chewing and closed his eyes when Megan scratched the scruff of his neck. He raised his head as though he was sniffing the air and gave a tiny, contended growl. "Do you know, if I didn't think Tab would try to scratch his eyes out, I'd take him myself," said Megan. "Honestly, I would. He's just beautiful."

She stared at the puppy for a long time, then got to her feet. "I'm not sure, but I think I *might* know just the person to give this little pup the most fantastic home. Can you leave it with me, and I'll bring him in tomorrow afternoon? Do you think you'll be able to keep Boxer until then?"

Liam breathed a visible sigh of relief and held up a pair of crossed fingers. "Megan, if you can vouch for someone who'd be prepared to take Boxer on and give him the home he deserves, I'll make sure no one else takes him before you've brought your friend in tomorrow."

"That's great. I'll see you then!"

ooooooo

Back at Kismet Cottage, Megan opened the door of the cat box, made a fuss of Tabastion, and let him out of the back door. As she suspected, he sped off across the lawn like a rocket—as free as a neutered tomcat—for the first time in over a week.

"Have fun, Tab," she called after him. She kicked off her shoes and flicked on the kettle to make a cup of caramel coffee, before scrolling through the contacts on her phone until she came to the one she was looking for and pressed 'Call'.

"Hi, how're things going? That's good. Look, are you free for a while in about half an hour? I want to come over and talk to you about something. You sure? No, I don't want to tell you over the phone, I'll tell you when I see you. Okay? See you in a bit."

Secrets, Lies, and Puppy Dog Eyes

CHAPTER 4

At the site of the old Bliss Bay School, at the top of a small hill in the middle of the village, Megan pulled into a parking space and surveyed the building site in front of her.

It had only been a couple of months since it was looking very likely that the school would be bought by a developer who was planning on knocking it down and building a hypermarket on the land. The very thought had sent the villagers into meltdown, resulting in protests and raucous meetings with the local authorities to prevent the sale from going through.

Until then, Megan had had no idea that her childhood friend, Jack Windsor, had been involved in a bidding war against the developer. It was only when he'd returned to Bliss Bay, and put in a winning bid for the school and its land, that all had been revealed.

Unlike the ruthless developer, though, Jack wasn't planning on taking a bulldozer to the school. He was planning a renovation that would make it his home, keeping as many features of the old school as he could. He had no interest in building an eyesore that would detract from the charm of the village. Rathermore, he wanted to create something that would sit well within it, in keeping with its surroundings.

Megan made her way across the uneven path to the school. There were tradesmen of every description hustling back and forth, like a colony of busy worker ants.

"You should have a hard hat on, love," called a man carrying a hod of bricks on a broad, tattooed shoulder. "There's debris flying all over the place in there."

"I'm only here for a minute. I just need a word with Jack."

The man stuck up a thumb. "Just a sec, I'll see if he's around. I saw him a while ago, so he can't be far. Don't come too close, will you?"

Megan looked around the site. Bricks and paving stones were stacked neatly, and the uneven ground had been levelled, ready for rolls of new turf to be laid. The outside of the school looked as it always had. The clock tower and big brass bell remained untouched, as did the entire exterior of the main building and the old Arts and Crafts block, which stood independently in the grounds. Close by was the old Willow tree, which Jack had point-blank refused to allow to be removed, so all the work was carrying on around it.

"The roots may cause you problems if you leave it there," the surveyor had said. "Just my opinion, but you might want to get rid of it while you've got the opportunity."

"I'll take my chances," Jack had replied, sticking a big yellow notice to the tree with the warning, 'DON'T TOUCH!' in large black letters, just to be on the safe side.

Little things like that made Megan adore Jack. With few exceptions, he cared about everything and everyone.

Since meeting up again, their relationship had developed into an easy friendship, with no awkward silences for either of them fill with needless words. Megan was thrilled he was back in the village. It was great to be in the company of a good man who was good fun. The fact there was no romance between them was an added bonus. Friendship suited them both just fine.

"Hey, Megan!"

She looked up to see Jack striding towards her, waving his hard hat in the air, his jeans smeared with cement and his white t-shirt clinging to him with sweat, emphasising the six-pack abs underneath. He rubbed a muscled forearm across his forehead and pushed his dark hair from his rugged smiling face.

It occurred to Megan that he was exactly the type of guy she'd seen in countless TV commercials whenever a tall, broad, clean-cut, drop-dead gorgeous hunky man was required to promote a product.

The image didn't last long, though. As clumsy as he'd always been, Jack caught the toe of his boot on the pile of bricks he'd jumped over, sending him sprawling face forwards into the mud before he could right his footing, his hard hat rolling along the ground.

"Oh, blimey, Jack. Are you alright?" Megan rushed over to find him spitting out mud and shaking with laughter. He rolled onto his back and clutched his sides.

Megan started to giggle, then laughed with him until the tears were pouring down her cheeks. "You always did know how to make an entrance, Jelly-Legs," she gasped, holding her ribs and referring to him by his childhood nickname.

"Sure did," he said, taking her hand and allowing her to help him to his feet. He looked at her, his face, t-shirt and jeans caked in mud, and said, with a completely serious expression, "Do you think anyone will notice I fell down?" which started Megan off all over again.

"You're such an idiot," she said, wiping away her tears and delving in her handbag for a pack of wet wipes. "Here, we can use these to clean you up a bit."

"Gee, thanks, Mom," he replied, in his deep voice, his American accent even more pronounced because he was over-emphasising the words.

She giggled again. "How's your day been? Looks like you're getting a lot done."

Jack nodded. "Yeah, we're doing okay. We've moved a lot of stuff."

"Still think you'll be finished by New Year?" Megan wiped the worst of the mud from his forehead.

"If it kills me," said Jack. "I want a big housewarming party with all the guys who've worked on the job, and I'd like to invite whoever wants to come from the village. And then I want to sit down to a big New Year's Day dinner at my own table, in my own kitchen, with Uncle Bill and Aunt Rita, and a few friends." He wiped his hands down the back of his jeans. "Anyways, what's up? Phil said you wanted to talk?"

Megan rubbed her last wet wipe against his chin. "There, I think that's the best I can do until you get in the shower."

He raised an eyebrow.

"Where you'll have to get the rest of the mud off *on your own*," she said, with a grin. "And, yes, I do want to talk to you, but I can wait till you've finished."

Jack looked at the sky, the light fading quickly. "We're pretty much done for the day.

If you hang on, I'll close up and then we can chat. Or, better still, why don't I go and get properly cleaned up and then I can come round to your place?"

"Have you just invited yourself to dinner?"

Jack winked. "I'll bring a bottle of something. I'll even cook, if you can wait for me."

Megan smiled. "It's okay, I'll cook. I'll see you when you're ready."

ooooooo

"Well, you scrub up very nicely, I must say." Megan opened the door to find Jack outside with a six pack of beer and a bottle of rosé wine. His dark hair was still wet from the shower, his grey eyes creased at the corners in a smile that reached up from his lips.

He followed Megan into the kitchen. "Mmmm, something smells good."

"It's just risotto, but it doesn't take long, so we'll be eating soon. Come in and make yourself comfortable. Did I hear a taxi dropping you off?"

"Yep. I wanted to chill out with a few beers, so I left the car at Bill and Rita's."

"Excellent idea," said Megan. "In that case, you can open something and pour me a glass."

Secrets, Lies, and Puppy Dog Eyes

"How was your day?" said Jack, putting a glass of rosé wine on the counter.

"Good. Des's baking went down a storm, as usual, and we were rushed off our feet." She tasted the risotto and added a couple of turns of black pepper. "Olivia came in and told us about something weird that happened, though."

"You mean the obituary?"

"Oh, you know about it?"

Jack nodded. "One of the guys working on the school is seeing a woman who works at the church. She called him this morning to tell him what had happened, and that she'd gotten the blame for it."

"It's creepy, don't you think?" said Megan, as she dished up the risotto into bowls and put a block of Parmesan cheese on the table.

"Not really. It was just a mistake, wasn't it? An unfortunate one, but they happen, don't they? We all make them."

Megan shook her head. "But that's the thing. Fern *didn't* make a mistake because she didn't do it, and neither did Julie. Whoever pinned that obituary to the noticeboard made it so it looked like it was an official church notice, but it wasn't. They put it there some time during Fern leaving yesterday, and Edmund and Annabel Hillier finding it this morning, right next to the notice about

Edmund's former wife's memorial service. All things considered, not the best start to their day."

"You're kidding?" Jack forked risotto into his mouth as though he hadn't eaten for a week. "Well, in that case, yeah, it is a bit creepy. I bet it really freaked them out."

"Yeah, it did, apparently. And it's just enough of a mystery to get Des's sleuthing instincts on the go again. When I left him today, he was talking about trying to find out who was responsible. I mean, I know he's only looking out for the community, but I can't help but worry about him sometimes. I'm sure there's nothing *to* worry about, but he's not twenty-five any more, even though he thinks he is."

Jack chuckled. "Your uncle Des has got a lot up here." He tapped his head with his finger. "He's not stupid enough to get involved in something that's going to put him in any danger. Not that this is that kind of situation anyway, I'm sure, but you know what I mean. I really think it's just a stupid prank." He put down his fork. "That was delicious. Is there any more?"

Megan jerked a thumb over her shoulder. "In the pan. You might have to add another spoonful of stock and heat it up a bit if it's thickened up too much."

Secrets, Lies, and Puppy Dog Eyes

Jack ladled two more spoons into his bowl and sat back down at the table. "It's fine just as it is. So, what is it you want to talk to me about?"

"Well, you remember you said that you wanted to get a dog when your place is finished?"

Jack nodded. "Yeah. What about it?"

"Were you serious?"

"Yeah, deadly serious. We never had one when I was young, because we moved around so much because of Dad's job, but I always wanted one. And when I left home, I was always working, so it wouldn't have been fair on the dog. It's different now, though, so once I'm settled, getting a dog is my number one priority, and my place is going to be the perfect home for one when it's done. Why?"

Megan leaned forward and told him about Boxer. "I didn't originally think of you because I didn't think you'd want a puppy, but when I saw him I knew I had to tell you about him. What d'you think?"

"Well, it's a bit earlier than I'd planned, because I won't be around during the day until the job's finished, but I can take a look. If he likes me, and vice versa, maybe Aunt Rita could look after him for me while I'm working, and I can take over when I get home? Thing is,

I really wanted a rescue dog. There are so many of them that need a home."

"Well, he *is* a rescue dog," said Megan. "He was rescued from those two-year olds. But you need to see him for yourself before you go making any plans. Do you think you'll be able to come with me tomorrow when you've finished work? Around six?"

"Course I will. Let's hope we'll hit it off."

"Yes, let's," said Megan, and touched the wooden kitchen table.

ooooooo

The following morning, Police Constable Fred Denby settled his police helmet firmly on his head and pressed the doorbell outside the Hillier home.

The whole village had heard about what had happened the previous day, but Edmund hadn't lodged an official complaint with the police until an hour ago. Subsequently, Fred's sergeant had sent him off to find out what he could about 'The Obituary Incident', as it was being referred to at the station.

He heard footsteps approaching, followed by Annabel opening the door and welcoming him in with a smile. Her slim athletic build belied her sixty-three years and her blonde hair was still thick and naturally glossy, usually worn loose and falling to her shoulders. Today, though, it was pulled back into a loose chignon.

"Fred, it's so nice to see you. Come in and take the weight off your feet. I'll put the kettle on and get out the biscuits. We've got a new tin that our granddaughter gave me for my birthday. They're artisan—probably cost her all her pocket money, bless her. Anyway, listen to me, wittering on. Come on, come into the living room." She led the way and pointed to a reclining armchair. "Right, you sit there and I'll be with you in a tick. Tea or coffee?"

"Tea, please, Mrs Hillier. That's very kind of you. Is Mr Hillier not here?"

Annabel nodded. "He's just in the shed, sorting out the leaf blower. I love the autumn—all the beautiful shades of red, yellow and orange—but it makes such a mess of the garden. I'll give him a shout to let him know you're here once I've made the tea. I'm sorry you've had to come out. I told Edmund not to make a fuss, but he wouldn't listen."

"It's no trouble," said Fred, with a beaming smile. "All part of the service, in fact. Are you feeling alright? It must have been quite a shock."

Annabel took a tray to the table and set it down. "I'm absolutely fine. A few jitters, maybe, but nothing more. Here we are, you pour yourself a cup and help yourself to a biscuit. I'll just give him Edmund a shout. I won't be a sec."

Edmund arrived presently, leaving his gardening clogs on the doormat and pushing his feet into a pair of fleecy slippers. He strode into the living room, tall and straight-backed, his gunmetal hair blown slightly out of place by the breeze. He didn't even acknowledge Fred's presence before he launched into a tirade.

"I want to know what you're going to do about finding the person who put that obituary on the noticeboard? And, before you say anything, I know no one was hurt, and it's not a major crime, but it was a terrible shock for us to find it. Annabel's putting on a brave face, but can you imagine how she must have felt to see it? She's only smiling because she's not the type of woman to let something like this spoil her day. She's a real trooper."

Fred wished he hadn't just taken a large bite of a pistachio and lemon biscuit. "Well," he said, covering his mouth with his hand, "I'll call in at the church office and see if they still have the note, and make enquiries to see if anyone saw anything."

Edmund's eyes shot skywards. "You mean you haven't done that yet? What sort of police force are you? If you sit on your backsides and do nothing, you'll never find out who's responsible, will you! My wife has been the victim of intimidation, which is a crime, is it not, PC Denby?"

Fred grimaced. "Well, technically, that's true, but..."

"But nothing!" said Edmund. "I want you to find whoever did this and bring them to justice."

"I told him it was probably just kids playing a joke," said Annabel, patting her husband on the shoulder, "but he wouldn't listen."

"Honestly, I don't know how you're managing to be so calm about it, sweetheart," said Edmund. He turned to Fred. "This has affected our whole family, you know, not just us. Our daughters, Teresa and Polly, were here yesterday evening and they're as worried about it as I am. Our son Barnaby's working away at the moment, so he can't be here, but Annabel spoke to him last night and he was shocked to hear the news.

"We've even had to explain what happened to our nine-year old granddaughter in case she hears about it from someone at school. You know how children can over-dramatise things, and the last thing we want is for her to be scared to death that something terrible's going to happen to her grandmother. She had a very overactive imagination, so goodness only knows what must be going through the poor girl's mind."

Sherri Bryan

Fred sighed inwardly and took his notebook from his pocket. "If you could tell me exactly what happened yesterday morning, please." When he'd finished making notes, he asked, "And do you have any idea who might have had reason to do this? Anyone with a grudge against either of you?"

Edmund shook his head. "No idea at all. As you know, Annabel and I are very active members of the community—especially since my retirement from the bank—and I'd like to think we're well-thought of. I certainly can't think of anyone who'd want to do something so ghastly. And I'd like you to arrange to take the entire family's fingerprints or a DNA swab, or whatever it is you do, so that you can exclude our prints from the note."

Fred stood up and put his helmet back on. "Okay, leave this with me, Mr and Mrs Hillier, and I'm sure we'll find whoever's responsible before too long. I'll be sure to keep you informed of any developments."

"Yes, please do," said Edmund. "No, it's alright, Annabel," he said, as she stood up, "I'll see PC Denby out." He followed Fred to the door. "I hope to hear from you very soon," he said loudly, before looking over his shoulder and stepping outside. "One more thing, PC Denby." He lowered his voice to a whisper. "In case you think I'm over-reacting to this fake obituary business, can I remind you that my first wife died when Teresa and Barnaby were quite young, and—even after all these years—I *still* have no idea what happened to my second wife, Dawn. All things considered, the fact that a potential threat has been made against Annabel is of great concern. I hope you can understand." He fixed Fred with a stony glare.

Fred stood up a little straighter. "Of course, Mr Hillier. Rest assured, I'll get on the case right away."

Chapter 5

At Kismet Cottage, Megan sat on the couch, talking to her mum, and taking care not to ladder her tights.

It had been so long since she'd dressed 'for work' she kept forgetting she was wearing anything on her legs, as her usual dress since coming back to Bliss Bay had been tracksuit bottoms, jeans, or summer skirts which suited bare legs.

Claudia Fallon had called for a quick chat from the deck of the cruise liner she was on while she watched her husband play quoits. "Darling, we're having so much fun, I almost don't want it to end. Were it not for the fact that I couldn't bear to be this far away from you and Lizzie for too much longer, I'm sure I could get used to cocktail hour, and a permanent life on the proverbial ocean wave.

"And I'll tell you something else. That advice Olivia gave me was fabulous! She said whenever her mum and dad go on a cruise, they always take clothes with expanding waistbands, because there's food available twenty-four hours a day. Of course, you never intend to take advantage of it all, but it's very hard to resist. I'm so glad I listened to her, because I think I must have put on at least half a stone. It's our second honeymoon, though, so every time I take an extra canapé or profiterole, I just tell myself I deserve it. It's not like I overindulge all the time, is it? I'll just have to work it all off when I get back home."

Megan heard the unmistakable gentle clatter of ice cubes against glass, and heard her mother take a sip of her drink through a straw.

"Anyway, is everything okay with you, Meggie?"

"Everything's fine, Mum. In fact, you'll be pleased to hear that I'm leaving in about twenty minutes to see a client for a party planning job. It's the eighteenth birthday party I told you about for the daughter of the detective who was in Bliss Bay recently. Remember?"

"Of course I remember!" said Claudia. "Congratulations, darling, that's wonderful! Haven't I always told you and Lizzie that you can do anything you want if you put your minds to it, and have some belief in yourself, even if the odds are against you? Haven't I always said that, love?"

Megan smiled. "Yes, Mum. Ever since we were about four, I think."

"It's never too early to start drumming good advice into your children's heads," said Claudia. "It stands them in good stead for what's ahead. Of course, with the best will in the world, parents can't foresee horrendous husbands and feckless fiancés in the future, but we do our best. I just knew that you and Lizzie would be little marvels the first time I set eyes on you. Well, I won't keep you if you're on your way out. I just thought I'd call for a little chat while I was able to pick up a signal. Everything okay with everyone else?"

"Yes, well, it is with us," said Megan, "but Edmund and Annabel Hillier are having a bit of a rough time. And Sandra Grayling's taken to her bed, apparently, she's so upset."

"Why? What on earth's going on?"

Megan quickly filled her mother in on the events of the past few days and heard the catch in her breath.

"Oh, good grief, that's awful! Why on earth would someone do that?"

"Don't ask me," said Megan.

"And what about Annabel? How's she taking it?"

"She's not thrilled, as you can imagine, but, now she's over the initial shock, she's not too bad, apparently."

"Oh, I am glad to hear that," said Claudia. "What a horrible thing to have happened for the whole family. It must have hit Teresa and Barnaby especially hard. Their own mum died when they were very young, then Dawn died, and now this. Poor things, they must be in a terrible state. Has Barnaby come home? I don't think he's been back to Bliss Bay for years."

"He's still not back, as far as I'm aware," said Megan.

Secrets, Lies, and Puppy Dog Eyes

"You know, I always used to feel so sorry for those two. Teresa found it terribly difficult to communicate with people after her mum died. You could hardly get her to say boo to a goose, she was such a shy little thing. Still is, actually. You only have to look at her and she blushes and looks like she wants the ground to open up and swallow her. I think that's why I always think of her as being much younger than she is, although there's probably only about ten years between us."

"Yes, I've noticed she's a bit awkward at times," said Megan. "Probably down to a lack of confidence. Or do they call it lack of social skills these days? I used to work with a girl whose face went bright pink every time she met a new client—she had no control over it, and it used to really embarrass her."

"And Barnaby, poor chap," Claudia continued. "His dad used to give him *such* a hard time when he was younger. The poor lad couldn't do anything right in Edmund's eyes. His schoolwork wasn't good enough, his friends weren't good enough, and he wasn't sporty enough. He tried so hard to make Edmund proud, but he never seemed to manage it. With Edmund for a dad, it's little wonder Barnaby took the chance to get away from Bliss Bay as soon as he could. Living with Edmund constantly nagging at him must have worn him down. Mind you, whatever Teresa and Barnaby lack in confidence, Polly makes up for. That girl's got more confidence than she knows what to do with. I would imagine she's taking everything in her stride, even though Annabel's her mum?"

"I think so," said Megan. "I heard she's just getting on with things, but she and her husband are telling Beatrice as little as possible about it."

"I'm going to sit bolt upright on my sun-lounger, so I don't fall asleep" said Claudia. "I must tell your Dad about all this when he finishes his game. I know Annabel from the WA, but I've never had much to do with Edmund, apart from if we ever needed to see him about something at the bank. Your dad knows him quite well, though, so he'll be sorry to hear he's having a hard time.

"I remember him being very unpopular right after Dawn died, because everyone was so fond of her, and a whole crowd of the villagers took him to task over his relationship with Annabel. There was a lot of animosity towards them for ages, especially as it came out not long before she died that Dawn had been taking medication for depression. We were all so sad for her. And I'm not surprised Sandra's taken what's happened so badly because it's probably brought up lots of old feelings. She thought the world of Dawn, you know. Anyway, I'd better shut up, or you'll be late for

Secrets, Lies, and Puppy Dog Eyes

your appointment. Good luck, and take care okay?"

Megan looked at her watch. "Yes, I'd better get going. And you take care, too. And give my love to Dad, won't you? And don't drink too many cocktails."

"I will, I will and I won't," said Claudia. "Love you, darling."

"Love you too. Bye for now."

Megan took one more look at herself in the full-length mirror and gave her reflection a nod of approval before grabbing her bag, her phone and her keys.

After losing her job as a corporate event organiser when the company she'd worked for relocated to Sweden, Megan had missed the hustle and bustle it had brought to her life on a daily basis. To her, it had been the perfect job and she'd been devastated when she'd lost it.

However, when her parents had asked her to organise their wedding vow renewal ceremony, the villagers had seen for themselves that Megan was able to put on a party that people would talk about for a long time to come.

In fact, it had gone down so well, word had got as far as the ears of the Detective Inspector who'd come to Bliss Bay recently to investigate a series of murders. Before he left, Sam Cambridge had asked Megan if she'd be interested in organising his daughter's eighteenth birthday party in November, and she'd accepted the job immediately.

To be able to do what she loved, in the company of her family and friends, was almost perfect. If it wasn't for the fact that her pig of an ex-husband and his witch of a wife also lived in the village, it would be *absolutely* perfect.

She threw a cat treat to Tabastion and ruffled his fur. Since his operation, she'd been sure to make an extra-special fuss of him and he seemed to have forgiven her, because he lay on his back with his legs outstretched and batted at her gently with a paw, his claws well and truly retracted.

"I'll be back later, Tab. Wish me luck." She gave him one last fuss before closing the front door behind her and setting off to meet her first proper paying client since arriving in Bliss Bay.

As she pulled off the drive, she remembered she was down to her last five-pound note, so took a detour via the bank to use the cash machine.

She fished her bank card from her purse on the short walk to the bank, only to be confronted with an OUT OF ORDER sign across the keypad. Her heart sank. Unless there was no other option, she avoided the

Secrets, Lies, and Puppy Dog Eyes

bank like the plague because Kelly worked as a senior cashier there.

Can I manage on £5.00 to get me through the day? Megan hesitated outside, trying to work out if that would be enough before realising with a sigh that it wouldn't be. If she needed to pay for parking, there was no way five pounds would cover it, and not every machine accepted payment by credit card. She would just have to go into the bank and avoid eye contact with Kelly.

She might even have the day off, she told herself, hopefully, as she pushed open the heavy glass door, but no such luck.

Kelly sat behind the first counter sporting her current hair colour; deep violet with ash-blonde highlights. She was talking and smiling at the customer at the window, counting out their cash and sliding it to them in the tray. As soon as she saw Megan, though, the smile vanished and her face contorted in a hateful expression.

Megan joined the queue, praying she'd be called to another counter. But this obviously wasn't her lucky day.

Cashier number one, please, said the recorded message, when it came to her turn.

She made her way to the counter and dropped her bank card into the tray under the window. "Hello, Kelly. The cash machine isn't working, so I'd like to withdraw fifty pounds from my account, please," she said, as pleasantly as she could.

Kelly glared at her through the glass for what seemed like an age before leaning forward and speaking very quietly, but very clearly. "Do you have any idea how upset Julie was after your interfering uncle stuck his nose in where it wasn't wanted?"

Megan frowned. "I'm sorry, I don't know what you're talking about."

"I'm talking about your uncle backing up what that stupid cow Fern was saying about Edmund and Annabel; that someone else had pinned up that obituary because they might have a grudge against them, when it was obviously her mistake that she didn't have the guts to own up to."

"Oh, right." Megan stared at her bank card, which was still sitting in the tray. "Well, all he was doing was agreeing with Fern—I did too, actually. He's known her for years, and he believed her when she said she hadn't had anything to do with it. Julie obviously thought otherwise, though. It's not a crime for people to disagree with each other, you know."

Kelly looked a little taken aback, as though she couldn't believe Megan had spoken up. "Yes, I'm aware of that," she hissed, "but she was in tears by the time she got to my place because your uncle shouted at her, and he was bullying her in a very threatening way. He's lucky she hasn't pressed charges against him."

"*What*? Oh, for heaven's sake!" said Megan. "Des certainly *didn't* shout at her, and he didn't threaten her, either. If anyone was raising their voice, it was Julie, not Des. And if she really *was* crying by the time you saw her, it's probably because she deliberately poked herself in the eye to make you think she was upset, because she certainly wasn't crying before. For your information, *she* was the one who was saying vile, hateful things—no one else. If anyone was doing any bullying, it was her." Megan pointed to her card. "Look, I'm on my way somewhere, so I don't have time for this. Do you have any intention of giving me my money, or should I go to another cashier?"

Kelly's painted lips smiled thinly. "I'm sure I don't need to remind you that it wouldn't be a very good idea to upset any of my friends again. We're a very close group, as I'm sure you'll remember, and we don't take kindly to people ganging up on us."

"Did you listen to a word I just said?" Megan met Kelly's gaze through the window, matching her steeliness. "*No one* ganged up on Julie. And is that a threat?"

Kelly shrugged. "Call it what you like. You haven't been back in Bliss Bay for long, so I'm just letting you know the way things work around here. I've already had to warn you off my husband, but I didn't think I'd need to do the same for my friends."

"You know what? You really are unbelievable." Megan wasn't sure if it was because there was a glass screen between them that gave her the courage to stick up for herself against Kelly, but once she'd started, she found she couldn't stop.

"How *dare* you accuse my uncle of bullying after all you put me through when we were younger?" she whispered, her voice shaking with anger. "Everyone else in the village might have forgotten about it, but I *never* will. You and your group of cronies were the biggest bullies around and you went out of your way to make my life as miserable as you possibly could. Well, I'm not standing for it now, Kelly—not from you, or Julie, or any of you. You're forty years old—don't you think it's about time you grew up and stopped behaving like a stupid, spiteful schoolgirl?"

So far, the conversation between them had been reasonably quiet. The counters were far enough away from each other to ensure that other customers couldn't eavesdrop but, suddenly, Kelly said in a voice loud enough for everyone in the entire bank to hear,

"I can't take much more! You've been chasing after Laurence ever since you got here. *I'm* married to him now, not you, but you can't get over the fact that he left you for me, can you?" She took a deep breath and her voice trembled. "I've tried to accept that you've come back to Bliss Bay, and I was hoping you'd be civil enough so we could all live in the village together without any trouble but, obviously, I was wrong. Please, Megan, please leave my husband alone—I'm begging you!"

Megan realised the bank had gone completely silent and she shuffled uncomfortably on the spot. "I don't know what you're playing at, but you know very well that's not true," she whispered. "I've already told you that I have absolutely no interest in Laurence whatsoever. Now, if I could just have my money, please?"

Kelly stared back at her, then covered her face with her hands and burst into tears. Except they weren't real tears. Megan had seen Kelly's old trick enough times when they were young to know they were crocodile tears. Lots and lots of noise, but not a single tear.

The dramatics were enough to drum up the sympathy vote, though. Every customer in the bank—some of whom Megan knew—was glaring at her, furious that she'd upset their favourite cashier.

"I think you should make yourself scarce, don't you?" said another grim-faced cashier through the window, as she patted

Kelly on the back and handed her a box of tissues.

"Nothing would make me happier, believe me," said Megan, "but I'm still waiting for my fifty pounds." She picked up her bank card and waved it in the air.

Begrudgingly, the cashier took the card and gave Megan her cash. As she put it in her purse, a woman at the front of the queue said, "You should be ashamed of yourself, upsetting poor Kelly like that."

"I never had you down for a trollop, Megan," said another, shaking her head.

Megan opened her mouth to reply, then decided it wasn't worth the effort. As she turned to leave, she caught Kelly's eye, and saw the brief spiteful smile she sent her way, before she continued with the amateur dramatics and disappeared from view behind a crowd of well-wishers.

ooooooo

"And I want loads of pink and red sparkles—crystals and stuff like that. And a three-tier red velvet cake with white icing and edible pink glitter on it. And can you arrange life-sized pink and red fluffy unicorns so we can just have them dotted around the house? Ooh, and I'd like pink and red full-face masks to be handed out to people as they arrive. D'you know the type I mean?"

Secrets, Lies, and Puppy Dog Eyes

Megan nodded and smiled across the table at Zoe Cambridge. She scribbled notes in her book before flicking through the supplier manual from her corporate days, stopping at a page filled with masks of every description. "Something like this, you mean?"

"Oh, wow! Yes, *exactly* like that. Ooh, I like this one best; the one with the sparkly bits around the eyes."

Megan grinned. "I wouldn't expect anything less. Anything else?"

"Um, oh, yeah. Would you be able to get a chocolate fountain?"

"With pink or red chocolate?"

Zoe's eyes widened. "Are you being serious? You can seriously get a chocolate fountain with, like, actual pink or red chocolate?"

Megan nodded. "If that's what you want. I mean, I'm only guessing, but I assume you're quite fond of pink and red?"

Zoe giggled. "Am I that predictable? They're my favourite colours. You'll have to come and see my bedroom before you go. It's got two pink walls and two red walls and a pink and red spotted carpet and curtains."

"I don't go in there often," said Zoe's mum, Jillian, with a grin. "Not unless I want a migraine."

"Anyway, d'you think you'll be able to do all that?" said Zoe.

"I don't think it'll be a problem," said Megan

"Seriously? Dad said there was no way you'd be able to do the unicorns." Zoe clapped her hands. "This is going to be SO awesome!"

Megan ran through the list of requirements for Zoe's party one more time. "Okay, if that's everything, I'll get started on organising things. And if you change your mind about anything, or want anything else, can you let me know as soon as possible, because there may be some things that might be difficult to change at very short notice."

Zoe nodded and flicked her pink and red highlighted hair over her shoulder. "Thanks, you've been amazing. I'm kind of disappointed about the eighteen pink and red kittens, but I suppose it's not such a good idea after all, is it?"

Megan resisted the urge to roll her eyes. "Er, no, it's not. If kittens were supposed to be pink and red, they'd already be those colours. And I never agree to requests for animals or birds at any event I organise. Can you imagine how distressed they must be in the middle of a party with loud music, flashing lights and people who've had too much to drink? I just won't have any part of it, however much money I'm offered. I'd turn a job down before I got involved in that."

"Yeah, I get it now," said Zoe. "I'd just never thought of it like that before. I mean, it's a shame, but I wouldn't want to be responsible for scaring an animal, so it's probably for the best."

"*Definitely* for the best." Megan closed her notepad and slid a card across the table. "Here's my number if you need to call me about anything, okay?"

Zoe nodded. "Thanks. I'm going to go and call Suki. She's going to be so jealous!"

Megan turned to the woman who'd sat through the meeting, listening to everything, but saying little. "I'll put together a quote and give you a call, Mrs Cambridge. Likewise with Zoe, if you have any questions, or concerns, just give me a call."

Jillian Cambridge gave her a wide grin. "Please, call me Jillian. My mother-in-law is Mrs Cambridge, not me. How on earth you do this job, I have no idea. Dealing with requests for fluffy unicorns and sparkly things would drive me round the twist. And don't even get me *started* on the kittens! If *you* hadn't said no, *I* would have."

Megan laughed. "Believe me, unicorns and sparkles are nothing compared to some of the things I've been asked for. I have a feeling Zoe's birthday party is going to be a pleasure to organise."

Sherri Bryan

The front door opened and a familiar voice called out. "I'd recognise that beaten up old Mini anywhere." DI Sam Cambridge strode into the kitchen, kissed his wife and held out an arm to shake Megan's hand. "I can't believe it's still going."

"That Mini will probably last longer that you and me," said Megan, with a chuckle. "It's good to see you again."

"Likewise. Dare I ask how much the bill is for Zoe's shindig?" Sam pulled a face and put his fingers in his ears.

"I'm going back to Bliss Bay to make some calls and work on some figures, and then I'll give you a call. If it reassures you to know, I'm pretty sure the budget you've set is going to be more than enough."

Sam grinned and let out an exaggerated breath. "That's the best news I've had since I heard the words unicorns and crystals. When you've got a figure, just give Jill or I a call, okay? Jill works in Social Services, so we're both in meetings a lot of the time. If you can't get one of us, try the other." He took off his jacket and slid it over the back of a chair. "Do you have to rush back, or have you got time for a cuppa? I can't stay long myself, but I've got a spare half an hour, so I thought I'd pop home to say hello."

Megan nodded. "I've got time."

"So, how're things in Bliss Bay?" said Sam.

"Well, we're all out of murderers since you left, thank goodness, although we had a strange thing happen a couple of days ago." She told Sam about the obituary.

Jillian shivered. "Oh, that's horrible! The poor woman. Is she alright?"

Megan nodded and sipped her coffee. "She seems to be. She seems to take everything in her stride. Her husband didn't take it very well at all, though." She turned to Sam. "What do you make of it?"

Sam stared at his coffee. "Well, I don't want to worry you, but that doesn't sound good to me. It could be a bad joke, but someone who's going to all that trouble sounds to me like they might be building up to something bigger." He held up his hands. "I could be totally wrong, of course, but that's my gut opinion without knowing anyone, or anything else about it. It doesn't sound like a kid's prank, put it that way."

"You mean like someone's out for vengeance?" said Jillian.

Sam shrugged. "Possibly. There are plenty of reasons for someone to start a campaign of harassment. Not that I'm saying that's what this is, of course."

"Blimey, I hope you're wrong," said Megan, with a look of alarm. "It's all been pretty peaceful since you left the village, and that's just the way we like it."

"In that case," said Sam, "forget I said a word about it. It's probably nothing like that." He changed the subject. "How's old Fred doing? He was quite deflated when the team and I left Bliss Bay. He told me how much he'd enjoyed working on that last murder investigation, and he wishes there were more cases like that for him to get involved in. A village bobby's life isn't usually so exciting, you know."

"Yeah, and thank goodness for that," said Megan, taking another sip of her coffee. "Fred Denby might be yearning for the all-action life, but I'm very happy that things are back to normal, thank you very much. It's bad enough that my Uncle Des is itching to get back into crime busting."

Sam chuckled. "Now there's a character. If I have half his savvy when I'm his age, I'll be a happy man." His phone rang and he gulped down the rest of his coffee. "Duty calls, I'm afraid, so I must be getting back. I'll be seeing you." He grabbed his jacket and turned back before leaving the room. "By the way, just because I'm curious by nature, what was the name of the woman involved?"

Secrets, Lies, and Puppy Dog Eyes

"In the obituary, you mean?" said Megan. "It was Annabel Hillier."

Sam nodded and tapped his forehead. "Righto, that's stored up there in the old grey matter now. Not that I'll ever need it, I'm sure, but old habits die hard. I'll speak to you soon, no doubt."

Chapter 6

At the village police station, PC Fred Denby dropped heavily into his chair and rubbed his aching feet and his full stomach.

He'd spent the entire morning working on 'The Obituary Incident', which had involved door to door visits to all the houses in the vicinity of the church, and a great deal of Bliss Bay hospitality. It was virtually impossible to knock on a villager's door without being invited in for a chat, a cup of tea and a slice of cake. It was one of the reasons Fred loved doing house to house enquiries, but he'd had to add an extra two holes to his belt since he'd come to the village.

As he cast his eyes over the piece of paper Fern Rudd from the church office had given him that morning, he didn't mind admitting that the hairs on the back of his neck had stood up when he'd read the obituary someone had gone to so much trouble to write, and pin to the noticeboard after dark.

It is with great sadness that the family of Annabel Hillier announce her sudden passing at the age of 61.

Annabel will be sadly missed by the entire community, but especially by her surviving family members;
her loving husband, Edmund, their daughter, Polly, her stepdaughter, Teresa, her stepson, Barnaby, her granddaughter, Beatrice, her

son-in-law, Gary, her daughter-in law, Caroline, her parents, Joseph and Violet Hemsworth, her sister, Pamela, her brother-in-law, Dominic, and her nephew, Kilby.

Rest in Peace, Annabel.

Luckily, Fern had had the foresight not to dispose of it but, instead, had filed it in a plastic wallet. However, it was unfortunate that, prior to that, it had been ripped from the noticeboard by Edmund Hillier, who'd passed it to Annabel before thrusting it into the hands of Reverend Patrick Beale when he arrived in response to Edmund's irate phone call, who'd passed it to Julie, who'd eventually handed it to Fern.

And as if that wasn't bad enough from an evidence gathering point of view, Fred also learned that it had then passed through the hands of most of the villagers who, upon hearing about the scandal, had popped into the church office for a gossip with Julie, and a first-hand look at the notice that had caused so much hoo-ha.

"Edmund wants us to arrange a fingerprint and swab test so we can exclude the family's DNA from any other that's found on the note," he said to his sergeant, Glen Tibbs, who had just walked down the stairs from his office on the top floor. "It's not going to be an easy job to pin down whoever was responsible, though, because it's been handled by half the village." Fred scratched his head and yawned. "And no one I've spoken to saw a thing."

"Well, we need to keep on top of it," said Glen. "Edmund Hillier is a very influential man, and he donates very generously to various police charities, among others."

Fred nodded. "I know, Sarge. We'll find whoever's responsible before too long, you mark my words."

ooooooo

Megan drove back to Bliss Bay, feeling a lot calmer than when she'd left it.
The incident with Kelly had turned her insides to jelly but she was proud of herself for standing up to her. Little by little, the confidence that had been knocked out of her over the years was coming back.

In need of a little human contact with someone who didn't want to rip her head off, she steered the car in the direction of her uncle and aunt's house.

"Hello, love," said Des, dropping a kiss on Megan's forehead and clasping his arms around her in a hug. "I wasn't expecting a visit from you today. Did everything go okay with your first client?"

"I just wanted to see you, that's all, and, yes, everything went fine." Megan walked through to the kitchen to find
Aunt Sylv wearing a pair of work goggles and a headlamp, and wielding a welding iron. In the

Secrets, Lies, and Puppy Dog Eyes

Harper household, Des shopped and cooked, and Sylv did everything else.

"Hello, sweetheart," she said, squeezing Megan in a hug that sent the air hissing from her lungs. "You want some lunch? We've just had ours, but there's some left. Des made some hotchpotch soup, and it's lovely with a bit of crusty bread."

The thought of a bowl of Des's soup, which contained just about everything he could find in the fridge and kitchen cupboards, made Megan realise how hungry she was. "Yes, please. That sounds great. By the way, Uncle Des, I saw Kelly in the bank and she told me that Julie said your behaviour was very threatening the other day, and you really upset her." She rolled her eyes. "Of course, I told her you *didn't* threaten her, and she *wasn't* upset, but you know what that lot are like. I thought I'd better let you know in case Julie makes a complaint. I'm sure she won't, but you never know."

Sylvie took off her goggles, her eyes bulging in their sockets. "That bloody woman! If I could get my hands on her, I'd wring her scrawny neck! What a nerve she's got. Des wouldn't hurt a fly."

"Well, I think the whole village know that," said Megan, "so I doubt anyone would believe her, but I thought you should know, just in case."

Des nodded. "Thanks for telling me, love. Funnily enough, when I spoke to Patrick earlier about Fern, I also told him that Julie's attitude had a lot to be desired, so he already knows what happened. I'm pretty sure if she were to make any accusation, he'd believe my version of events."

"I hope so," said Sylvie, the frown between her eyebrows getting deeper by the second, "or *I'll* be paying Julie Cobb a visit at the church office to tell her a few home truths. *I'll* give her threatening behaviour," she muttered.

Des chuckled. "I'm sure it won't get as far as the police, so don't worry, Sylv. Speaking of which, Megan, we had a visit from Fred not long ago. He was doing house to house calls. He went to the Hillier place this morning and then he went to the church to see if he could get his hands on the obituary."

"And, did he?"

"Yes. He showed it to us, didn't he Sylv? It looked just like the real thing, so I doubt it was kids playing a joke."

"Well, I happened to see Sam Cambridge earlier when I went to meet his daughter, and he said a similar thing when I told him what had happened. He said his gut reaction is that it could be a harassment campaign against the Hilliers. Obviously, he's only speculating, but he said that's what it sounds like it could be."

"Honestly, I don't know why some people don't find better things to do with their time," said Sylvie.

"I spoke to Mum earlier and told her what's been going on," said Megan, dunking a doorstep of bread into her soup. "She said everyone loved Dawn Hillier. What did you think when she died?"

"Same as everyone else, I should think," said Sylvie. "It was a terrible shock, especially as there was a rumour going around for a while that she might have committed suicide. She was such a lovely woman, very kind and full of fun most of the time, but she used to get very down every now and then. I never asked her why, because I felt it would have been too intrusive. It wasn't long before she passed away that some blabbermouth at the doctor's surgery let it slip that she was taking antidepressants. Some people wondered if she'd taken her own life, although the police eventually decided it was a suspicious death.

"And then Edmund took off with Annabel, which made the whole situation even worse." She clicked her tongue. "You can imagine the gossip, can't you? Mind you, between you and me, I never thought he and Dawn were well-suited. She needed someone who was going to sweep her off her feet and tell her how much he adored her, and that definitely wasn't Edmund. He was far too reserved for that. She craved affection, but he didn't even seem to notice. And then he got promoted at the bank and he took his job so seriously, he and Dawn hardly saw each other." Sylvie scratched her nose and frowned. "All this was a long time ago, though, love, so some of my facts might be a bit wonky."

Megan nodded. "And what about Annabel? What's your opinion of her now?"

"She's very pleasant. It took a while for us to take to her, but you can't help but like her. Not all the villagers are quite so accepting of what happened, though. Some of them still think badly of her and Edmund to this day."

"You mean people like Sandra Grayling?"

"For one, yes. She was horrified." Sylvie drummed her nails on her welding iron. "And when Edmund stood at Dawn's graveside and threw a rose onto her coffin, he clearly said, "I'm sorry", which upset a lot of people. Some of the mourners thought he was saying sorry because Dawn was dead, but most of them thought it was an apology to her because he'd wasted no time in finding someone to take her place."

"I suppose emotions were running high," said Megan, "seeing as Dawn was so well-liked, so I can understand why there was so much animosity flying around."

"She obviously wasn't well-liked by everyone, though," said Des, thoughtfully, "or she'd probably still be alive."

Megan shuddered and spooned the last of her soup from the bowl. "Thank you, that was delicious."

"What are you up to later?" asked Des.

"I'm taking Jack to the vet to see a Boxer puppy. He's been talking about getting a dog for a while, and I think this pup might be the one. If he takes him, he'll be leaving him with his Aunt Rita during the day until he's finished work, so you can pop over the road to say hello to him."

"Oh, that'll be nice," said Sylvie. "How are you and Jack getting on these days, by the way?"

Megan smiled. Sylvie never took off her matchmaking hat. "Just fine, thank you. No romance, and no church bells ringing, so you don't need to buy a new outfit."

"Not yet," said Sylvie, with a knowing smile.

"Not ever!" replied Megan. "I've told you a million times that Jack and I are just friends, so please stop thinking we're about to walk down the aisle and provide you with a huddle of great nieces and nephews, or whatever the relationship would be." She looked at the time. "Right, I'll wash this bowl up and then I'd better make a move"

She hugged them both and turned back to Sylvie as she stepped out of the front door. "Oh, and if Jack proposes while we're at the vets, you'll be the first to know."

ooooooo

"Let's go in my car," said Jack. "Not that I don't love Vinnie the Mini, but mine's a little more comfortable for me from a legroom point of view."

Megan shrugged. "Okay. Can we stop off at the shop on the way, though, because I'm running a little low on cat food until I do a proper shop? I just want to pick up a couple of trays."

"No problem. Actually, I need some bananas. I never get a chance to stop when I'm working, so I can eat them on the go."

Jack pulled up on the small forecourt and nodded to the swing chair with its striped canopy that had stood outside the village shop for years. "If it wasn't for that chair, we might never have met up again," he said, referring to their first meeting.

"I think we probably would have," said Megan. "After you bought the school, the entire village was talking about you, so I'm sure we'd have bumped into each other at some point."

They were about to go into the shop when a couple came out and passed them on the forecourt. "Teresa?" said Megan.

The blonde woman with the ruddy complexion turned, her friendly face breaking into a wide smile when she saw Megan. "Hi! How are you? William, you know Megan, don't you? Megan, this is William Longhurst."

Tall, with cropped hair, and piercing dark eyes in a gentle-looking face, William put the cigarette he was holding into his left hand and gave Megan and Jack a firm handshake.

"We know of each other, but it's been a long time."

"I don't know if you know Jack Windsor?" asked Megan.

Teresa shook her head, blushing furiously. "Not personally, but we've heard of you, obviously. Nice to finally meet you in person at last."

Megan touched Teresa's arm lightly. "I was sorry to hear about what happened."

"Likewise," said Jack.

"The obituary, you mean?" Teresa frowned. "It's been horrendous. Annabel's trying to deal with it rationally but Dad's being so over-protective, he's treating her like she's made of eggshells, which is driving her crazy. I've been trying to keep Dad's spirits up, and Polly's just breezing through the days as though nothing's happened."

She rubbed her brow and sighed. "Of course, I suppose she has to be like that for Beatrice's sake, because we don't want her to know too much—she's only nine. And Barnaby's not around—it would be a lot easier for me if he was, because it'd take some of the pressure off—but it's hard for him to get away from work. And Dad's not very impressed that PC Denby's been dealing with it. I think he thought a team of detectives were going to come roaring down to the house with their lights flashing and their sirens wailing. He was quite miffed that he ended up with the village bobby. Anyway, we've talked of nothing else since it happened, so could we change the subject, please?"

"How about we talk about the Christmas concert?" said William. "Will you be coming? It's in the market square on Christmas Eve."

Jack shrugged. "Hadn't given it a thought. Didn't even know about it until just now. Are you selling tickets?"

William shook his head and took a deep drag on his cigarette, blowing the smoke up in the air, above their heads. "Sorry, filthy habit I know. It'll probably kill me one day, but we all have to go one way or another, don't we? Anyway, what was I saying? Oh, yes, the

Secrets, Lies, and Puppy Dog Eyes

concert. No, there are no tickets—it's free admission—but we're organising it, so we're spreading the word. That's why we've just been in the shop, to ask Olivia if she'll put up a couple of posters for us. It's going to be fantastic."

"William's creating a giant Christmas snow scene for the backdrop, aren't you?" Teresa said, proudly. "He's an extremely good artist, but very modest. He'll tell you that Annabel and I have done *loads* to help, but all we've done is make lots of tea, make encouraging noises, and help organise the choir. He's doing all the arty stuff. He's been working on the scene day and night, and it looks amazing so far. I can't wait until it's finished."

"Well, let's just say it's a joint effort," said William, "because Beatrice designed the posters, and Edmund and Polly have been helping to spread the word." He opened the bag he was carrying, which was filled with pieces of rock, wood, leaves and tree bark. "I've just been down on the beach collecting all this. I use it in lots of my pieces to add texture, and it's particularly effective in what I'm working on at the moment. If I do say so myself, I think it's going to look really good when it's done."

He took another drag of his cigarette. "And we're trying to get Dirk Boulder—you know, the lead singer from the heavy metal band, Nails Down a Chalkboard—to open the concert. He's playing a gig not far from here the day before, so we're waiting to see if he can drop by on his way home.

"It's a long shot, but it'd be great if he could come. You might think he's a strange choice to open a Christmas concert, but at his band's Christmas gigs, they always have a proper traditional carol. In fact, their version of The Holly and the Ivy is the best I've ever heard." He looked at Teresa. "Why are you staring at me like that?"

She shook her head. "William! You're *such* a bigmouth! That was supposed to be a surprise!" She looked at Megan and Jack. "Please don't tell anyone about that, will you?" She shot William an irritated glare and shook her head. "It'd be nice if we can keep *some* things up our sleeve until the concert."

Megan drew a finger and thumb across her lips. "We won't say a word, will we, Jack?"

Jack saluted. "Scout's honour."

"Sorry about that," said William. "I'm just excited about the concert, and things slip out." He looked at Megan and Jack through narrowed eyes. "Didn't you come back to Bliss Bay just recently? This'll be your first Christmas in the village for a while, won't it?"

They nodded.

Secrets, Lies, and Puppy Dog Eyes

"I thought so. Well, you're in for a treat. We've been holding the concert in the market square since it was revamped a few years ago, and each year's better than the last, isn't it, Teresa?"

"It really is," she gave an enthusiastic nod. "The trees are all lit up, and there are lights and candles everywhere. If we're lucky, we'll get a bit of snow, too, and it'll be just perfect. You must try to make it if you can. The whole village turns out for it."

"I'll definitely be there, said Megan. Mum and Dad will be home by then, and my sister will be here with her boyfriend, so it'll be a real family Christmas."

"Will your daughter be here, too?" asked Teresa. "You *have* got a young daughter, haven't you, or am I confusing you with someone else?"

Megan gulped. "Yes, I do have a daughter, but she'll still be away on her gap year. She'll be here in spirit, though." She forced a laugh so she didn't burst into a flood of tears at the thought of being without Evie at Christmas. "And she's twenty, so probably a bit older than you thought."

"Oh, right. Yeah, she's quite a bit older," said Teresa. "Anyway, we have to dash. We've got to get dinner on the go and then we've got a practice with the choir." She smiled and buttoned up her coat. "No doubt we'll see you around." She grabbed William's arm and they strode off, marching hard against the cold.

"Yeah, be seeing you," said Jack, as they stepped into the shop.

"Hi, Olivia," said Megan, looking at a pile of Christmas calendars Olivia was pricing. "You don't look very full of Christmas cheer."

"That's because I'm bloody well not," said Olivia. "I've just got off the phone from our poultry supplier and he said he might not be able to deliver the organic turkeys that people have placed orders for until December the 27th. I ask you, what good is a flipping' turkey on December the 27th? I asked him what I was supposed to tell my customers and d'you know what he said? He said to tell them they'll have to go vegan, or they'll have to wait a couple of days before they can 'gobble' up their Christmas dinners. He thought it was hilarious, but I wasn't impressed." She pointed to her face. "See? This is my 'not impressed at all' face." She stuck a price ticket on the back of a calendar and scowled.

"I'm going to see if Rob has more luck than me. When he gets back from the wholesaler, I'll ask him to give the supplier a call, and I bet he'll give Rob a different story. He talks to me in such a patronising tone, I'm sure he thinks I'll just accept whatever he tells me because I'm a woman." She punched a fist into her palm. "He won't be thinking that if he doesn't deliver my flippin' turkeys on time, I can assure you."

Megan chuckled and took a couple of trays of cat food from the shelf. "Well, I'm sorry for the trouble, but he only said he *might* not be able to deliver them on time, didn't he? He's probably telling everyone that to cover himself."

"Hmpf, well, if that's the case, he's going to have a Christmas mutiny on his hands. I take it you know that one of the turkey orders is for your Mum? She placed it before they went on their cruise."

Megan's face fell. "No, I didn't. Oh blimey." She shrugged. "Well, we'll just have to eat something else, won't we? It's not the end of the world."

"Not for you, maybe," mumbled Olivia. "Anyway, where are you off to? "

"We're going to meet Jack's new dog... sorry, his *possible* new dog. He's gorgeous. Anyway, we'll see you soon. And good luck with the turkey guy."

ooooooo

"You go in and I'll park," said Jack, when they got to the vet. "It's a bit of a tight space, and I don't want to block anyone in."

Megan nodded and walked into the waiting room where, Nell, the receptionist was reading from a celebrity magazine.

Sherri Bryan

"Oh, hi, Megan," she said. "You've come to see Boxer, haven't you?"

"Yes, and I've brought my friend with me. I'm hoping he's going to fall in love with him as much as I did."

"If you take a seat, Liam's just finishing up with a client. He won't be long." Nell carried on with her magazine. "Here, listen to this, *The sound of hearts breaking all over Ascot in Berkshire must have been deafening as Jack Windsor left the county behind to make tracks for his new home in the village of Bliss Bay in Devon.*

Mr Windsor—who, until recently, was one half of the international advertising agency, Windsor McQueen—is reported to be looking for a quieter life, having lived on the sharp edge of the marketing industry for the best part of two decades.

Having put in a winning bid for the old Bliss Bay School, Mr Windsor will be making it his permanent home once it's been sympathetically renovated.

Ascot's loss is Bliss Bay's gain!"

Nell turned to Megan and held up the magazine. "Oh my, just *look* at him. He's like a Norse God—Thor springs to mind—except he's got dark hair. I saw him in the high street the other day and I walked into a lamppost because I couldn't take my eyes off him. "She looked down again at the picture of Jack and sighed. "Absolutely flippin' gorgeous. I wouldn't mind putting my slippers under his bed, if you know what I mean," she said, with a wink.

Nell was so obvious, there was no doubt in Megan's mind as to what she meant.
"Hmm, there's definitely something about him, isn't there?"

The bell above the door buzzed and Nell looked up to greet her next client, the smile suddenly frozen on her lips.

"Hey, I'm with Megan," said Jack. "I've come to see the Boxer puppy." He frowned and waved a hand in front of Nell's face.
"Hello. Are you okay? Megan, is she okay?

"What?" Nell came out of her trance. "Oh, yes, I'm fine. I was just dreaming about you. I mean, I was *reading* about you. Yes, that's it, I was just *reading* about you. *Dreaming* about you! Hah! As if. Yes, I was just reading about you and who should walk in but you!" she gabbled. "I was just explaining to your Megan... I mean your girlfriend... *Is* she your girlfriend, by the way? No! Sorry, you don't have to answer that, it's none of my business. OMG, listen to me! Anyone would think I'd never seen a Norse God before. I mean..." Her shoulders dropped and she stared up at Jack's bemused expression.

Megan grinned. Nell's reaction to Jack was similar to her own when she'd returned to Bliss Bay and come face to face with him for the first time. Tall, broad, and incredibly handsome, he also possessed the nature of a mischievous cherub, which made almost everyone he met warm to him. The fact that he was completely unaware of the effect he had on some people only made them love him more.

"I think what Nell's trying to say is that you look, and sound, a little different to a lot of people around here. You do dress a little differently, and you certainly sound different from the locals."

Nell snapped her fingers. "Yes! That's it! That's exactly what I meant." She sent Megan a grateful smile and waited until Liam had called them both into a side room before she rolled her eyes and banged her head against the magazine on the desk.

"Well, here he is," said Liam. He stood back and Jack took his first look at the Boxer pup.

He was still chewing on his rope toy but he looked up with his big blue eyes and fixed his gaze on Jack.

Jack bent down to stroke him. "Hey, little guy. I hear you're looking for a new home?" He picked him up and held him close to his chest, and the puppy blinked his sleepy eyes and licked him on the nose.

Secrets, Lies, and Puppy Dog Eyes

"Well?" said Megan.
"Where do I sign?" said Jack.

CHAPTER 7

The next morning, a kerfuffle on the village green woke Megan.

She pulled on her dressing gown and looked out of the bedroom window to see a number of the women from the WA gathered around the church notice board.

"Oh, no, what now?"

She pulled on a pair of leggings and shoved her feet into her boots, before running across the green to the church.

"What's up?"

"We were just on our way to a WA committee meeting in the village hall," said Dora Pickles. "And we saw this." She pointed to a notice on the board.

It is with much sadness that the family of Edmund Hillier announce his sudden death at the age of 77.

An upstanding member of the community, known for his generous donations to numerous charitable causes, Edmund will be sadly missed by the entire Bliss Bay community.

He is survived by his loving wife, Annabel, his children, Teresa, Barnaby and Polly, his granddaughter, Beatrice, his daughter-in-law, Caroline, and his son-in-law, Gary.

Rest in Peace, Edmund.

"I assume Edmund's still alive and kicking?" said Megan, a brow rising in a perfect arch.

Sylvie nodded. "He was when I saw him in the newsagents this morning."

"Honestly, this is awful," said Megan, with a shiver.

"If only it were true," said Sandra, her voice cutting through the tense atmosphere.

"Sandra! You really shouldn't say things like that," scolded Sylvie. "This is a terrible thing for everyone, not just the Hilliers. What if someone posted an obituary about you? You wouldn't like it, would you?"

Sandra looked away. "Well, we should take it down before anyone sees it." She reached out to open the cabinet and unpin the notice.

"No!" said Megan. "We should let the police take it down. The other one was covered in fingerprints because so many people had touched it, so we should leave this for someone official."

Sandra shrugged. "Suit yourself. Come on, ladies, it's about time we got this meeting underway. As it's the first one I've attended for a while, I don't want us to be distracted by trivial matters like this."

As Sandra strode off, Megan noticed that her eyes were shining, and she looked as though she was trying to hold back tears. It crossed her mind that seeing an obituary for the man she'd once felt so much for might have hit Sandra hard, despite her indifferent attitude.

"Well, we can't just leave it there," said Dora.

"I'll call the police," said Megan. "Go on, you go and have your meeting."

Sylvie patted her on the cheek. "You're a good girl, love. I'll be round after the meeting to see what PC Plod said. Will you be in?"

"I should think so. Pop round whenever you want. Bring Dora, if you like."

Sylvie winked. "Will do."

Megan went back to the house for her phone. She dialled the station number and Fred answered within two rings.

"Hi, this is Megan Fallon from Kismet Cottage on the village green. I'm calling to let you know that there's another obituary on the church noticeboard, but this time it's for Edmund Hillier. Yes, I know, it's not good, is it? Yes, of course, I can stay by it until you get here. Okay, thanks."

She walked back to the noticeboard and lounged against it, sending a text to her sister, Lizzie, straightening up when the sound of heavy puffing and blowing took her attention away from her phone.

"Oh, hi, Uncle... er, Sherlock," she said, as Des pulled to a stop, and swung his leg over

Secrets, Lies, and Puppy Dog Eyes

his bike, wearing his usual padded anorak and jeans, all topped off with a deerstalker hat, complete with earflaps.

"Sylv asked Dora to call me to tell me about the obituary—you know she doesn't like to use her phone unless it's to play games—so I grabbed my gear and came straight over to survey the crime scene."

"What exactly is that on your head?" said Megan

Des touched the hat as though he'd forgotten he was wearing it. "Oh, this. It's rather snazzy, isn't it?"

"If you say so," said Megan, trying to be kind.

"Don't you like it?" Des gave the hat an affectionate pat. "Be honest, now."

"Honestly... not really," said Megan. "But if you like it, that's all that matters."

"Oh," said Des, looking forlorn. "I thought it made me look rather distinguished, in a country gent sort of way. I was looking for a new hat, and I thought this was just the jobbie."

"What's that under your jacket?" said Megan.

"What?" Des's cheeks turned slightly pink. "Oh, that's my notebook. You know I always carry one in my shirt pocket these days. You never know what's going to happen next, so it pays to be prepared."

Megan shook her head. "No, not that side, the other side." She poked at the bulge under his jacket and felt something hard in the inside pocket. "What is it?"

Des sighed as he unzipped his jacket and pulled out a large magnifying glass.

"Blimey, couldn't you get a bigger one?" Megan rolled her eyes "That must only be, what, a foot long?" She tapped her chin with an index finger. "I could be wrong, but I'm pretty sure I remember you saying something about staying "under the radar"?

"Yes, that's right." Des nodded and peered through the magnifying glass to study the obituary at close quarters, one eye clamped shut.

"Well, if you don't mind me saying, there's absolutely nothing "under the radar" about the way you look at the moment. In fact, I'd bet money that if a group of tourists came by right now, they'd be more interested in snapping *you* with their cameras than they would anything else."

Des pulled his most indignant face, just as Fred Denby's car appeared.

"Morning, Des, Megan," he said, as he stepped onto the pavement. "I hope you haven't touched anything?"

"Oh, no, just reviewing the evidence," said Des, turning to Fred, his eye looking as big as a saucer behind his giant magnifying glass.

Fred recoiled slightly. "Right, well, stand back so I can get a good look."

Des stood aside and continued to peer through his new piece of equipment, examining the grass and pathway near the noticeboard for clues.

"Dear, oh dear," said Fred, as he read the obituary. "Dear, oh dear, oh dear. This is not good. This is not good at all."

He unpinned the notice and put it into an evidence bag. "Who the heck is doing this?" he wondered aloud.

Megan shook her head. "No idea, but it's getting a bit personal now, don't you think? And it's not clear whether it's a scare tactic, or a threat. Whatever it is, it gives me the creeps. I dread to think what the Hillier family are going to say when they find out about it."

Fred nodded and scratched his nose. "I have a feeling Annabel isn't going to take the news of this one so well."

ooooooo

"I want police protection! I want a car outside the house 24/7! And I want a full investigation by detectives from Central HQ."

Edmund paced his living room at a rapid rate, his steps almost silent against the deep pile of the carpet. The only other noise in the room came from Annabel, who was curled up on the couch with a duvet, and sobbing quietly.

"Look at my wife! Just look at her! What are you going to do about it? I want answers, Denby, not just the brush-off. And why isn't your superior here? I would have thought this would warrant his involvement."

"He'll be calling round later today," Mr Hillier," said Fred, trying to calm the situation. "And we're doing all we can to find whoever's responsible for this, I can assure you. Look, why don't you sit down and I'll make a nice cup of tea, shall I?"

"Tea?" spluttered Edmund. "We don't want any bloody tea, man! We want the police to find out who's doing this! And pronto!"

Fred stood up and put on his helmet. "I'll get right back to the station now, Mr Hillier, and, er, step up the investigation. We'll keep you informed along the way, of course."

"Be sure that you do," said Edmund, giving him a sceptical look. "And make sure your Sergeant calls round ASAP. I want you to drop everything else and make this your priority, do you understand?"

Fred nodded. "I'll see myself out," he said, sending a sympathetic smile in Annabel's direction. As he made his way back to the station, he passed Teresa and William on the pavement and pulled in to the kerb. "Have you heard the news?"

"What news?" said Teresa.

Secrets, Lies, and Puppy Dog Eyes

"Another obituary was found pinned to the church noticeboard this morning," said Fred. "And this one's for your dad. I'm sorry, I don't mean to alarm you, but I thought you should be forewarned if you're on your way round to his place."

"Oh my God!" Teresa dropped the bag of shopping she was holding and took off down the road at high speed.

"It's not a good situation, is it?" said William, bending to pick up the bag. "I take it you're no closer to catching the culprit?"

Fred shook his head, a glum expression on his face. "Not at the moment, but I'm sure we will."

William nodded. "I don't doubt it. Be seeing you, PC Denby."

ooooooo

At precisely ten-past one, the doorbell rang at the Hillier house and Edmund opened the front door to find Fern Rudd on the doorstep.

"Fern? What are you doing here?"

"I'm sorry to turn up unannounced," she said, "but I wanted to talk to you and Annabel for a minute. I'm sorry if it's inconvenient, but I won't take much of your time."

Edmund showed her into the living room and Annabel breathed a sigh of relief when she saw Fern. "Oh, thank goodness," she said, kicking off the duvet. "After what happened this morning, I was frantic it might be someone coming to do Edmund harm. I begged him not to open the door, but he's gone all vigilante." Annabel smiled weakly. "I didn't feel too bad after seeing the notice about me, but I simply can't deal with the prospect that Edmund might be in danger. Anyway, come in and sit down. Can I get you a cup of something?"

"No thanks," said Fern, perching next to Annabel on the couch. "I've come out in my lunch break, so I don't have long." She clasped her hands together and took a deep breath. "Look, I know this might sound odd, but I wanted you both to know that I had nothing to do with those obituaries. I know some people think I had some involvement in the first one being put on the board, so it wouldn't surprise me if rumours start circulating that I had something to do with the second one, too."

"Don't be silly, Fern," said Annabel. "Why on earth would we think you were involved? We don't, do we Edmund?"

"No, of course we don't," he said, in a gruff voice.

Fern heaved a huge sigh of relief. "That's alright then. I know how stressful it must be for you, but I couldn't bear it if you heard rumours and thought it was me, so I had to let you know it wasn't."

Annabel pulled her into a hug. "Silly girl. We would never think that. Now, how are you and that lovely Colin getting on together? You are still together, aren't you?"

Fern nodded. "I'm really hoping he stays in Bliss Bay but I don't want to keep on at him about it in case I scare him away. He was only planning on being here temporarily."

"Yes, I know." Annabel ran her hand through her hair. "I remember him telling me when he came to fit our new kitchen units. He's a jolly good handyman, I'm glad we took a chance on him. When he first came to the village looking for work, we were among his first customers. I'd like to think we had a little bit to do with him being asked to work on the old school renovation. We've told everyone we know how good the quality of his work is."

"I know, and he's very grateful," said Fern. "Thanks for that. It's kept him here a bit longer, that's for sure."

"Why don't you bring him round for supper one evening? We love to entertain and it'd be lovely to have you."

"Oh, well, we wouldn't want to impose…"

"Nonsense!" said Annabel. "You wouldn't be imposing at all." She scribbled her mobile number down on a piece of paper. "Here, when you've talked to Colin, and you've decided on a suitable date, call me and we can arrange something."

Fern nodded and stood up from the couch feeling much better than when she'd arrived. Speaking to Annabel and Edmund had lifted a huge weight from her shoulders. "Thank you, I'll be in touch then."

"Make sure you are," said Annabel, smiling and waving as Edmund showed Fern to the door.

As soon as Fern was out of sight, the smile dropped from Annabel's face as she curled up again on the couch, and disappeared under the duvet.

ooooooo

Back at the station, Fred flopped down in his chair and looked at the second obituary.

"How the heck are we going to catch the bugger who's doing this?" he said to Glen. "Perhaps we should take it in turns to keep a night watch from one of the houses with a good view of the church. You're still calling round to the Hillier place later, aren't you, Sarge? Edmund's chomping at the bit for a visit from you." He sniffed. "Didn't seem to think I was good enough."

"I am, but something else has just come up that could delay me," said Glen. "I've just had a call from Jack Windsor."

"That American chap?"

Secrets, Lies, and Puppy Dog Eyes

    Glen nodded. "They were ripping out the old school lockers, and they found a textbook shoved behind them with a note inside that gives the identity of Dawn Hillier's killer."

Chapter 8

Police Sergeant Glen Tibbs took the notebook from Jack and dropped it into an evidence bag.

"And you say it was behind the lockers?"

"Yeah. A couple of the guys pulled them away from the wall and it just dropped out. It was pretty dusty and covered in cobwebs, so they were going to throw it in the trash, but Colin flicked through it out of curiosity, and that's when he saw the note. It's been affected by damp at some point, so the bottom of the book has disintegrated and taken some of the note with it, but what's left of it is still pretty readable."

Glen nodded. "We'd like to speak to the men who found it, please."

"Sure." Jack pointed across the room. "Colin's the guy in the yellow shirt and Pete's the guy with him in the green overalls. And they were both wearing work gloves, so they shouldn't have contaminated it any more than it already is. You don't mind if I get back to work, do you? Just shout if you need me, I won't be far away. Oh, and you should have hard hats on while you're in here. I'll get them for you."

ooooooo

Secrets, Lies, and Puppy Dog Eyes

"The original has been sent to forensics, Mr Hillier," said Glen, "but this is a copy of the note that was found."

4th October 1977
To the police.
My name is Curly. I know I should use my real name but that will identify me and, for obvious reasons, I'd rather keep that secret for now.

Dawn Hillier was killed recently. It was an accident but she died, all the same. She wasn't the victim of a robbery gone wrong.

She was a good woman and I'm sorry she's dead. Not that that makes the situation any better, but I want you to know that I really am sorry.

It wasn't a bag snatch—you'll know that when you find the bag, because none of Dawn's money was taken. I can't tell you exactly where it is, all I'll say is that it's not far from the cliffs in the bay.

Dawn was pushed, and she lost her balance, but it wasn't deliberate. I don't think even Red would have done that on purpose.

You're probably wondering who Red is? Well, Red is the person you need to speak to in connection with Dawn's death.

I suppose this note is to ease my conscience. Believe me, I wish I was brave enough to own up to the police in person, but I'm not. You must understand that Red isn't a good person to have as an enemy, and I've been threatened with terrible things if I ever breathe a word of what happened.

So, if you want to know who killed Dawn, you need to speak to Red, whose real name is

"Is what?" said Edmund. "Whose real name is what? Who is this 'Red'?"

"I rather hoped you'd be able to help us with that," said Glen. "As I explained when I called you, the lower half of the note has been exposed to the elements—water or damp, in this case—so the name of the person involved is missing. If you cast your mind back, can you think of anyone who might have been known as Curly or Red?"

"Curly or Red? What sort of nonsense is this?" said Edmund. "They sound like cowboy names in bad westerns."

"Well, they're obviously nicknames," said Glen, "so I wondered if you could think of anyone they may apply to?"

Edmund looked at Annabel, and Teresa and Polly, who'd come straight over when he'd called them to say some crucial evidence had been found during the old school renovation.

"There were some redheads at school, Dad," said Teresa, her cheeks flushed with excitement as she recalled their names. "There was that geeky guy... What was his name? David Bridges, that's it. Do you remember, his nose was *constantly* running. And Maria Connolly. Her hair was so red, it was like someone had painted it on." She frowned. "And there was another guy I can't think of... Hang on, his name will come to me in a minute... I'll get on the phone to Barnaby in a sec, and ask him if he can think of anyone I might not remember."

"For God's sake, Teresa!" bellowed Edmund. "This isn't a joke! I hardly think we're looking for a child. We need to be thinking of *adults* who had red hair." He glared at Glen. "Surely, in light of this new evidence, the case will be re-opened?"

"Actually, that's not my decision," said Glen, "but I've been in touch with Central HQ and that will certainly be my recommendation. They'll take into account the new evidence, and the evidence from the original case, and make their decision based on that."

"And what are you doing about finding Dawn's handbag?" snapped Edmund. "I assume you *are* doing something about it?"

Glen visibly bristled. "Yes, we are. We've already cordoned off the bay, and are in the process of arranging for officers to conduct a search. Without knowing exactly where the bag was buried it'll take time but, if it's there, we'll find it."

"Is Dawn's original case file at Bliss Bay?" asked Annabel.

"No, Mrs Hillier," said Glen. "All the records pertaining to the case would have been transferred to the archives at HQ. If the evidence that was collected back then can be forensically tested, hopefully it'll tell us something we don't already know."

"Well let's bloody well hope so, because you don't seem to know much at the moment!" said Edmund. "Although that shouldn't surprise me after the way I was treated when Dawn died. The police didn't have a shred of evidence against me, yet I was hauled off to the station and treated like a common criminal. You can imagine how that looked in the eyes of the villagers, can't you? It's taken a long time to regain my position in the community, and the trust and respect I lost. Even to this day, I'm sure some people *still* think I was involved in Dawn's death."

"I'm very sorry about that, Mr Hillier." Glen gave an awkward cough. "Anyway, rest assured, we'll be doing all we can. I give you my word."

Edmund rolled his eyes. "How very reassuring," he said, with a droll expression.

Glen's cheeks flushed and he stood up to leave. "Well, if that's all, I'd better head back to the station. Do you have any more questions before I leave?"

Secrets, Lies, and Puppy Dog Eyes

"Did you say the original notebook and the note have already been sent for forensic testing?" said Annabel.

"Yes, that's right, but it will take some time for the tests to be completed. If you have any questions in the meantime, you know how to contact me."

Edmund rubbed his face with both hands. "I want to know the minute you find anything. The sooner we can get some closure on this, the better."

"Yes, of course." Glen nodded a goodbye and made his way to the front door.

Teresa and Polly stood up, too. "We'd better get going as well. We'll see you out, Sergeant Tibbs." They kissed Edmund and Annabel and told them not to worry.

"Teresa, I hate to ask," said Annabel, "but I don't suppose you could stay for a few days, could you? I feel a bit jittery and I think I'd feel better if someone else was here when your dad goes out to play golf and do his Freemasons' stuff. I can't ask Polly. She's so busy with Beatrice and all the PTA stuff she's involved with."

"I don't see why not," said Teresa. "I can do my copywriting from anywhere there's an internet connection, so that's no problem. I'll have to actually work, though, I can't just sit around chatting and drinking tea." She chuckled and Annabel squeezed her hand.

Page 131

"Of course, I understand," said Annabel, the smile coming back to her face. "Thank you, you're a good girl." She turned to Glen. "She's like my own daughter, you know."

Teresa rolled her eyes and smiled. "I'll have to go back home and grab some things and then I'll be back."

"Tell you what," said Annabel. "To make up for the inconvenience, why don't you ask William to come round for dinner whenever he likes, and I'll put on a real spread? I'd suggest you invite him to stay, too, but he's working on that thingy for the Christmas concert in his studio, isn't he? We wouldn't have the room for it here."

"Don't worry," said Teresa. "Even if you did have room for it, I think he'd rather stay in the studio. He's got all his stuff around him there and he doesn't have to worry about making a mess like he would if he came here. But dinner would be great. There's no way he'll turn that down. Give me an hour or so, and I'll be back."

On the way down the garden path, Teresa said quietly, "Dad doesn't mean to be so hard on you, Sergeant Tibbs, it's just that when Dawn died, it was so awful for him. I know how Barnaby and I felt, so he must have felt much worse. I know you'll find that hard to believe, seeing as he got together with Annabel so soon afterwards, but Dawn's death really did hit him hard. Just give him a bit of time to come to terms with everything that's happening at the moment."

"Yeah," said Polly, checking a chip in the varnish on her fake fingernail. "Obviously, I wasn't around then, but I know that Dad really loved Dawn. I didn't know her, but he still talks about her now, so I kind of feel like I do."

Glen nodded. "Unfortunately, I'm quite accustomed to dealing with people who've been on the receiving end of bad news, so I've learned not to take it personally. I quite understand that your father is upset by this development after so long, so I hope we'll be able to bring this case to a close once and for all, and give the former Mrs Hillier the justice she deserves."

Polly nodded. "Of course, we all hope she gets justice but, between you and me, I think Mum deserves a mention, too. I think she's coping brilliantly, under the circumstances. I mean, with all the focus on one of Dad's former wives, you'd think it'd be hard on her, wouldn't you, but she just lets it all go over her head. I'm not sure I'd be quite so understanding. Anyway, see you later."

"Please keep us in touch, won't you Sergeant Tibbs?" said Teresa. "And I know it didn't go very well today, but if you have any news over the next few days, it might make it easier for you to talk to Dad if I'm there. Annabel and I get on very well, you see, and having me there will help take her mind off things. If she's happy, Dad's happy, and that will have a big effect on his mood. Just a thought." She waved over her shoulder as she walked off up the road. "See you soon."

ooooooo

"Can you believe it!" said Glen, slamming down the phone in his office. He ran down the stairs to find Fred standing at the filing cabinet.

"What's up?"

"Central HQ can't find anything on the Dawn Hillier case. All the evidence that was gathered from the scene has gone missing."

"How the heck's it gone missing, Sarge?"

"During the move from their original offices, it seems that a number of old case files were misplaced, so they can't tell me anything about the evidence that was gathered at the time." He rubbed the pads of his fingers against the knotted muscles in the back of his neck. "We might not know much at the moment, but I'll tell you one thing I *do* know. I am *not* setting foot in the Hillier house again until I have something more positive to tell Edmund."

"Well, the evidence that was found today was pretty positive, I'd say, Sarge," said

Secrets, Lies, and Puppy Dog Eyes

Fred. "It's the biggest clue to Dawn's killer yet."

"Yes, *I* know that, and *you* know that, Fred, but nothing happens fast enough for Edmund Hillier." Glen sighed. "I would have preferred not to mention that note to him until we'd had some contact from HQ, but in view of the fact that all the workmen at the old school probably saw it, I didn't want word of it getting back to the Hillier family without having told them about it first."

"Did HQ say how long they think it'll take to find the missing files?"

Glen shook his head. "Let's just say that soon won't be soon enough. In the meantime, rather than sit here and twiddle our thumbs, we might as well try to find out the identity of these 'Curly' and 'Red' individuals, because if there's any truth to that note, someone known as 'Red' pushed Dawn Hillier down that incline."

"I suppose, as you and I weren't here then, Sarge, that means more house-to-house enquiries?" said Fred, wearily, loosening his belt.

"Exactly," said Glen. "There are still a lot of people in the village who might remember who had those nicknames going back forty years."

Fred nodded. "Only thing is, Sarge, back then, they probably weren't particularly unusual nicknames for people with red hair *or* curly hair. We could end up with a list as long as your arm."

"We'll just have to whittle it down until we've found the two we're after, then, won't we?" said Glen, irritably. "I'm sure someone will be able to cast their mind back that far." He put on his hat. "Right, come on. We need to get started and there's no time to waste. There's a killer out there that needs to be caught, and we're going to catch him."

Chapter 9

"You wanted to speak to me about something, Chief?" DI Sam Cambridge stuck his head around the door.

"Ah, yes, Sam, come in." In his office at Central HQ, Detective Chief Superintendent, Rick Wakefield, waved a hand to a chair beside his desk. "I'll come straight to the point. It's a rather sensitive matter, so I wanted to be sure to brief you about it myself." The DCS cleared his throat and clasped his hands on his desk. "I just spoke to a rather irate Bliss Bay resident who called to complain that, in his opinion, the officers at the station aren't taking the investigation into his former wife's death seriously enough. We're members of the same golf club, so we have a tenuous social connection, which is why, I assume, he thought he could get on the phone to me and I'd kick some backsides."

Sam nodded. "And what's that got to do with me?"

"Well, he donates to a lot of worthy causes, Sam, particularly police charities, so I think he'd appreciate a visit. Call it a PR exercise, with a view to allaying his concerns, of course. He just needs someone other than his local officers to explain that forensic testing takes time, and that if there's sufficient new evidence to justify re-opening a case, that's what will happen."

"Can't you give it to someone else, Chief?"

"Actually, he specifically asked for you. Said he was very impressed with the way you and your team handled the recent murder investigations in Bliss Bay. And you don't have anything major on at the moment, do you? Nothing that someone else can't take on, surely? DS Harvey Decker, for example, is very capable."

"Well, that's true, but—"

"Wonderful! That's settled, then." The DCS gave Sam a big grin. "Speak to my assistant on the way out, and she'll give you all the details. She'll also get in touch with PS Tibbs to let him know you'll be visiting the village, but perhaps you could call in at the station anyway as a courtesy." He raised an eyebrow and sent Sam a cautionary glance. "And please remember, Sam, I want Mr Hillier to feel reassured. I wouldn't like him to decide that his generous donations to the police charities could be better spent elsewhere. Do we understand each other?"

Sam nodded. "Whatever you say, Chief. I'll— Sorry, did you say his name was Hillier?"

"That's right. Edmund Hillier."

ooooooo

Sam pulled up outside the Hillier home. It was too much of a coincidence that this was a different Hillier family to the one Megan had mentioned to him, so his interest was piqued.

He wasn't one for turning on the charm. Sam hadn't got to where he was by kissing babies and shaking hands. He'd done it through sheer hard work. Nevertheless, if the DCS wanted him to reassure a concerned member of the community, that's what he'd do. He put on his best smile and Edmund welcomed him in and told him the whole story.

"My entire family are going through hell at the moment. As if the obituaries aren't enough to deal with, we have the upset of Dawn's death being brought up again. I'm sorry to trouble you with this, DI Cambridge, but in view of the new evidence which has come to light and, as you handled the recent murder investigations in Bliss Bay so competently, I wondered if you'd be able to use your influence to bring matters to a swift conclusion."

Sam nodded. "If you're happy to leave it with me, I'll make some enquiries."

"I'd appreciate that very much," said Edmund. "I know that calling DCS Wakefield might have gone above a few heads, but I appreciate how limited the resources are in a village police station. Now there's a chance we might be close to finding out who was responsible for Dawn's death after all these years, I'd like to get a result as soon as possible.

"I understand from Sergeant Tibbs that he's in the process of liaising with someone to locate all the old evidence for the case, to see if it can be tested for DNA, and he tells me the original note that was found today has also been sent for forensic tests." Edmund harrumphed noisily. "Between you and me, I don't have a great deal of confidence in him. I ask questions, but he can rarely give me answers. All he can tell me for sure is that items have been sent for forensic testing and we'll have to wait for results."

"Well, as you've already mentioned," said Sam, "the resources at Bliss Bay *are* extremely limited and, even if they weren't, there's very little Sergeant Tibbs would be able to tell you simply by looking at the new evidence that's come to light. I appreciate it's frustrating, but the reason he keeps repeating that items have been sent for forensic testing is because that's exactly what has happened. I don't doubt that he's well aware of your need for answers, Mr Hillier, but reviewing the evidence in any investigation takes time."

"Yes, yes, I understand that," said Edmund. "I suppose I'll just have to wait. As I mentioned, though, the note that was found also discloses the location of Dawn's handbag, so if there's anything at all you can do to help move things along in getting that found, I'd be very grateful."

Sam nodded. "As I said, I'll make some enquiries. I should tell you that in the light of new evidence—especially that which may reveal the identity of a killer—there's every possibility the case would have been re-opened anyway, particularly if usable DNA samples are retrieved."

"I never understood why the police just stopped the original investigation so soon," said Annabel. "It really didn't go on for very long at all."

"I don't know for sure," said Sam, "but I would imagine that the Senior Investigating Officer who was in charge of Dawn's case simply had to make a decision to stop the investigation in the light of no new leads.

"I know it sounds harsh when a death is involved, but there's only so much the police can do once they're out of suspects, evidence and leads. I know things aren't moving as quickly as you'd like, but I can assure you, everyone involved will be doing everything they can to get results. Leave it with me, though, and I'll see what I can find out.

ooooooo

As soon as Sam got back in the car, he popped an indigestion tablet into his mouth and called Detective Sergeant Harvey Decker to give him a quick update.

"You've got a friend in forensics, haven't you?"

"Yeah, Cheryl Foley. Why?"

"Will you get in touch with her and ask her to let you know if she hears of any evidence coming in that relates to an old suspicious death case in the name of Dawn Hillier?"

Harvey nodded. "Will do, boss. Is it a new investigation?"

"Not for us," said Sam. "Not yet, anyway. Right, I'll see you later. I'm off to smooth the waters with Glen Tibbs who, I would guess, isn't overly impressed that I'm here. Speak soon."

ooooooo

"So the DCS asked you to come?" said Glen, after he'd given Sam a rundown of recent events in the village.

Sam nodded. "But only to show Mr Hillier that his concerns are being taken seriously all the way along the chain. It's no reflection on you, Glen, or you, Fred. You know as well as I do that some people think they can jump the queue because of their social standing within a community, and Edmund Hillier strikes me as being one of them."

"You could say that," said Glen, as his phone vibrated across the desk. "'Scuse me, I'd better take this. What? That's brilliant! Thanks for the call." He punched both fists in the air.

Secrets, Lies, and Puppy Dog Eyes

"Fantastic news! They've found Dawn's handbag, and it's been taken to forensics."

"That's great, Sarge," said Fred.

"What a breakthrough, eh? Along with the tests that are being carried out on the notebook and the note, I have a feeling we might actually be close to finding out what happened to Dawn at long last." Glen smiled for the first time in days.

"In that case, as I'm here, I'll pop down to the site to show my face," said Sam. "Will you keep me in the loop? Just so I know what's going on with everything."

"Will do. And if you could track down the missing file and all the evidence, that would be a huge help," said Glen shaking Sam's hand.

"I'll see what I can do. Good to meet you, Glen, and good to see you again, Fred. Take care."

ooooooo

"You're kidding!" said Megan.

"Nope. Colin found the book behind the lockers, and the note was inside."

Jack sat at Des and Sylvie's kitchen table, wolfing down a third slice of apple and cinnamon cake. "Anyways, I know you like to do a little sleuthing, Des, and I guessed you'd be interested, Megan, which is why I called to ask you to meet me here, so I could tell you both together."

Des's pen sped across the pages of his notebook. "And you say the two names mentioned were Curly and Red?"

"Yeah. Weird, huh? It's a real shame there was damp behind the wall, or I'd have been able to tell you the *actual* name of the killer. This is awesome cake, by the way."

"Can you think of anyone who had red or curly hair back then?" said Megan.

"Loads of people, love," said Sylvie. "Perms were very popular, you see, particularly with women, although I seem to recall that quite a few men had them, too. You didn't see many kids with them, but plenty of adults had perms."

"So there were plenty of people who could have had the nickname, 'Curly', said Megan. "What about people with red hair?"

Sylvie shrugged. "Again, are we talking about natural red hair, or dyed? Loads of people used to colour their hair in those days. Even your mum and me had red hair at one point, although I do remember some natural redheads. Millicent from the baker was a proper redhead, but she's passed away now. And Dougie from the garden centre had a real mop of ginger hair, but is he a killer? I doubt it."

"And what about Felicity Larabie and Tony Trotter," said Des. "They had red hair, didn't they?"

Secrets, Lies, and Puppy Dog Eyes

Sylvie nodded. "Felicity's always had terrible trouble with her bunion, though—right from when she was a teenager—so she'd still have been hobbling away from the crime scene when the police arrived. And didn't Tony emigrate to Holland after he married that lovely Dutch girl, Lotte?"

They sat, drinking tea, Des clicking the end of his pen in and out until Sylvie said, "Oh, my goodness! I can't believe we forgot Sandra and Walter. They both went grey so early, I completely forgot about them."

"Sandra and Walter had red hair?" said Megan.

Des slapped his hand on the table. "Yes! Sandra's was poker-straight, but Walter's was curly!"

"Walter's was more of a reddy-brown," said Sylvie, "but Sandra's was a proper auburn."

"Surely they can't be Curly and Red?" said Megan. "I thought you said Sandra was devastated when Dawn died."

"That's true, she was." Sylvie nodded. "Yes, I think we're barking up the wrong tree with those two. Neither of them is the murderous type."

"But what *is* 'the murderous type'?" said Megan. "We didn't think the *last* murderer in Bliss Bay was 'the murderous type' either, did we? Remember?"

Sylvie shuddered. "I'd rather not, if it's all the same with you. Anyway getting back to Sandra and Walter. I can't explain it, but I really don't think they could have been involved in what happened to Dawn. At worst, Sandra was a little standoffish at times, and Walter was a bit of a jobsworth, but murderers? I really don't think so."

"Hmm, that's why I'm not so sure they're as innocent as they seem," said Des, tapping his nose and giving her a knowing wink. "It's often the ones you least suspect that have committed the biggest crimes."

Sylvie rolled her eyes. "There speaks the voice of experience—Professor Desmond Harper, Criminologist and baker extraordinaire."

Jack snorted. "I'd better get going. Thanks for the cake." He scratched the back of his neck and looked a little embarrassed. "You know, I've never been into the whole village gossip thing, but it was all the guys could talk about this afternoon, so I just kind of got reeled in. Some of them were quite shaken up."

"Did Sergeant Tibbs ask you not to say anything?" said Megan. "Seeing as it's pretty sensitive information."

"No, but seeing as most of the guys saw the note, I guess he didn't think there was any point," said Jack.

Secrets, Lies, and Puppy Dog Eyes

"Well, I'm glad you came round, Jack," said Des, rubbing his hands together. "I've been waiting for a proper chance to get out and do some investigating, and you've provided the perfect opportunity."

"Megan raised an eyebrow at Jack as she saw him to the door. "Yeah, thanks a lot for that."

"Any time," he said, with a grin. "I'll see you around."

"Anyway, Megan," said Des, when she came back into the kitchen. "How about we go round to Sandra and Walter's place to see if we find out anything. When would be the best time for you?"

"Er, how about *never*," said Megan. "For a start, the Grayling's place is like the bogeyman's house in horror movies that everyone warns you to stay away from in case you get dragged in and never seen again. Anyway, if they *were* involved with Dawn Hillier's death, they're hardly going to confess, are they? And what if they get suspicious if you ask too many questions and do us in?"

"Oh, don't be such a scaredy cat," said Des. "Sandra Grayling's bark is worse than her bite and Walter's a nice bloke.
What d'you think they're going to do? Give us poisoned tea and bury us under the floorboards in broad daylight?"

"Des does have a point," said Sylvie. "We knew Sandra long before Dawn Hillier moved to Bliss Bay, and she was quite nice. And Walter's always been okay." She looked at Des. "Although it pains me to say it, I think the old fool's probably right."

Des blew her a kiss. "Thank you for that vote of confidence, my little scorpion." He clapped his hands. "So, what d'you say Megan. Nothing ventured, nothing gained, and all that."

Megan sighed. "Alright, we'll go, but only if you promise me you won't wear that ridiculous hat, and you'll leave the magnifying glass at home. Promise me!"

"But those flaps keep my ears warm," Des protested. "It'll be bloomin' windy up on that cliff."

Megan sighed. "Alright. But can you please leave the magnifying glass here? It'll be bad enough turning up on the doorstep of someone we don't even like, let alone with that thing sticking out of your pocket. I mean, what would you say if one of them asked you what it was for?"

"Oh, for heaven's sake… Alright, I won't take it," grumbled Des, "but I don't know what the point of having it is if I'm never allowed to use it."

Megan exchanged a wink with Sylvie. "So, when d'you want to go, then?"

Secrets, Lies, and Puppy Dog Eyes

"How about now?" said Des, his tone decidedly brighter. "Nothing like striking while the iron's hot, as they say."

Megan shook her head. "Oh no, I'm not going now. It's almost seven o'clock, and it'll be dark soon. I am *not* wandering about on the cliffs when it's pitch black."

"Alright, point taken," said Des. "How about tomorrow morning, then? Say, around ten? I'll cycle round to your place and we can walk from there?"

Megan nodded and pushed herself up from the table, shoving an arm into her coat. "Okay, I'll see you then. And if you haven't heard from us after an hour, Aunty Sylv, will you call out a search party?"

Sylvie chuckled. "I'll set my stopwatch. Now, no more talk of murder tonight, if you don't mind, Des, or you'll drive me round the bend."

Chapter 10

The discovery of Dawn's handbag provided a fresh topic of gossip for the villagers who were inclined to do so and, at The Cobbles Café and Flower Shop, they were making the most of the news.

"Isn't it amazing that they've found it after all these years," said Chris Joyce, the Manager of Fairbrothers' Shoes, as he finished his coffee before setting off to open up the shop.

"I wonder if they'll find any fingerprints?" said Terry, who'd popped in from the fishmongers for a takeaway coffee.

"Let's hope it's covered in them," said local resident, Eleanor Cooper. "We don't need to be sheltering any more killers in Bliss Bay."

"I still think Edmund had something to do with it," said Alison Berman, the village librarian.

"I agree," said Myrtle Finch, who'd popped in for a cuppa on her way to work at Peel's Ironmongers. "If you ask me, her death was a bit too convenient. I mean, what sort of man ends up marrying the woman who's organising his wife's funeral?" She shook her head and rolled her piggy blue eyes. "Lord's sake."

"What do you think, Petal?" said Dora Pickles, munching on a raspberry muffin.

Secrets, Lies, and Puppy Dog Eyes

Petal shrugged. "Don't ask me, I didn't know anything about it until that obituary was found. You've got a few years on me, remember, Dora."

"It wouldn't surprise me if it's one of those mysteries we'll never find out the answer to," said Sylvie, stirring her coffee and watching the world go by out of the window. "There are lots of cases that are never solved, and... Oh, my goodness, it's Sandra!"

The bell above the café door jangled and the chatter stopped as Sandra Grayling walked in, a pair of dark glasses covering her eyes.

"Morning, Sandra," said Amisha, as she cleared a nearby table. "We haven't seen you for a while."

"That's because I haven't been in for a while," snapped Sandra, as she headed for her favourite table in the corner, "but if I'd been aware that you were keeping track of my movements, I would have stopped by to keep you informed." She settled herself in her chair. "Are customers expected to check in at regular intervals these days? Is it something new you've started since I was last here? That being the case, Walter's gone for a walk, and he should be in the vicinity of the market square in about two minutes." She threw Amisha a scowl.

"No, I didn't mean it like that," said Amisha. "I just meant that I know you haven't been feeling too good since all that hoo-ha on the anniversary of Dawn Hillier's death. I hope you're feeling better."

"Well, I seem to recall that you weren't here that day, so how on earth you'd know how I was feeling, I have no idea," said Sandra, oozing hostility. "And—not that it's any of your business—but I had to post a letter, so I thought I'd drop in on the way home for a change of scene. And, while I'm here, I'll have a pot of tea and an Eccles cake. I assume they're back on the menu now that normal service has been resumed?"

"Yes, we have them. I'll bring your order over in a sec," said Amisha, with a beaming smile, which disappeared as soon as she turned her back. "That woman would test the patience of a saint," she whispered to Lionel behind the counter.

"You handle her very well," he whispered back. "And, remember, she's had a bit of a shock, so we can't blame her for being a bit off."

"Yeah, but she's been a bit off ever since I started working here in 2010." Amisha picked up the order and set it down on Sandra's table. "Give me a shout if you need anything else."

"I shall do no such thing," said Sandra, pursing her lips. "You are a waitress, are you not? It is not up to *me* to shout if I need something, it is up to *you* to notice if I do. Now go away and leave me in peace."

Amisha took a deep breath and bit her tongue as she turned on her heel.

"Anyway," said Alison, "I remember Dawn being on tranquillisers. I always wondered if she just fell down the bank because she was drowsy."

"But if she just fell, who took her handbag?" said Myrtle. "And it was antidepressants she was taking, not tranquillisers."

"Oh, yes, that's right," said Alison. "Sad, isn't it, to think that someone so young had reason to take medication to help her get through the day."

"If you ask me, Dawn Hillier must have been loopy," said Myrtle, heaving her big bottom out of the chair. "She had a lovely job, a lovely husband, and two lovely stepchildren, so what did she have to be depressed about?" She twirled her index finger around at the side of her head. "Loopy."

There was a clatter as Sandra got up from her chair so quickly, it fell backwards onto the floor. "How dare you say things like that without knowing all the facts! Dawn was *not* loopy. She was a wonderful woman who had more about her in her little finger than all of you put together." She glared at Myrtle, threw some money onto the table, and stormed out.

ooooooo

At the forensics lab, Cheryl Foley was examining the evidence. "The handbag is weatherworn, obviously," she said, "but the contents have very little damage, considering how long the bag's been buried in the sand."

"What's in there?" asked her colleague.

"There's a cosmetics bag with a lipstick and eye pencil in it, a bottle of antidepressants prescribed to a Mrs D Hillier, a notebook and pen, a comb, a purse full of money, and two photographs in the transparent plastic compartments; one's of a baby, and the other's a wedding photograph." Cheryl sighed. "You know, even after doing this job for all these years, some things still get to me. You'd think I'd be hardened to it by now, wouldn't you? I just look at that baby, and think that some poor kid lost its mum, sister, aunt, godmother, or whatever the woman who died was to it."

"You're too soft for this job, Cheryl," said her colleague.

Cheryl nodded distractedly as she finished what she was doing, then picked up the phone to call Harvey Decker.

"Harve, it's me. Just letting you know that I've got Dawn Hillier's handbag. It still has to be tested, but I thought you might be interested to know what was in it."

Secrets, Lies, and Puppy Dog Eyes

ooooooo

With furious tears in her eyes, Sandra Grayling marched all the way to the police station, not stopping until she flung open the door.

"Sergeant Tibbs," she said, "I wish to speak to you about Dawn Hillier."

Glen rewrapped the bacon sandwich he'd been about to devour and took the pen from behind his ear. "Dawn Hillier?"

"Yes, that's right. I can't bear to think of the gossip and untruths that are flying around the village, so I have to tell you, just to set the record straight."

"Let's go and sit down in my office, shall we?" said Glen. "He opened the door to the room at the top of the stairs and offered her a chair. "Now, what is it you'd like to get off your chest, Mrs Grayling?"

Sandra pursed her lips. "It's *Miss*."

"Sorry, Miss Grayling." Glen looked at her expectantly, his pen poised.

"People are saying the most terrible things about Dawn," said Sandra. "People who didn't know her like I did are talking about her as though there was something wrong with her, just because she was taking antidepressants, and I won't stand for it, do you hear me? I won't!" She banged a fist on Glen's desk before composing herself. "The reason for me coming here, Sergeant Tibbs, is to tell you the truth, so that if you hear any of the disgusting rumours, you can ignore them. Apart from Walter, you're the only person I've ever told about this since Dawn told me. Not even Edmund knows."

Glen arched a brow. The prospect of learning something about Dawn that even Edmund didn't know had him intrigued. "And what is this secret, Miss Grayling?"

"Dawn was taking antidepressants, it's true, because she needed help to cope with a situation in her life that caused her great distress. A situation that she shared only with me after she came to Bliss Bay."

Glen nodded. "I see. And what was that?"

"She had a child before she married Edmund Hillier. A child that her parents forced her to give up for adoption."

ooooooo

"So, you say that an old friend of Dawn Hillier's claims that Dawn had a baby before she married Edmund, who he knows nothing about?" said Sam, when Glen called to tell him about Sandra's revelation.

"That's what she said," said Glen, "but I haven't told Edmund. I'm not telling him anything else unless there's absolute proof."

"That's very wise," said Sam. "Very wise indeed."

Secrets, Lies, and Puppy Dog Eyes

CHAPTER 11

Sandra and Walter Grayling's family home—The Roundhouse—stood on a clifftop, about ten minutes' walk from Kismet Cottage in the opposite direction from the village, on the edge of a coastal path that went down to the beach.

"Just look at it" said Megan, shivering in her coat, the wind whipping her long brown hair out around her face. "It even *looks* like a place where bad things happen."

"The trouble with you is that your imagination's too vivid," said Des, tapping her on the head. "It looks a bit grim, because it's always exposed to the elements. It's weather beaten, that's all, and I don't suppose it's had a fresh lick of paint since Sandra and Walter's parents passed away, which was a long time ago. It's no wonder it looks a bit sorry for itself. Now, come on, look lively, and try to smile. I know it's going to be difficult, but just try, okay?" He strode forward and rapped on the door. A minute passed before Walter opened it, blinking as though he was unaccustomed to daylight.

Megan shuddered.

"Des, Megan," he said, seemingly at a loss as to what else to say to his two rare visitors.

"Walter, lovely to see you," said Des, pumping his hand up and down in a vigorous handshake. "We were just passing and we thought we'd pop in to see how you and Sandra were keeping. Didn't we, Megan? *Megan!*"

"Hmm? Oh, sorry, yes, we just popped in on our way back from, er, a walk. We know that Sandra hasn't been herself since that day in the café, so we thought we'd pop in and see how she's getting on."

"Oh, well, I suppose you'd better come in then." Walter shuffled off, leaving Megan and Des to follow him through the gloom. "Sorry it's so dark in here, but ever since Sandra had that funny turn, she's preferred to keep the shutters closed. She says it's because she's become sensitive to the light but, between you and me, I think it's because she'd been crying a lot, and her puffy eyes are less noticeable in the dark. Recently, she's only left the house for WA meetings, or if something urgent needs doing."

"Walter!" Sandra called from upstairs. "Are you talking to someone?"

"Yes, Sandy. It's Des and Megan. They were just passing and they thought they'd pop in to say hello."

There was a pause before Sandra said, "*Who?*"

"Des Harper and Megan… sorry, what's your surname?"

"Fallon."

"Megan Fallon."

Secrets, Lies, and Puppy Dog Eyes

"What do they want?"

Walter sighed. "Why don't you just come down and speak to them? It'll do you good to have some company." He motioned to Des and Megan to sit down. "Make yourselves comfortable. I'm sure she'll be down in a minute." He stared at them, then said, "Can I offer you some tea?"

"That would be lovely, thanks," said Des, making his way over to an armchair and bumping into a couch in the dark.

"This is really creepy," grumbled Megan. "Why did I let you talk me into this? They're probably vampires, or something. That's why it's so dark."

"Just sit down and stop whining," said Des, squinting as he put on his glasses and took out his trusty notebook and pen.

"That's a bit ambitious in this light, isn't it?" hissed Megan. "We can't see two inches in front of our noses, so I don't know how you're going to write anything."

"I'm sure I'll manage," said Des, tapping his pen on the arm of the chair. "Actually, this is probably a very nice house," he said, gazing around. "This room is huge, so I'm sure the rest must be, too, and I bet they still have all the original features. Shame they keep it to themselves."

"Yes, I suppose," said Megan.
"It's probably great for parties, especially in

the summer. And in the winter, it could be lovely and cosy if they had a fire burning in the fireplace." She screwed up her eyes. "That *is* a fireplace, isn't it? Or is it just a big hole in the wall?"

"No, it's a fireplace," snapped Sandra, who'd appeared in the doorway of the living room, a pair of dark glasses covering her eyes. "And a jolly nice one, too." She shuffled in and sat down in a chair across the other side of the room next to a shuttered window. She took her time to settle herself, the shawl around her neck, and her cardigan. "Well?" she said. "What do you want? It's terribly bad manners to call round to someone's house unannounced you know."

This is ridiculous, thought Megan. *I didn't come here to be lectured on social etiquette by Bliss Bay's rudest resident.* She could just about make out Sandra's silhouette across the room. "Look, we're sorry if we've disturbed you, and if you'd really rather not, please say, but do you think we could open a shutter, please? Just one, so we can see a bit better. If Uncle Des or I trip over something, we could hurt ourselves really badly. It's alright for you and Walter, because you know where everything is, so you can avoid it, but we can't."

"No one asked you to come," grumbled Sandra. She didn't move for a while, then said,

Secrets, Lies, and Puppy Dog Eyes

"You can open this shutter." She pointed to her left." Just this one, though."

Megan made her way slowly across the room, her arms outstretched and her feet feeling for the edge of any rugs which could be trip hazards. She let out a breath when she reached the window and undid the catch on the shutter. When she opened it, the light flooded in and she gasped in awe.

"Oh, wow! This view! This view is incredible! I thought the view we had from Kismet Cottage was good but this is miles better. It's amazing how different the landscape is because you're higher up and closer to the sea. It's so rugged and natural, and you can see far more of the sea than we can. It's absolutely amazing. I could look at it for hours."

"It's even better if you open all the shutters," said Walter, who'd come in from the kitchen with the tea. "It's a panoramic view."

"I'm sure it's beautiful," said Megan. "You're lucky to have such a wonderful home." She made her way back to her chair and waited for Des to get started.

"Well?" repeated Sandra. "What do you want?"

"Look, I'm going to come straight to the point," said Des. "There's some funny business going on around here, and we'd like to try to find out who's behind it. Fake obituaries and strange shenanigans. As concerned residents, we think it's in all our interests to do what we can to get things resolved."

"And how do you propose to do that?" said Sandra, pointing at the notepad on the arm of Des's chair. "Don't tell me you're one of those voluntary policemen these days?"

"If you mean a PSCO, no, I'm not," said Des. "I'm a concerned member of the community, and you should be, too. Like I said, we're just talking to a few people who we think might be able to help give us some information that'll help to find
who's responsible for what's been going on. Which is why we've come to see you."

"What sort of information?" said Walter.

"Is it going to upset you to talk about Dawn Hillier, Sandra?" said Megan, "Because if it is, we won't."

Sandra's jaw clenched, then relaxed. "What do you want to know?"

"Just whatever you can tell us about her," said Megan.

Sandra took off her glasses and rubbed her eyes. "Dawn was the most wonderful person," she said, her voice shaking with emotion. "She was kind and generous and so thoughtful. After I lost my fiancé, I didn't know how I was going to carry on. My parents didn't understand how I felt, and Walter was no help whatsoever." She looked up and sent a weak smile her brother's way. "No offence, Walter, but you really didn't understand what I was going through. If it hadn't been for Dawn, I don't know how I would have got through those dark days."

"She was a big help, was she?" said Megan.

"That doesn't even begin to describe what she did for me," said Sandra. "It sounds stupid to say it now, but I'm convinced that talking to Dawn actually soothed my soul. It gave me peace. She was like an angel on earth, that's the only way I can describe her. She understood tragedy, you see, because she'd experienced it herself. That's why she was so empathetic."

Des flipped over a page in his book and cast Megan an excited sideward glance. "Tragedy? What kind of tragedy?"

Sandra hesitated, her lips pursed. "Her baby."

"Her *baby*?" Des stopped writing. "But she and Edmund didn't have any children."

"No, *they* didn't, but *she* did. She had the child before she came to Bliss Bay. That's why she came here—to make a fresh start."

"Oh, that's terrible," said Megan. "She lost a child?"

"No," said Sandra. "Although, yes, I suppose she did, but not in the sense you mean. She gave it up for adoption. Under the circumstances, I appreciate it may seem out of character for me to be defending her. I'm sure the whole village is well aware of my opinions about such things as children being born out of wedlock, but because Dawn was so good to me I could have overlooked anything she did that went against my personal morals.

"She didn't want to give it up, but she was still living with her parents and they told her there was no way she could keep it, because she was single. There was a terrible stigma attached to unmarried mothers in those days. *And* she got pregnant right in the middle of her teacher training course, which her parents were furious about. They'd always wanted her to be a teacher, and there was no way she'd have been able to do that with a baby. After it was born, they just wanted to get Dawn out of their hometown as soon as possible to stop any gossip, which is how she ended up in Bliss Bay. They found out that the school needed a teacher, and Dawn got the job. She never got over giving up the child, though, and she used to be overwhelmed by these terrible dark depressions."

"Does Edmund know?" asked Des.

Sandra shook her head. "She never told him, and she asked me not to, so I've never said a word to him about it, and I never will. He asked her once what she was so miserable about and she said it was something that had happened before she met him. She was about to tell him when he said she couldn't keep living in the past so whatever it was, she should get over it and move on."

Her eyes flashed with anger. "He was never the right man for her. I thought it then, and I still think it now. I just hate myself for not telling her what I thought of him. She could have been so much happier with someone else. Someone who'd bothered to take the time to find out what was troubling her. I could have told her what I thought, but I didn't say a word. And the reason I didn't say anything was because I thought if I told her what I felt, and she listened, she might have ended up leaving Bliss Bay. I couldn't bear the thought of her not being here any more, so I said nothing.

"I wish I'd told her how *I* felt," said Walter, quietly.

"Sorry, what was that?" said Des.

"I wish I'd told her how I felt," repeated Walter. "I loved her for years. *I* would have made her happy."

"*What*! Walter! You've never told me! That's disgusting!" said Sandra. "You were married!"

Walter gave a resigned nod. "That doesn't mean that someone else won't come along one day and take your breath away when you least expect it. Dawn made me rethink my entire life, Sandra, and if I'd only had the guts, I would have let her know how I felt about her. I would have risked everything I had, but I knew she'd never look at me. Her husband was a bank manager. Why would she be interested in a school caretaker?" He pulled on his earlobe self-consciously, aware that everyone was looking at him. "I've got some newspaper cuttings if you'd like to see them?" he said, changing the subject to take the attention off him.

"Newspaper cuttings of what?" said Des.

"Of when Dawn died. You know, about the police investigation."

"*Walter*! I despair!" admonished Sandra. "You were a married man! What on earth did you think you were doing showing such an interest in another man's wife?"

He sighed. "I just told you, Sandy. I loved her. Alive or dead, Dawn was the only woman I've ever loved with *all* my heart."

"Did Janice know?" said Sandra, referring to Walter's wife.

"Of course not. I did love her, too, you know, I just loved Dawn more." His lips moved slightly in a melancholy smile.

"And why did you never mention to *me* that you'd kept these newspaper cuttings?" said Sandra, a stern expression on her face.

Secrets, Lies, and Puppy Dog Eyes

"Because I knew this is exactly how you'd react. You would never have understood. Anyway, Des, would you like me to fetch them?"

"Yes, please," said Des. "I most likely read them at the time, but I can't remember them now, so it would be great to see them again. We'd love to see them, wouldn't we, Megan?"

She nodded. "Yes, we would. Thank you."

Walter disappeared, leaving the three of them sitting in awkward silence.

"So, will you be going to the Christmas concert, Sandra?" said Des.

"I have no idea," she said, shortly. "Unless they're for the WA, I never make any plans for Christmas. From a personal point of view, it's a dreadful time of year for Walter and I. Our parents both passed in December, a year apart, and a few years after that, Walter's wife passed away on New Year's Eve. You probably heard about it at the time, but people don't remember these things unless they affect them directly."

"Oh, I'm sorry," said Des. "My condolences. Yes, you're right, I'm sure Sylvie would have mentioned it to me." He twiddled his thumbs and stared at the carpet.

"Here we are," said Walter, reappearing, and Des breathed a sigh of relief.

"*I* don't want to see them, thank you very much," said Sandra, pursing her lips.

"You don't have to. We'll look at them here, on the dining room table," said Walter, opening a large buff-coloured envelope. "There's more room here than on the coffee table, anyway. Come over here, Des, Megan, and I can spread everything out. Sit down, sit down."

They made their way carefully across the room. However, even with one shutter open, there wasn't enough light to see the small newspaper print.

"I knew I should have brought my magnifying glass," grumbled Des.

Walter nodded. "It *is* very difficult to read in this light, isn't it?"

"You're not putting the electric on at this time of day," said Sandra. "It's a waste of money."

"Well, we can't see a thing," said Walter, "so I'm going to open the shutters. I'm giving you fair warning, so you can go back upstairs if you want to. We should be making the most of the natural daylight, not shutting it out. You can sit there in your dark glasses if you don't want to be bothered by it."

Sandra opened her mouth like a fish, then shut it again, but stayed put in the chair. "Oh, just do what you like."

Secrets, Lies, and Puppy Dog Eyes

Walter opened all the shutters and the light came streaming in, illuminating the huge room, and Megan felt the breath catch in her throat. "Oh, Walter! That view just gets better. It's crying out to be painted—it's magnificent! If ever an artist was looking for the perfect seascape, this is it. If I lived here, I'd keep the shutters open all the time. It's literally breathtaking."

"Never mind the bloomin' view, Megan, look at all this!" said Des, nudging her in the ribs, his fingers deftly sorting through the newspaper cuttings.

"This one's from the local paper," said Walter. "You may remember this reporter was like a dog with a bone. Once he got a lead, he wouldn't let it go."

Suspicions Surface Over Claims that Woman's Death Followed Bag Snatch

By Mike Zamora

The death of Dawn Hillier has not only shocked the close community of Bliss Bay, but it has forced the residents to look more carefully at their neighbours, and the people they thought they knew.

It is possible, of course, that her killer could be from outside the village—someone passing through who saw her standing at the bus stop and snatched her handbag, leaving her to die after she fell down the incline—but my instinct tells me that her murderer is closer to home.

It must be very difficult for Mr. Hillier at this time. As well as dealing with his own grief, and that of his teenage children, he will now have to assume the role of both father **and** mother.

Or will he?

There have been reports that Mr. Hillier has recently been seen enjoying the company of Annabel Hemsworth, one of the employees at the company organising Dawn Hillier's funeral. In itself, there is nothing unusual about that. One would expect regular contact to be necessary at such a time.

However, are the funeral arrangements really so complex that it's necessary for the two of them to be discussing them over dinner at a cosy table for two in a dimly-lit bistro? The photograph below will show that this is, indeed, where they were yesterday evening—at the romantic restaurant, 'All for Love', in the nearby village of Honeymeade.

Whatever the reason, we should bear in mind that Mrs Hillier has yet to be buried and, as a mark of respect to her, I will keep my full opinions on this matter to myself for the time being.

Rest in Peace, Dawn. May you have sweet dreams.

I pray we do not have to wait too long for your killer to be brought to justice.

"Goodness, he doesn't sound like he was a fan of Edmund Hillier," said Megan.

"You can say that again," said Walter. "Every piece he wrote *inferred* that he thought Edmund had been involved in Dawn's death, although he never actually said as much."

"I wonder what he meant when he talked about his 'full opinions'?" said Des. "I'd love to know what they were."

Walter nodded. "Yes, so would we but, unfortunately, Mike Zamora lost his job soon after he wrote that piece because Edmund wrote a stinking letter to the editor, demanding he be fired. He said all his reporting was tantamount to defamation of character without being in possession of all the facts."

"Annabel was also fired," said Sandra, suddenly, from the corner of the room. "Quite right, too. The way she and Edmund were carrying on was a disgrace."

"I have to agree with Sandy on that point," said Walter. "And it put Edmund in a very bad light. He hadn't long been promoted to Assistant Manager at the bank, so he really didn't need the bad publicity. We don't know for sure, but we think his manager gave him a dressing-down after that newspaper article was published. He didn't want anything to bring the name of the bank into disrepute, so he told Edmund to make sure nothing like that ever happened again. After that, everything went quiet between Edmund and Annabel until the bank manager retired a couple of months later, and Edmund got promoted. No prizes for guessing what the first thing he did was."

"He married Annabel?"

Walter nodded. "Of course, that put a lot of noses out of joint because so many people thought the world of Dawn but, as there was only one bank in the village at the time, Edmund wasn't too worried that he'd lose any customers over it."

"They must have had Polly very soon afterwards," said Megan. "She's just a year younger than me, I think. They sent her to a private school, didn't they? I know she certainly wasn't at Bliss Bay School when I was there."

"Yes, Edmund was earning a good wage by the time she got to school age, so he and Annabel were able to pay for her to go to a private school." Walter rolled his eyes. "For all the good it did her. What a waste of money that was. Whatever Polly's academic qualifications are, she certainly hasn't made use of them since she left college, and she didn't go on to university like her parents hoped she would."

Secrets, Lies, and Puppy Dog Eyes

"I wonder if that reporter's still around?" said Des. "That Mike Zamora chap."

"If he is," said Walter, "you'll probably find him propping up the bar at The White Bear in Honeymeade. I remember hearing that's where he used to spend most of his spare time."

Des exchanged a glance with Megan and she shook her head, knowing exactly what was going through his mind.

"Well, this has been very useful," said Des. "I've made so many notes, I think I'm going to need a new pen—this one's almost run out of ink. I used to use pencils, but I kept breaking the leads. Sylvie started calling me the Pencil Predator."

"The Pencil Predator! Hah! That's a good one!" said Megan, with a forced laugh, suddenly seeing an opportunity to glean some useful information from the Grayling siblings. "Um, speaking of nicknames, did either of you two ever have one? When you were young, maybe?"

Walter shook his head. "No, I don't think we did. Nothing that I can remember."

"Yes, you had one," said Sandra. "We used to call you Walter Wombat when you were little."

Walter blushed. "Well, none apart from that one."

Megan smiled and turned to Sandra, who was sitting straight-backed in the chair, the grim expression still on her face. "Look, I hope you don't mind me asking, but would you consider telling the police what you've told us?"

Sandra turned her head and look out of the window. "I've already told them."

"Oh, right, well that's great," said Megan. "Hopefully, the information will be of use in the investigation. Something you've told them could trigger something, which could provide the answer to a question they've been looking for, which could help solve a puzzle they've been scratching their heads over. You know what they say, even the smallest piece of information, regardless of how insignificant it may seem, could be the missing detail the police have been waiting for."

Sandra completely ignored her.

"Well, I suppose we'd better be off, then," said Des. "Thanks for the tea." He looked down at the table and, realising he hadn't even touched his tea, picked up the cup and gulped down the tepid liquid in seconds. "Mmmm, lovely. Nothing like a nice cup of tea," he said, with a grimace. "Anyway, goodbye, Sandra, Walter. Thanks very much for your time."

"Yes, thanks," said Megan.

Secrets, Lies, and Puppy Dog Eyes

"And thanks for coming," said Walter. "I think your visit might have been just what Sandy needed to give her something else to focus on."

As they settled themselves into the car, Megan didn't say a word. She knew it wouldn't be long before Des blurted out what he'd been holding back for the last few minutes.

"So, what d'you think about that, then?" he said, eventually.

"About what?"

"About going to find this Mike Zamora chap?"

She looked at Des, all fired up and raring to get to The White Bear, and nodded. "I suppose you want to go today, do you?"

"Well, we might as well, love, don't you think? No time like the present, as they say." He looked at his watch. "We're a bit early yet, though, so we'll go home first and give Sylvie an update. She pretends she's not interested, but she's just as fond of village gossip as the next person." He grinned and pointed ahead. "Come on, let's go home and we'll set off for the pub in an hour or so."

Chapter 12

"Well?" said Sylvie, switching off her welding iron.

"No way," said Megan. "I'd be very surprised if they're the 'Red' and 'Curly' we're looking for."

"I agree," said Des. "Sandra adored Dawn, and Walter confessed that he'd been in love from the minute he set eyes on her. He loved her so much, I doubt he'd have harmed a hair on her head, let alone killed her."

"*Walter was in love with Dawn?*" said Sylvie. "But he was married." She shook her head and tutted. "It just goes to show, you think people are happy with their lot, but you never know, do you? What about the obituaries? Do you think either of them had anything to do with them?"

"I really don't think so," said Megan, "even though you could say they had motive to. Neither of them can stand the sight of Edmund and they don't sound too keen on Annabel, either."

Sylvie nodded, thoughtfully. "I hope neither of them are involved in anything nefarious. Even though Sandra's not my favourite person, I really would be disappointed to learn she'd been responsible for any of what's gone on recently." She looked at Des and Megan. "And, seeing as neither of you have taken your coats off, I assume you're not staying? Where are you off to now?"

"We're going to see if we can find the reporter who spent a lot of time investigating Dawn's death. Mike Zamora, his name is. He thought Edmund was the prime suspect."

A frown appeared between Sylvie's brows. "Hmm, I think I remember a reporter who had a bee in his bonnet about Edmund Hillier being responsible for what happened to Dawn. Mind you, he wasn't the only one. Half the village thought he had something to do with it. Anyway, I'll be interested to know what you find out. And don't forget, Des, if I'm not here when you get back, it's because I've gone to lunch with Dora. They've got salmon fishcakes, chips and mushy peas on special for £2.99 at The Duck Inn. She and Archie had them last week and they're to die for, apparently." She dropped a kiss on the end of Des's nose. "I'll see you later."

ooooooo

It had just gone midday when Des and Megan arrived at The White Bear, a quaint inn which dated back to the 16th century and which was every inch the quintessentially traditional British village pub.

The smell of a log fire, and a cheery smile from the landlord, greeted them as they walked in from the cold.

"Afternoon, both. Chilly out there, today, isn't it? You'll be needing something to warm you up. What can I get you?"

"I'll have a hot chocolate, please," said Megan.

"Make that two, if you would," said Des.

"Would you like to see a menu?"

"Er, I don't know, we hadn't thought about it," said Des. "Shall we have a look at a menu?"

"Yes, please," said Megan. "The smell of a log fire always makes me hungry."

The landlord passed them a menu and busied himself with the drinks. "Are you on holiday, or just passing through?" he said. "I know most people who come in, apart from tourists, of course, and I don't recognise you."

"We're from Bliss Bay," said Des. "Actually, we're looking for someone. I don't know if you'll be able to help us."

The landlord immediately gave him a suspicious look. "Well, that depends who you are, and who you're looking for, doesn't it?"

"Oh, we're no one sinister. We're just hoping to speak to someone we were told we might find in here," said Des. "We're researching the history of Bliss Bay, and we were told that Mike Zamora might be able to help us with some information we're missing, seeing as he used to be a reporter back in the day."

"Would you happen to know him?" said Megan.

The landlord relaxed and nodded. "Oh, I know him, alright. He's a character and a half." He put down two steaming cups of hot chocolate on the bar. "He usually comes in between one and two o'clock, so I'll let him know you're here when he does. Meanwhile, choose a table, and let me know when you're ready to order your food."

"'Researching the history of Bliss Bay'?" said Megan, with a grin. "That was impressively quick thinking."

Des tapped the side of his nose. "You've got to be able to think on your feet when you're investigating, haven't you? And it's not entirely a lie, is it? More of a tiny fib."

They ate their lunch, chatting as Des went through his notes. "I hope he still remembers the case. A long time's passed since then."

Megan nodded as she noticed the landlord lean across the bar and speak to a squat man with a bald head who'd ordered a pint. They glanced over and Megan knew the man had to be the reporter they'd come looking for.

"I think Mike Zamora's just walked in," she said. "Let's see if he wants to talk to us."

They didn't have to wait long before he made his way over.

"I hear you wanted to speak to me?"

"Mr. Zamora?" said Des.

"That's right," said Mike, shaking Des's hand. "You're doing some kind of research on Bliss Bay, I understand?"

"Well, that's not strictly true," said Des. "We didn't want to say too much to the landlord, but we want to talk to you about the investigation into Dawn Hillier's death."

"Are you reporters?" asked Mike.

"Oh, no," said Megan. "We're just Bliss Bay residents who are trying to find out a bit more about what happened to her. I'm Megan Fallon, by the way, and this is my Uncle, Des Harper. We'd be really grateful if you could spare a while to chat with us."

Mike looked them up and down before pulling out a chair at their table, his eyebrows raising when Des took the pen from behind his ear and sat, poised to write. "What is it you want to know?"

"Anything you remember about the case," said Megan.

"I remember almost *everything* about the case," said Mike, taking a sip of his pint of beer. I just wish I could have seen it through to the end, but Edmund Hillier didn't want me anywhere near it."

"Did you think he was involved?"

Mike nodded. "At the time, I thought he was involved up to his neck in it, but after I was fired from my job, and given a police warning to back off, I stopped looking for answers." He took another sip of his pint. "To be honest, getting fired probably did me a favour. I'd been arguing with my boss for ages because a lot of the stuff I wanted to put in the paper was too controversial, in his opinion. He was forever trying to get me to tone things down. Basically, he wanted me to change the way I wrote, and I wasn't prepared to do that. He'd been looking for an excuse to get rid of me and that was it.

"It all turned out okay, though. I hadn't been married long, and my wife wasn't happy that I was spending so much time away from home on the case, so she was over the moon when I got fired. To tell you the truth, if I hadn't been, I doubt we'd still be married." He chuckled.

"What did you mean in one of your articles when you said you'd be keeping your 'full opinions' on the matter to yourself?" said Des.

"My, my, you have been doing your homework, haven't you?" said Mike. "Well, what I meant by that is that I'd hoped to be able to prove without any doubt that Edmund had killed Dawn. Right from the start, he never struck me as a convincing grieving husband. It was just a gut instinct, but he didn't come across as genuine to me at all." He put his elbows on the table and leaned forward. "And I found it very odd that his first wife died in mysterious circumstances, and so did Dawn."

"What happened to his first wife?" asked Megan.

"She was killed in a hit-and-run, and neither the driver, nor the vehicle responsible was ever found."

Des nodded. "I remember that being mentioned during the investigation into Dawn's death, but it never crossed my mind that Edmund had anything to do with it. I knew his first wife had died, but I thought it was an accident."

Mike shrugged. "Maybe it was, but when I did a bit of delving and found out that Edmund was seen out partying with other women, while a neighbour looked after his kids, just a few weeks after his wife's death, it struck me as a bit suspect. I know Edmund thought I was on a witch-hunt, and he was right—I was—but maybe now, you can understand why. I mean, it's not a crime to be a playboy, but his behaviour raised a few eyebrows, I can tell you. He shouldn't have been surprised that I thought it was suspicious."

"I must have only been around sixteen or seventeen when his first wife died, so I don't remember a lot about it," said Des, "but it does seem coincidental that he was off having fun with other women so soon after she died, *and* that he got together with Annabel so soon after Dawn passed away."

"Exactly," said Mike. "It's a terrible fact, but you don't have to do too much research to see that there have been plenty of men over the years who've murdered their wives for the simple reason that they've tired of them, and want to move onto someone new."

Megan frowned and nodded. "In Edmund's defence, though—and I'd never defend anyone I knew was guilty of violence towards women—he *has* been with Annabel for a long time, hasn't he? Has there any been any evidence that he's cheated on her since they've been married, Uncle Des?"

"Not to my knowledge but, like I said, he's not really a friend of mine. Seeing as he worked at the bank until he retired, though, I'm sure someone in Bliss Bay would have found out if he was ever seen playing away from home. You know what the gossip grapevine's like. It would have been all over the village before long."

"Sounds a bit like Honeymeade," said Mike. He rubbed his chin, a frown appearing at his brow. "You know, you've just jogged another memory. When I was nosing around, asking questions in the village, a woman told me she'd seen Dawn with Annabel Hillier—or Hemsworth, as she was known back then—

together in the market square, the week before she died. I asked her if she was positive, and she swore it was Annabel and Dawn."

"Didn't you tell the police?" said Megan.

Mike nodded. "I told one of the detectives, but he didn't take very kindly to the news."

"Why not?" said Des.

"Because Annabel Hemsworth was his girlfriend. He'd just started going out with her and he wouldn't hear a word said against her. He told me the witness must have been wrong."

"Is he still around?" said Des, excitedly. "We can tell the police and they can interview him."

Mike shook his head. "No chance. He died the same day I spoke to him. In those days, the pub was where detectives got together to discuss a case. They were long days, and some of them were hard drinkers. Ted Leyton was one of them, I'm afraid. He went home after a session, fell asleep in the bath and drowned. Too much to drink and not enough sleep isn't a good combination for anyone."

"Oh, that's awful," said Megan. "Poor guy."

"Wasn't Annabel upset?" said Des. "She *was* going out with him, after all."

Secrets, Lies, and Puppy Dog Eyes

"They'd only had one date," said Mike. "She was a proper looker in those days. Legs right up to her neck, long blonde hair and the most beautiful eyes. I wasn't surprised Ted didn't want to jeopardise his relationship with her. Anyway, after he kicked the bucket, I told another detective, but I never heard anything else about it. I don't know if Annabel was ever interviewed, but I was fired not long after that, so I lost touch with everything."

Des frowned. "That witness must have got it wrong. I'm sure Dawn and Annabel didn't know each other."

Mike shrugged. "The woman was adamant. She swore it was them she saw. She said Annabel was very distinctive, so she wouldn't have mistaken her for anyone else, and Dawn was wearing a bright purple coat, which stuck in her mind."

"How do you know for *sure* that they didn't know each other?" said Megan, suddenly. "It was reported that Annabel didn't know *Edmund* until after Dawn died, but how do we know if she knew Dawn? Even if it was just as an acquaintance, or to say hello? We don't, do we? If she was involved in Dawn's death, maybe that's why she's denying knowing her. If they really *were* seen together, that must prove something, even if it's just that Annabel was lying about knowing her. And if she's lying about it, there must be a reason why."

Des's eyes sparkled with excitement as his pen raced across the page of his notebook. "I know it's a big ask, Mike, but I don't suppose you can remember the name of the witness, can you? If we mention it to the police, they can see if they can find her."

"I'll never forget it," said Mike. "It was a Polish name, and it stuck in my head. It was Magdalena Kozlowski."

"Oh no!" said Megan, suddenly deflated. "That was the woman who used to live a few doors down from my parents' house. She passed away recently."

"Oh," said Des, his shoulders slumping. "The one who used to feed Tabastion, you mean?"

"Yeah, that's the one."

Mike looked at his watch. "Well, if there's nothing else, I'd better be getting back to my pals. We're up for a game of darts, see." He stood up and shook hands. "I hope our chat's been of help with your 'research'," he said, with a wink, and went on his way.

ooooooo

"We should tell Fred," said Des, on their way back to Bliss Bay.

"Or Sergeant Tibbs," said Megan.

"If the information Mike gave the detective about a witness seeing Annabel and

Secrets, Lies, and Puppy Dog Eyes

Dawn together was never acted upon for some reason, the police definitely need to know about it now," said Des.

Megan pulled up outside the police station to find Glen Tibbs pacing up and down.

"It helps to clear my head," he said. "There's a lot going on, you see. Anyway, what can I do for you?"

"Do you have a minute?" said Des. "We've got some information on the Dawn Hillier case that might be of interest."

Glen's ears pricked up. Anything that might help him solve the case and get Edmund Hillier off his back was of interest. "Come up to my office. Where did you get this information? I hope it was from a reliable source."

"I'd say so," said Des, as he settled himself in one of the chairs in front of Glen's desk. "We've been talking to Mike Zamora, who was a reporter on the case for a while. It's information that was given to him by a member of the public which may not have been processed by the detectives who were working on the case."

"Not processed?" said Glen, with a frown. "What kind of information is it?" he asked, leaning back in his chair.

"Well, it's the name of a possible suspect."

Glen sat forward so quickly, he almost slid off the seat. "Who?" he snapped, his hands clasped on the desk as he thought about how impressed Edmund Hillier would be when he told him they had a break in the case at last.

"It's Annabel Hillier."

Glen's bubble burst as Des and Megan continued with their story.

"So the witness claimed to have seen Dawn and Annabel having a conversation in the market square the week before Dawn's death, but Annabel claims not to have known her?" He leaned back and narrowed his eyes. "That means that either the witness was mistaken, or Annabel Hillier is lying."

"Yes, that's what we thought," said Megan.

Glen chewed on his bottom lip. "Okay, thank you, leave it with me. We'll need to take a statement from each of you."

As he led them back downstairs, Glen sighed as he realised today wasn't going to be the day he got back into Edmund Hillier's good books.

ooooooo

"Come in, Sergeant."

Having just got back from Honeymeade, where he'd gone to meet Mike Zamora for himself, Glen followed Annabel Hillier into the living room.

"I'm afraid Edmund's not in just now. He shouldn't be long, though."

Secrets, Lies, and Puppy Dog Eyes

"Not to worry," said Glen, with an inward sigh of relief. "It was you I wanted to speak to actually."

"Oh. Well, I'd be happy to help, if I can. Would you like some tea?"

"No, thank you, Mrs Hillier. Just a few moments of your time."

The sound of footsteps on the stairs was followed by Teresa's head poking around the door. "Hi." She nodded to Glen and looked at Annabel with a frown. "Everything alright?"

"I hope so, although I don't know why Sergeant Tibbs is here, yet." Annabel settled herself in the armchair and crossed her long legs. "You don't mind if Teresa's here, do you? She's staying for a few days."

Teresa flopped down on one end of the couch. "Yeah, until one of your lot finds out who's got it in for us."

Glen cleared his throat and opened his notebook. "Mrs Hillier, I just wanted to clarify something with you regarding the investigation into Dawn's death."

Annabel's shifted in the chair and looked at Teresa. "Oh? What would that be?"

"Well, it's been brought to my attention that there was an account of you being seen with Mrs Hillier in the days before her death. I wanted to clarify this with you, because you've said before that you didn't know her."

"That's right. I didn't. I knew *of* her, but not well enough to speak to. Whoever gave that account is wrong, Sergeant." Annabel held his gaze, her mouth set in a determined line.

"Who said that Annabel was seen with Dawn?" said Teresa. "And why has this only just come to light, after all this time?"

"I can't divulge the source of the information, I'm afraid," said Glen, "but I had to clarify it. Witnesses sometimes give statements that are confused, partly accurate, or completely incorrect, but we still have to check every one of them. Sorry to have bothered you. Thanks for your time."

As he walked off down the path, Teresa put her arm around Annabel's shoulders.

"Why would anyone think *you* had anything to do with Dawn's death?" she said, as Annabel dabbed at the tears on her cheeks. "I think we should tell Dad to make a complaint."

Annabel shook her head. "Don't worry, it's just the police doing their job. Don't ask me why the information's only just come to light after so long, but Sergeant Tibbs was only trying to validate its authenticity. I'm not worried about it, because I know it wasn't me who was seen with Dawn, but it's upset me, because it's come on top of everything else that's happened recently. We can tell your

Secrets, Lies, and Puppy Dog Eyes

Dad, but there's no need for him to complain about it."

ooooooo

"I'm sorry to call you direct, DI Cambridge," said Edmund, as he attempted to keep calm. "You did give me your contact number, so I assume it was alright to use it?"

"No problem," said Sam, the phone tucked under his chin as he reached for his notebook and pen. "What can I do for you?"

"My wife is very upset following a visit from Sergeant Tibbs and, quite frankly, we don't need the aggravation. He called at the house this afternoon to tell us about an ancient witness statement which has been dragged up from goodness knows where, which seems to infer that Annabel has been lying about her relationship with Dawn. I can assure you, she *didn't* know her, but this witness statement claims she was seen with Dawn the week before she died.

"After my last conversation with you, I was quite prepared to wait for someone to get in touch to keep me up to date with developments, but the visit from PS Tibbs this afternoon has left me with no alternative other than to contact you to voice my concerns. The last thing I wanted was for Annabel to be more upset than she already is, but Sergeant Tibbs soon put a stop to that."

"Have you made him aware of that?" asked Sam.

"Believe me, I'd love to," said Edmund, "but Annabel has begged me not to make a fuss. Please, DI Cambridge, whatever you can do to ensure that neither my wife nor I are implicated any further in Dawn's death will be much appreciated."

"Okay, leave it with me, Mr Hillier. Yes, goodbye."

"Everything alright, boss?" said Harvey, who was leaning on the edge of Sam's desk.

"It's this Hillier case. Obituaries, cryptic notes, evidence which seems to indicate Dawn Hillier had a baby her husband knew nothing about, and a witness statement that seems to infer that the current Mrs Hillier is lying through her teeth."

Sam drummed his fingers against his forehead, before reaching for his indigestion tablets and then picking up his phone. "It's about time I found out what's happening about Dawn Hillier's original file being found. There's something about this whole case that seems off, but I don't know what, so it's about time we did a bit of digging to find out."

Chapter 13

"You'd better be careful," said Megan, warily. "You know how Tabastion can be with human strangers. I've no idea how he's going to react to Boxer... I mean, Blue. Sorry, it's going to take a while to get used to his new name."

"Well, I don't see any claws yet," said Jack, as they sat on the village green, attempting to acquaint their respective furry family members.

"Yeah, but Tab has a habit of getting them out when you least expect it, so don't get too cocky, or Blue will end up with a scratch down his nose." The words were no sooner out of Megan's mouth than Tab had slid out of her arms and was making a beeline for the puppy. She grabbed at him but Jack held up a hand.

"Hang on, let's see what happens. He doesn't look like he's being aggressive, so let's just give him a minute."

Blue leaned forward in Jack's arms and sniffed at Tab, who stood stock-still, even letting the puppy lick his ear.

"I'm going to take a chance," said Jack, keeping a hold on Blue's lead, but setting him down.

To Megan and Jack's amazement, Tab curled up on the grass and Blue curled up beside him. Within seconds, they were both asleep, a deep purr issuing from Tabastion and a gentle snore from Blue.

"Well, would you look at that!" said Jack. "They're best buddies already. Who'd a thunk it?"

"Am I dreaming?" said Megan. "Will you pinch me?" She shook her head. "I've seen Tabastion cause actual bodily harm to two people, so the fact that he's happily curled up with a dog is unbelievable!"

"You still want to come with me when I take him for a walk?" said Jack.

"Of course I do. Let them enjoy each other's company for a bit, though." Megan leaned back on her palms and squinted against the morning sunshine. "How's your Aunt Rita been getting on with Blue while you've been working?"

Jack rolled his eyes. "Oh, they're getting on like a house on fire. She's so attached to him, she wants me to leave him at her place when I move out. Even Uncle Bill's taken to him."

Megan chuckled. Jack's uncle Bill was the gruff old seadog who operated the ferry service across the bay, and he wasn't known for his soft side. "Well, that's saying something. How's Blue getting on with their Labrador?"

"Great" said Jack. "Fitz is ancient, but Blue's bought out the puppy in him again.

Secrets, Lies, and Puppy Dog Eyes

It really warms your heart to see it. You should come visit one day and see them playing together."

Megan nodded. "I'd like that. It's a date."

"You still enjoying being back in the village?" said Jack, nodding across the green towards Kismet Cottage.

"I am," said Megan, "but I really should be looking for somewhere else to live. Not that I don't love Mum and Dad being around but, once they're back, I have a feeling we're going to get under each other's feet after a while. And, anyway, I'd like to have some independence, so I don't want to get too comfortable living back at home."

Blue opened his eyes and yawned. He pushed himself to his feet and pulled at the lace on Jack's tennis shoe, pawing it with his huge foot. Tab opened a wary eye and assessed the situation before slinking off back to his favourite spot: the wall outside Kismet Cottage where he liked to sit, sunning and preening himself.

Jack stood up and groaned. "I hate when your joints tell you when you're getting older. Right, come on, Blue, let's go get some exercise."

They walked through the village, Megan and Jack chattering about anything and everything and Blue trotting along beside them, stopping to sniff whenever they passed something of interest. He picked up a stick and held it between his teeth until something else caught his attention, when he dropped it and picked that up instead.

"He's started taking stuff home and burying it in the garden," said Jack. "The other day, he found a stick that was almost as big as him. He carried it all the way home and went straight to the end of Aunt Rita's vegetable patch and buried it there."

Megan laughed. "He's going to be a fantastic companion for you, isn't he? He's such a good-natured little dog."

Blue dropped the stick he was holding and put his nose in the air.

"He's got the scent of something," said Jack. "Maybe there's a cat nearby."

"Maybe," said Megan, turning her face up to the autumn sun. "Anyway, what do you want to do today? Seeing as Sunday's the only day of the week you're not working on the school, and it's a glorious day, why don't we make the most of it?"

Jack nodded. "Sure. What did you have in mind?"

"How about we stop somewhere for a coffee and read the papers, then have lunch at The Ferry Inn, and I'll cook dinner later?"

"Sounds like an excellent plan, but only if coffee and lunch is on me... Can you smell

Secrets, Lies, and Puppy Dog Eyes

smoke?" Jack looked down at Blue, whose nose was still up, sniffing the air. "Do you think someone's started a bonfire?"

"I'd be surprised at this time of the morning," said Megan, "but if it is, goodness knows what they're burning. It's a really acrid smell."

"Look, you can see the smoke now." Jack pointed to a faint plume of smoke in the near distance. "We'll probably pass it any minute."

They turned into the next street to see a fire engine, a police car, and a small crowd of people on the pavement outside a cottage, smoke still rising from the fire which had been extinguished. The front seemed untouched by the flames, but the small extension at the back looked to have been badly damaged by the fire.

"Oh my goodness!" said Megan, to a woman in curlers, a dressing gown and furry slippers. "We thought it was a bonfire."

The woman shook her head. "It took hold during the night, or early this morning, whichever way you want to look at it. We were all asleep, though, so it was a while before the smell woke anyone and the fire brigade was called."

"Was anyone in there?" said Jack.

"I don't know. After the fire engine arrived, PC Denby turned up, then PS Tibbs, but we haven't seen anyone since, so we don't know if William or Teresa were in there, or if they're okay if they were."

Megan's eyes widened. "This is *their* place?"

The woman nodded. "Oh yes, didn't you know? They used to live in Danecroft Road, but they moved here a few years ago. They only added the art studio recently, though—that's the bit that caught fire. Actually, I'm not sure if Teresa's there at the moment, because I saw her the other day and she was off to stay at her dad's place for a while. Apparently, Annabel's a bit upset over that obituary lark." The woman shook her head, with a disapproving click of her tongue. "Can't say I blame her."

A man in a football shirt and a pair of tracksuit bottoms piped up, "William's been working on the stuff for the Christmas concert day and night," he said. "If it's got frazzled, he's going to be devastated."

"You can say that again," said the woman. "We had to take our grandson to A&E last week after he got his grandad's dentures stuck in his mouth—don't ask—and by the time we got back, it was quarter-past two in the morning, and William was still hard at work. He's put so much effort into it."

"Well, I'm sure he'll be disappointed, but as long as he and Teresa are okay, that's the most important thing, isn't it?" said Megan.

Blue sniffed at the small patch of grass in the front garden, picked up a large branch from the rose border and settled himself down, looking around at the assembled crowd with his big blue eyes.

"That's a cracker of a dog you've got there," said the man. "He's going to be a big 'un. Look at the size of his paws."

Jack grinned. "Yeah, he's going to be a big boy, I reckon."

Fred Denby suddenly appeared from the back of the house, a roll of police crime scene tape in his hand. "If you could all move back, please. And could you get your dog off the grass, please, Mr Windsor? I need to cordon off the area."

Jack whistled and Blue came trotting over with the branch between his teeth. "If they're cordoning it off, it must be a crime scene, so I guess the fire must have been set deliberately."

"What's going on?" the woman in curlers asked Fred. "Was there anyone in there? Are William and Teresa alright?"

"I'm afraid I can't tell you anything yet," said Fred, with stern-faced authority. "But you'll find out soon enough, I'm sure."

"Come on," said Megan to Jack. "I don't feel right, hanging around outside."

Sherri Bryan

They walked off, stopping when a car drove past and pulled up outside the cottage.

"Hey, aren't those the detectives who were here before?" Jack nodded to Sam and Harvey who exchanged comments with Fred as they climbed into their white forensic overalls, before making their way to the back of the house.

"Yes, that's them," said Megan, with a frown.

Jack glanced at her, an eyebrow raised. "I'm no expert, but I'd say that's not a good sign."

"I'm no expert, either, but I'd agree with you, said Megan.

ooooooo

"Police have launched a murder investigation after a cottage annexe in Nicholson Road was burnt to the ground in the early hours of this morning, and firefighters recovered the body of a fifty-six year old man from the severely damaged structure.

"Chief Fire Officer, Brian Phelps, confirmed that the blaze had been brought under control soon after they attended the call, but they were too late to save the victim. Mr Phelps also confirmed that the fire had been started deliberately, the spread of which was hastened by a number of highly flammable items in the immediate vicinity of the blaze.

Secrets, Lies, and Puppy Dog Eyes

"Meanwhile, the detective in charge of the murder investigation, DI Sam Cambridge, has been quick to reassure Bliss Bay residents that his team will do all they can to ensure the perpetrator is caught as soon as possible.

"If anyone has any information which may help the police in their investigation, please call Crime Busters, or the incident room at Bliss Bay Village police station, where a team of detectives are waiting to take your call. The numbers will remain on the bottom of your screen for the duration of this news programme.

"In other news..."

Megan's fork paused halfway to her open mouth as she tasted the sauce for the chicken and asparagus tray bake. "Jack! They found a man's body in the cottage. It must have been William's."

Jack's face appeared in the serving hatch between the kitchen and living room, then disappeared just as quickly. "God, that's awful. No one else found?"

"Just the man, apparently. I can't imagine how Teresa must be feeling. That family have had bad luck coming from all sides recently."

"Who'd want to set fire to William's art studio?" said Jack, as he rolled around on the rug with Tabastion and Blue.

"I have no idea," said Megan, crossly, banging lids onto pans and slamming the oven door shut. "Why anyone would want to set fire to *anything* deliberately is beyond me, *especially* if they knew someone was inside. Honestly, what's wrong with people?"

She stomped into the living room and curled up on the couch with a frown.

"I wonder if it's connected to the obituaries?" said Jack, from the floor, where Tabastion was stretched out across his chest, and Blue was chewing on his shoelace.

"Why would it be?" said Megan.

Jack spread his hands. "I don't know. Maybe it isn't, but the obits have been directed at the Hilliers, and William's girlfriend was Teresa Hillier. Maybe whoever set the fire is the same person who's been harassing the family, but now they've taken things up a level?"

Megan's frown deepened. "You know, that's what DI Cambridge said could happen when I spoke to him. He said harassment campaigns sometimes escalate, and it certainly looks like this one might have."

"Well, his team figured things out last time, so there's no reason they won't do the same again," said Jack. "Try not to worry about it. Let DI Cambridge and his guys take the strain. That's what they get paid for."

"Hmm, I guess you're right," said Megan. "He looked under pressure, didn't he, DI Cambridge, when he got out of the car? Did you notice?"

"I should think he is." Jack propped himself up on his elbow. "A murder investigation and an eighteen year old daughter's birthday party to pay for. Who wouldn't be under pressure?"

Chapter 14

The next morning, Megan bought a bunch of flowers from Petal's shop and took them to William's house to place outside by the front wall.

There was already a number of bouquets on the pavement, the largest of which had just been set down by Teresa, who was accompanied by Edmund, Annabel and Polly.

"I'm so sorry for your loss, Teresa," said Megan. "And to all of you."

Teresa nodded and wiped her eyes, the tissue she was using no match for the river of tears that flowed out of the red-veined eyes staring out of her blotchy red face. "What has our family ever done to anyone? Why is someone targeting us like this?" She blew her nose, trumpet-fashion.

"Thank you, Megan," said Annabel. "We can't understand who would do this. William had no enemies. None at all. He was such a good man."

"It must have been a random thing, Mum," said Polly, clinging onto Teresa with one hand and typing a message on her phone to her husband, Gary, with the other. "I reckon it'll end up being manslaughter, not murder."

Teresa began to wail and Edmund pulled her to his chest. "There, there, love, come on." He gave Megan a brief nod and a

Secrets, Lies, and Puppy Dog Eyes

cursory smile. "If you'll excuse us, we need to get home." He glared at Annabel. "Which is where we should have stayed, instead of coming out so everyone can gawp at us."

"Edmund, we came out because Teresa wanted to come and leave some flowers," said Annabel, sharply, returning his glare. "Not everything we do has to be what *you* want." She smiled at the small crowd of people on the pavement. "Thank you everyone, we appreciate your kindness in coming to pay your respects."

As they left, it occurred to Megan that it was the first time she'd ever seen Annabel Hillier come close to losing her composure. She turned to leave, and saw Fern Rudd walking up the road towards her, a small bunch of flowers in her hand.

"I can't believe it," she said, placing the bouquet against the wall. "I only just found out this morning."

"It was all over the news yesterday evening," said Megan. "Didn't you see it?"

Fern shook her head. "I smelled the smoke yesterday morning, but I didn't think anything of it. And I didn't watch any TV at all over the weekend. Colin's been in a bit of a strange mood recently, and when he'd finished work on Friday, he said he was going back to his place, and that's where he was all weekend. As he wasn't around, I thought it would be a good opportunity for me to catch up on all the films and series I love, but he hates, so I didn't see the news at all." She chewed on her thumbnail. "I don't know what's wrong with him. I asked, but he didn't want to talk much."

"I'm sure it's nothing serious," said Megan. "He's been working really hard on the school, hasn't he? Maybe it's taking its toll? I know Jack aches from head to toe at the end of every day."

"Perhaps," said Fern, with a shrug. "I wondered if it's because I've been coming on a bit too strong, so I'm backing off and leaving it up to him to get in touch." She looked at her watch. "Anyway, I'd better get to work. See you soon."

ooooooo

As the investigation into William Longhurst's murder gathered pace, and the team of detectives from Central HQ made themselves at home, Bliss Bay's small village police station buzzed with activity.

"As far as alibis go, Edmund, Annabel and Teresa Hillier all claim to have been asleep at the family home on the night of the fire," said Glen, "and we've got no evidence that disproves that. Polly, Gary and their daughter, Beatrice, were at their home, and Barnaby Hillier and his wife…" Glen paused to check his notes, "Caroline, were staying at a hotel where he's working in St. Eves."

Secrets, Lies, and Puppy Dog Eyes

Harvey took some sheets of paper from the printer.

"Boss, good news. Dawn Hillier's file and all the missing evidence have been found. They were locked in a basement with a load of other old case files. Here's the post-mortem report."

Sam pinched the bridge of his nose and blinked a few times. "Let's hope we're getting somewhere, at last." He took the report and looked through it.

"I'd say that dismisses the theory that Dawn might have committed suicide because she was depressed," said Harvey. "It says a whole peppermint was found in her mouth. Why would you start eating a sweet if you were about to kill yourself? We've seen where she died. If she really *had* been contemplating suicide, I doubt she'd have thrown herself down a small bank like that. In any case, look at what the report says about the fresh bruise just below her shoulder. She was pushed—she must have been—and it was just bad luck she hit her head on a tree stump when she landed. If she hadn't, she'd possibly still be alive today."

Sam nodded. "Possibly. What evidence has been found?"

"Dawn's coat, her shoes, a gold star that was stuck to her forehead, and a piece of wool that was found at the scene."

Sherri Bryan

"A gold star?" Sam raised an eyebrow and pushed himself up from his chair before putting on a tie in preparation for his TV appeal. "I'm keeping everything crossed that forensics can get something from it that'll bring this case to an end and give Dawn's family some closure."

"Not before time," said Harvey. "And speaking of Dawn's family, it's a good thing Teresa Hillier was staying at her dad's place on the night of the fire, or we could have been looking at a double murder."

"Hmm, and if William hadn't refused Annabel's offer to stay the night at the Hilliers' place after he'd been round for dinner, we probably wouldn't even be here, because he might still be alive," said Sam. "He must have been keen to get home, because it was bloody cold that night. Given the choice to stay in a warm house or walk home, I know what I'd have done."

"Yeah, me too," said Harvey. "He was working on something for the Christmas concert, apparently, and he wanted to get home to carry on with it."

There was a knock on the door and Fred poked his head into the office. "They're ready when you are, boss."

ooooooo

Jack had invited Megan, Des, and Sylvie for dinner at his Uncle Bill and Aunt Rita's

Secrets, Lies, and Puppy Dog Eyes

house which, conveniently, was just across the road from Des and Sylvie's.

"They're adorable together, aren't they?" said Megan, watching Bill and Rita's old Labrador, Fitz, bounding around like a dog half his age, trying to keep up with Blue.

"I'd move those if I were you, Megan," said Jack, nodding towards the boots she'd left at the end of the couch. "If Blue gets his teeth into them, you can kiss them goodbye."

"Don't be daft," said Megan. "His teeth are only tiny. He couldn't possibly do any damage to those. They're leather."

"Oh, you think they'll be safe because they're leather, do you?" said Jack, one eyebrow raised. "Just wait a minute." He ran upstairs and came back down holding a tennis shoe. "That darn dog is either burying stuff, or chewing it. This is what he did to my *leather* tennis shoe." He held up the tattered shoe, its sole flapping loose from the upper leather, like a gaping mouth.

Megan laughed and put her boots by the front door. "Well, he obviously knows when *not* to use his teeth, because he's been playing with Fitz for ages and he hasn't nipped him once."

"I 'ain't never seen nothin' like it 'efore," said Bill, munching on a mouthful of his favourite chewing tobacco. "I 'aven't seen Fitz move so fast since 'e was a pup. Look at the fun 'e's 'avin. It warms the cockles of yer 'art t'see it." He brought a grimy finger to his eye and wiped a tear from the corner. "Damn cookin' fumes, makin' my eyes water," he said, gruffly.

In the kitchen, where they were preparing dinner, Jack and Rita exchanged a knowing look. "Cooking fumes, my foot," said Rita, with an exaggerated eye-roll. "There's only one thing that'll bring a tear to that old seadog's eye, and that's Fitz."

Jack chuckled as he seasoned a tray of chicken drumsticks. "Can't disagree with that."

"When's dinner ready?" Bill called over the back of his armchair.

"Around twenty minutes," said Jack.

"So I got time t'watch the news?"

"If you really insist on having the TV on while we've got guests," said Rita.

"It'll only be fer ten minutes." Bill pointed the remote at the TV. "An' they're not guests, they're friends, so we don' 'av to stand on ceremony." He turned up the volume and gave Megan a wink. "I only do it to wind 'er up," he whispered, with a wheezy chuckle.

"That vegetable garden of yours is looking great," said Des, dragging his feet against the kitchen doormat as he came in from the garden with Sylvie. "I've got a good selection of fruit and veg down, but I really must make it bigger for next year."

Secrets, Lies, and Puppy Dog Eyes

"I think autumn's my favourite season for veg," said Sylvie, taking off her shoes and putting on the slippers she always took with her when she went visiting. "Des always makes the most wonderful soups and casseroles through autumn and winter."

"'ere, Des," called Bill. "I 'ope yeh brought yer 'armonica with yeh?"

Des patted his trouser pocket. "Course I did, Bill."

"Tha's good," said Bill, picking his teeth. "We can 'ave a proper knees up after dinner. Maybe even a sing song?"

"Look," said Megan, "it's DI Cambridge. There must be an update on William's death."

They all gathered around the TV to hear the latest.

"Good evening, I'm Detective Inspector Sam Cambridge and I'm the Senior Investigating Officer in charge of the investigation into the murder of William Longhurst.

"We are appealing to anyone who may have seen, or heard, anything suspicious between approximately half-past two and three o'clock last Sunday morning to please come forward and contact us. We know that the last sighting of Mr Longhurst alive was by a taxi driver who had just dropped off one of Mr Longhurst's neighbours, and recalls seeing him walking up the road towards his house at around twenty-past two that morning.

"Mr Longhurst was well-liked and we have found no evidence to suggest he had any enemies. Although it has been established that the fire was set deliberately in the annexe which Mr Longhurst used as an art studio, it wasn't the fire that killed him. At this stage, we believe he was killed prior to the fire being set, which the perpetrator hoped would hide their tracks and conceal the murder.

"One of the panes of glass on the door to the annexe had been smashed, which leads us to believe that someone broke in while Mr Longhurst was out earlier in the evening, and he surprised the intruder, or intruders, on his return home. We believe this to be the case, because the door was found to be open when the fire service arrived, and the breakage pattern in that particular pane of glass was different to those caused by the fire to other windows.

"At the moment, we are treating this as a random attack on an innocent man and, with this in mind, it is in the interest of the whole community that we find whoever is responsible for this terrible crime as soon as possible. Of course, we are doing everything we can to make sure we find the perpetrator, but we also need your help.

Secrets, Lies, and Puppy Dog Eyes

"In particular, we are appealing for any information which will help us to trace the murder weapon, which we believe to be a piece of wood, most likely unvarnished, and approximately four inches long on one of its sides. We believe this was used to inflict the fatal wound to Mr Longhurst before his killer set fire to the annexe. Although accelerants were used to start the fire, thanks to the quick response of the fire service, an area of the annexe remained relatively untouched by the flames, and it is in this area that we believe the murder weapon would have been found. However, there was no trace of it, which leads us to believe that the killer *may* have taken it with them when they fled.

"If you have any knowledge as to the whereabouts of this weapon, or to the identity of the person responsible for Mr Longhurst's murder, we would like to hear from you. You can get in touch with us at Bliss Bay police station, where detectives are currently working on the case, or at Crime Busters, the numbers for which are at the bottom of your screen.

"In addition, I would like to announce that, following the emergence of new evidence, we believe we have sufficient grounds to officially reopen the investigation into the death of local resident, Dawn Hillier, in 1977, with a new team of dedicated officers assigned to it.

Sherri Bryan

"Dawn was twenty-five years old when she was killed. She worked as a teacher at the old Bliss Bay School, and was a popular member of the community. The last reported sighting of her was by the caretaker at the school, at approximately quarter-past seven on the evening of Tuesday September 13th, 1977.

"When she failed to arrive home, her husband and stepchildren began a search. Dawn's body was found shortly afterwards at the bottom of an incline at the side of the bus stop she often waited at. A post-mortem concluded that there was evidence to suggest she'd been pushed, and that she died from a head injury sustained as a result of the fall,

"Her handbag, which had been missing since that day, has recently been found, and is currently undergoing forensic tests, as is the original evidence from the case, in the hopes that these will lead us to her killer.

"In the years since Dawn died, there have been significant advances in the way deaths are investigated, all of which give us the opportunity to better scrutinise the original evidence. Let me assure you that no serious crime is ever considered closed, despite the years which pass, and where there are chances to bring those who escape justice to account, we will do everything in our power to do so.

"At this time, may I also appeal to anyone who may remember anything about

Secrets, Lies, and Puppy Dog Eyes

the original case, but for whatever reason didn't speak to the police at the time, to come forward. All information will be treated in the strictest confidence.

"I would like to conclude by reassuring you that we are doing everything we can to bring the killers of Dawn Hillier and William Longhurst to justice. We look forward to hearing from you. Thank you."

Bill turned the TV off and scowled. "Tha's enough bad news for one night."

"It's about time they looked into Dawn's death again," said Rita, "and I hope they catch the bugger this time."

"Bloody terrible state of affairs, it is," said Des.

"Corporal punishment," grumbled Bill. "They should bring it back. Trouble is, criminals these days know they can get away wi' stuff, because the 'ole' justice system has gone soft, so there's no deterrent for 'em not t'commit crime. Bah!"

"He's a nice looking chap, that inspector, isn't he," said Rita, as she went back into the kitchen. "Very pleasant face. Craggy, without being saggy, do you know what I mean? A man like that would be a lovely catch for Megan, don't you think, Sylvie?"

"Hmm, he's a bit old for Megan," said Sylvie, "but that sergeant of his would be just the ticket. Young, but not too young, nice-looking, and very well groomed. I think he'd be more up Megan's street."

Megan treated them to her most indignant look. "Er, *hello*. I'm right here! And don't *you* start, Rita! What is it with the women in this village? It's bad enough that Aunty Sylv and Mum are determined to marry me off to any man with a pulse. And, for your information, DI Cambridge is about twenty years older than me, and he already has a lovely wife called Jillian. And Harvey's nice, but—" She looked at Jack, who grinned and carried on tossing the salad.

Megan stopped fussing over the dogs and crossed her arms. "In fact, why am I even trying to explain myself to you? Why do you *insist* on trying to match make? I had a horrible marriage to Laurence, and it's not been long since Hugh told me he wanted to break off the engagement and go and 'find himself' in Tuscany. Please, read my lips, both of you. I. Do. Not. Want. A. Boyfriend. Now, can we *please* just drop the subject."

"Just in time," called Jack, from the kitchen. "Dinner's ready."

ooooooo

"This is lovely chicken, Jack, it just falls off the bone," said Des, chewing on a drumstick.

Jack licked his fingers. "Thanks, but I didn't do much apart from stick it in the oven."

"And these vegetables are delicious," said Sylvie. "You can tell they're straight from the garden. They taste completely different to supermarket bought veg."

"'Ere. 'Ow d'they know that the murder weapon what killed William wasn't burnt to a crisp?" said Bill suddenly, as though he'd been pondering the answer for a while. He threw his chicken skin to Fitz and kept the bone to gnaw on himself. "Yeh'd 'ave thought it would've been, wouldn't yeh?"

"That detective said that part of the annexe was relatively untouched by the fire, didn't he?" said Rita. "And that's where they figured out the murder weapon would have been. Mind you, even if the *entire* annexe had been damaged in the fire, it's amazing the things they can find out these days, even when you'd think there was no evidence left to go on. Of course, Bill, if you ever stayed awake during CSI, you'd already know that."

"That's true," said Des, waving a chicken leg in the air. "It's not as easy to find evidence after a fire as it would be if there *hadn't* been one, but the fire department and forensics really can do some amazing work these days. For example, Detective Cambridge said they're looking for a piece of unvarnished wood with a four inch edge as the murder weapon. Now, how do you think they know that's what killed poor William after a fire swept through his art studio?" He looked around the table and jabbed at his dining companions with his chicken leg. "I'll tell you why, it's because forensics these days are incredible, and they must have found tiny fragments of wood inside the fatal wound."

"Oh, come on, Des, do you mind if we don't talk about this while we're eating," said Sylvie. "It doesn't seem very respectful."

"'Scuse me a minute," said Jack, pushing his chair away from the table. "I need to let Blue out. Be back in a bit."

"When are your mum and dad back from their cruise, Megan?" said Rita, changing the subject.

"December the 20th. I can't wait to see them again. I'm really looking forward to spending Christmas here, and Lizzie's travelling down on the 21st, so we'll all be together. Well, almost all of us." Megan looked round when she heard the kitchen door open, glad of a reason not to have to explain Evie's absence at Christmas to Rita. "Hi Blue," she said, as the puppy came trotting towards her, his nostrils twitching as the aroma of roast chicken teased them.

"Er, Megan," said Jack, leaning against the door.

"Yeah?" She glanced up at Jack, then jumped to her feet. "Are you okay? You look a bit weird."

"D'you remember when we took a walk past William and Teresa's place on the day of the fire?"

"Yes, why?"

"D'you remember the piece of wood that Blue picked up from the front yard?"

Megan crinkled her nose. "Not really. I remember him picking something up, but I don't remember what it looked like."

"Can you really not see where I'm going with this?" said Jack, looking at her intently.

Megan stared back at him, gasping suddenly. "Oh my God! You don't think the thing Blue picked up is what the police are looking for, do you?"

Jack took his jacket from the coat hook on the kitchen wall, and a torch from the shelf. "There's only one way to find out."

Megan jumped up and grabbed her coat.

"Where are you going?" asked Rita.

"I hate to tell you this, but the murder weapon that killed William could be buried in your garden. If it is, I expect Jack's digging it up right now."

They all put their coats on and followed Megan outside to where Jack was digging carefully through the patch of soil at the end of the vegetable patch.

"Hold the flashlight for me, will you, Megan? There are plenty of small sticks, and a big branch, but nothing else, I don't think," he said, looking disappointed. "I really thought there might be something here." He pushed the trowel gently into the soil once more, feeling it come into contact with something hard. "Aunt Rita, do you have a plastic food bag?"

With his hand inside the bag, he pulled a large, irregular-shaped piece of driftwood from the soil.

A piece of driftwood which, in the light from the torch, appeared to be stained with what looked very much like blood.

ooooooo

Sergeant Glen Tibbs wasn't at all happy to be sharing the station with detectives from the central police headquarters, and he was particularly peeved about giving up his office to the Detective Inspector. It wasn't a particularly big office, but the smaller one he'd been relegated to downstairs was barely big enough to accommodate a desk and chair.

Glen had never had to share the station with anyone before, other than Fred, and another police constable if circumstances warranted one. A temporary Sergeant had been posted at the station during the detectives' last visit, when Glen had been on an extended holiday, literally island-hopping his way through Greece with a broken ankle, sustained when he'd fallen off the last step down from the plane at Naxos airport.

He tried to shut out the noise the detectives made between them. They all talked too fast, walked too fast, and expected things to be done too fast. *Much* too fast for Glen's liking. He wouldn't admit it to anyone, but he was feeling more than a little displaced in his own station.

"Evening, both," he said, as Megan and Des walked through the door, letting in a blast of cold air. "Nice to see you again. Don't tell me you've been out gathering more witness statements?" He chuckled and nodded to Des's hat. "How can I help you?"

"Is DI Cambridge here, please?" said Megan. "We'd like to speak to him about William Longhurst's murder, if possible."

"I'm sure I can help you," said Glen.

"No disrespect, but we'd rather speak to DI Cambridge, if he's here, please." Megan smiled. "If he's not too busy."

Glen pursed his lips, turned on the heel of his highly-polished police issue shoe, and marched up the staircase. At the first door on the right, he turned and knocked on it smartly. "There's a lady and a gentleman downstairs, DI Cambridge," he said. "They want to speak to you about the murder investigation."

"Who is it?" Megan heard Sam ask.

"It's a Miss Fallon and a Mr Harper."

"Oh, right. Ask them to come up, will you."

Glen beckoned Megan and Des with a crooked finger and marched back down the stairs.

"Well, this is a surprise," said Sam, staring at the deerstalker pulled down over Des's ears. "Is this a social call, or are you here in your amateur sleuth capacities?" He gave a wry smile as he moved papers off chairs so they could sit down.

"Yes, it's a surprise for us, too," said Megan. "We were hoping you wouldn't have any reason to come back to Bliss Bay. We're still getting over the last time you were here."

"I'm not here by choice, I can assure you," said Sam. "Although it's quite nice to be away from Zoe's constant chatter about unicorns and all things pink, red and sparkly for a few days." He grinned. "Anyway, what can I do for you?"

"Well," said Des. "We saw your TV appeal. You said William Longhurst had already been murdered before the fire was started."

"That's right."

"And that the fatal wound was made by a piece of wood?"

"We believe so, yes."

Des took the plastic bag from his pocket. "This piece of driftwood was taken from William Longhurst's front garden the morning after the fire, before the police cordon was put up."

"My friend's dog picked it up," said Megan. "He's forever bringing stuff home to bury, and we had no idea what it was—or that it was even there—or we'd have come in earlier."

"It's only when we heard about the search for the murder weapon, and Jack remembered the dog had picked up something from William's garden that morning, that he thought it might be right under our noses," said Des. "So he dug up everything he'd buried and found what's in that bag. It looks like it's stained with blood, so it could be what you're looking for."

"Well, I'll be..." said Sam. He stood up and shook hands. "Thank you. This is exactly why appeals can make such a difference. I'm going to get this to forensics right away."

"Glad we could be of service," said Des. "And, of course, our lips are sealed. We won't tell a soul what we've found. You never know who's listening, do you?"

CHAPTER 15

Since Sam's TV appeal, the phones at the station had been ringing off the hook.

While some of the calls gave the hope of new leads, most of them were from people with sketchy recollections of the night Dawn was killed.

"We've had two calls from residents who are sure they saw Dawn get on the bus that night," said Harvey. "Another caller is convinced he saw her in a passionate embrace with a man at the school gates, and someone else claims that Dawn appeared to her in a dream last week with the name of her killer, but when she woke up, she couldn't remember what it was."

Sam raised an eyebrow.

The sound of footsteps on the stairs was followed by Fred's face around the door. "Sandra and Walter Grayling are here to see you, boss. They specifically asked to speak to you."

"The woman who told Glen that Dawn had a child adopted, and her brother?"

Fred nodded. "That's them."

"Well, you'd better ask them to come up."

ooooooo

"We're delighted that you've reopened the investigation into Dawn's death," said Sandra, her gloved hands tightly clasped in the lap of her tartan skirt. "I assume DS Tibbs will have already told you all about my recent conversation with him and the valuable evidence I gave him?"

"You're referring to information that Mrs Hillier was taking medication for depression at the time of her death because she'd given up a child for adoption?"

"That's exactly right," said Sandra. "And she didn't tell her rogue of a husband a word about the baby." She leaned across the desk towards Sam. "If you ask me, you could do a lot worse than to question Edmund again. I'm still convinced he was involved in her death somehow. It was very convenient that he knew exactly where to find her body, don't you think?"

Walter cleared his throat. "Well, it could have been that he genuinely stumbled across Dawn by accident, Sandra. He *was* out searching for her before anyone else, after all."

Sandra fixed her brother with a steely stare. "Whose side are you on, Walter? I thought we agreed to come to speak to the Detective Inspector to convince him that he and his team should be looking in Edmund Hillier's direction if they want to put Dawn's killer behind bars."

Walter blushed. "Yes, we did, but we should be careful about making accusations without any proof."

"Poppycock!" said Sandra. "That man is as guilty as sin." She shook a finger at Sam. "If you keep the pressure on, he'll crack eventually. I'm absolutely convinced that you'll find the answer to Dawn's death at the Hillier house."

oooooo

After Sandra and Walter had left the police station, Sam considered his next steps. He looked at the list of items which had been found in Dawn's handbag.

The purse had been full of money, which backed up the claim in the note found at the school that she hadn't been the victim of a robbery.

The medication indicated that she'd sought medical help for depression, which Sandra Grayling said Dawn suffered after her parents forced her to give up her child for adoption.

The baby photograph must surely be Dawn's child, although there was no indication as to whether it was a boy or a girl, because it was dressed in a yellow romper suit.

Sam ruffled his hair with both hands and leaned back in his chair.

"What d'you think, boss?" said Harvey.

"I think it's about time we asked Edmund about this baby to see what he's got to say about it."

oooooo

Secrets, Lies, and Puppy Dog Eyes

"A baby photograph?" said Edmund. "I have no idea who it could be. I certainly never saw it."

"It couldn't be hers, could it?" said Annabel.

Edmund fixed her with an incredulous glare. "I think Dawn would probably have mentioned that tiny detail at some point during our marriage," he said, sarcastically, before turning back to Sam.

"I can only assume it's a relative's baby, or maybe a friend's. Someone she knew from before she came to Bliss Bay. From teacher training college, perhaps. In any case, it's certainly no one she ever told me about, so I doubt it's of any consequence. I'd suggest you ask Dawn's parents, but they both passed away years ago and she was an only child, so there are no siblings you can speak to, either."

"The thing is, Mr Hillier," said Sam, "we've received information which indicates that Dawn had a baby before she came to Bliss Bay, but it was given up for adoption."

All the colour drained from Edmund's face. "Don't be preposterous, man! She wouldn't have kept something like that from me. Who gave you this information?"

"I'm afraid I can't say, but it was someone who Dawn apparently took into her confidence. I should stress that we have no proof, but it seems as though that may have been the case. I wanted to ask you about it in the hopes it may help shed some light on what happened to Dawn."

Edmund sat rigid in his chair and said nothing.

"I understand from Sergeant Tibbs that you knew your wife was taking antidepressants?" said Sam.

Edmund nodded. "Yes, I did. And it became common knowledge shortly before she died. I seem to recall the receptionist at the doctor's surgery had a very loose tongue, and most of the villagers had a propensity to gossip."

"But you don't know *why* she was taking them?"

"I have no idea. I'm sure I must have asked her at the time, but she was sometimes inclined to be tearful, and I probably wasn't very sympathetic back then. As I've already said, Dawn had everything she wanted, so why she'd feel the need to take that kind of medication is a mystery to me. Probably something to do with women's problems, which we never discussed."

"You don't think she might have been depressed because of the baby?" said Annabel.

"For heaven's sake!" roared Edmund. "There *was* no baby! I was her husband, Annabel. Tell me, what sort of woman would keep a secret like that from her husband?" He scratched his head in an impatient fashion. "So, what happens now, DI Cambridge?"

"Well, as we've discussed before, forensic tests are being carried out on the bag, and its contents," said Sam. "Of course, it's highly likely that DNA other than Dawn's will be found... on the money in her purse, for example, all of which will have been handled by other people before it ended up with her, but it's unlikely it will belong to whoever pushed her down the bank. When forensics have finished their tests, we'll let you know if they find anything conclusive, of course."

Edmund nodded. "Right, thank you. And what about the evidence that was found at the scene of Dawn's death?"

"I'm afraid I can't tell you anything about that yet, either, Mr. Hillier," said Sam, "but I can give you my word that you'll be kept informed every step of the way."

"I hope so. As you can imagine, this is a terrible time for my entire family. The sooner you can tell us something that will help us to understand why these dreadful things have happened, the better."

"Who is it, Dad?" Teresa appeared at the living room door, her eyes puffy and swollen and her greasy blonde hair hanging in strands around her tearstained red face. A dressing gown was tied tightly around her waist, covering her pyjamas and thick socks

"Oh, Teresa, sweetheart, what are you doing up? You should go back to bed," cooed Annabel.

"She's hardly slept since Will… Since the fire, Detective Cambridge," said Edmund. "Every time she manages to drop off, a nightmare wakes her up."

"Who are you?" she shuffled into the living room. "Are you going to find out what happened to William? And Dawn?" She sighed. "So many people, coming and going, so many questions." Her eyes filled with tears. "Why is this happening to us? What have we ever done to anyone? First Dawn, then the obituaries, and now William."

Sam watched as Edmund put his arm around his daughter. "I'm DI Sam Cambridge. I'm in charge of the investigation into William's death. As I just said to your dad, as soon as we have anything that will help us find out what happened to William, you'll be the first to know. I know that won't bring you much comfort now, but I want you to know that we won't stop until we can get you some answers."

Teresa nodded and shuffled from the room, Annabel at her side.

As Edmund watched them leave, he turned to Sam and said, "I can't lose anyone else. Please, whatever you have to do, do it quickly."

Secrets, Lies, and Puppy Dog Eyes

Sam nodded. "I'll see myself out."

Edmund sat in his armchair, a dark look on his face. He didn't want to believe it, but it all made sense.

Dawn's mood swings. Her tears. Her reluctance to have a child with him.

She'd been suffering so much and he hadn't once shown her any sympathy or compassion. Had he really been such a monster that his own wife hadn't been able to share her deepest secret with him?

As the realisation dawned, and the truth hit home, Edmund put his head in his hands and sobbed.

Chapter 16

"We've got a result back from forensics, boss," said Harvey. "It's from skin and hair that was found on Dawn Hillier's coat."

"Is it red hair?"

"No, it's blonde, and there were a couple with the root attached."

"And who does it belong to?"

"Annabel Hillier."

ooooooo

"For the last time, I am telling you, I had nothing to do with Dawn's death!"

"We're going round and round in circles, Mrs Hillier," said Sam.

"But why are you questioning me like this? I can't be here. I need to be at home with my family. Edmund needs me and Teresa needs me. What on earth is going on?" Annabel clutched at her solicitor's arm. "Miles, do something!"

"You haven't been charged with anything, Annabel," said Miles Gregory. "And you can't be held indefinitely unless you *are* charged. It's true that the police can apply to hold you for longer, but in the absence of any proof that you've done anything wrong, I doubt that will happen."

"Please, you have to get me out of here!" said Annabel. "I don't even understand what I'm being accused of. I've lost count of the number of times I've told the police that I

Secrets, Lies, and Puppy Dog Eyes

didn't even know Dawn." She ran her hands through her hair as she tried to compose herself. "Look, ask anyone. Ask my husband, my mother, my sister, my friends! They'll all tell you that I had no knowledge of Dawn until *after* she died."

"Yes, I see from statements you've given that you say you knew *of* her, but you didn't know her personally," said Sam.

"Exactly," said Annabel. "Even though Bliss Bay was a much smaller community back then than it is now, not everyone knew each other well. That's what I mean. I knew she was a teacher but we weren't friends. We might have said hello a few times—I really can't remember—but that's all.

"I see." Sam scratched his head. "I'm a bit baffled, then, as to why your DNA was found all over Dawn's coat?"

Annabel's face paled. "What? That can't be possible. There's no way it could have been. There must be a mistake. There *has* to be!"

Sam stared at her. "I'm afraid there's no mistake, Mrs Hillier."

Annabel gulped and shook her head. "I honestly have no idea how that's happened, but I swear to you, I had nothing to do with her death. DNA isn't a hundred percent accurate, is it?

"That's true, but samples of skin *and* hair that were found at the scene of Dawn's death are a match to the DNA you provided after the second obituary appeared. The DNA your husband insisted the entire family provided in order that it may be excluded from anything the police found when they were searching for the person responsible for the obituaries. So, to answer your question, yes, it's true that DNA isn't always totally reliable, but there is no doubt in this case that yours was found at the scene of Dawn's death."

"But I wasn't there!" said Annabel, frantically. "I didn't kill her! And I have no idea why I'm here, because I wasn't involved in anything."

"You see?" said Sam. "The circle has been completed. We're back where we started."

Annabel clutched her solicitor's arm again. "Please, Miles, *do* something!"

Miles Gregory drummed his manicured fingernails on the table. "Mrs Hillier, the presence of your DNA at a forty-year old crime scene does not prove you were the perpetrator. The police will have to prove, without any doubt, that you were responsible for Dawn Hillier's death."

Annabel gulped. "*Responsible for her death*? Oh good grief, I can't believe this is happening. Can I see my husband? What about William's funeral? I can't miss that. It's out of the question. Miles, *please!*"

Secrets, Lies, and Puppy Dog Eyes

Miles crossed his arms, and one expensively-suited leg over the other. "DI Cambridge, if you have nothing to charge my client with, may I suggest you release her? She's hardly going to leave the country so if you need to question her again, I'm sure you'll find her at home, especially in view of her current family circumstances."

Sam gritted his teeth. Despite the evidence which showed Annabel's DNA on Dawn's coat, he knew it wasn't enough to charge her with anything. He'd hoped her cool exterior would crack and she'd confess under pressure but, regrettably, no such thing had happened.

After Annabel had left the station, he spoke to his team.

"Right, listen please, all of you. Either Annabel Hillier is as guilty as sin and lying through her teeth, or she's really not involved and we're missing something that's right under our noses. In either case, we're going to go over every piece of evidence again. Every statement, every report, every interview log, every witness account. Everything from the original case and everything we've found out since. If we have to work 24/7 to solve this case, that's what we're going to do."

Chapter 17

Having offered his condolences to William's father, who was being comforted by friends, and Teresa who was being comforted by the entire Hillier family, Sam slipped away to pay his respects to William's mother.

"I'm very sorry for your loss, Mrs Longhurst."

Edna Longhurst gave Sam a brief nod and dabbed at the constant stream of tears spouting from her eyes. "Thank you, Detective, although I can't quite believe he's gone. It hasn't sunk in yet, you see. And my husband's gone completely to pieces. All his life, Cyril's been a great believer of the British stiff upper lip, but I'm afraid his has deserted him for the time being."

"Of course," said Sam. "I can understand why."

An elderly woman appeared from a nearby huddle of mourners and sat down next to Edna. "I keep telling her that it'll take time to accept what's happened, but I know it's not making her feel any better," she said, taking Edna's hand. "And I know what I'm talking about, because I lost two of my boys when their tank went over a landmine. That was years ago, and the only way I get through it is to tell myself that they were doing what they loved when they died—they'd both wanted to join the army all their lives, you see." She shook her head.

"It's not the order of things. Parents shouldn't have to bury their children, but what can you do?" She shrugged her bony shoulders. "You never get over it, but time does help to ease the pain a little. I just thank God I still have my other son and my daughter."
She stuck out a wrinkled hand to Sam. "I'm Deborah Kent, by the way. I'm William's aunt. I've travelled all the way from Chester to be here. I'll be staying with Edna and Cyril for a while."

"It's good to meet you, Mrs Kent," said Sam. "And I'm very sorry for your loss, also."

As other mourners arrived to pay their respects to Edna, Sam ignored the black looks being sent his way from Edmund and Annabel Hillier and said his goodbyes to Megan, Des and Sylvie.

He was about to leave the room when a deep voice called out to him. He turned to see a short man in an ill-fitting suit, an extra-large knot in his tie, and his blond hair falling over his eyes at the front and past his collar at the back. He extended his arm.

"DI Cambridge. I'm Barnaby Hillier. I just wanted to introduce myself and say thank you for all you're doing to find the people responsible for Dawn and William's deaths." A brief smile crinkled the skin at the side of his eyes. "Even though I've only been a couple of hours away, we've been working to such a tight deadline, I couldn't spare the time to get here before now. At one point, I wasn't even sure if we were going to make the funeral, but we managed to get finished in time. I'm glad we made it. Everyone's in a terrible state. My place is here at the moment, not miles away."

"Sorry to meet you under these circumstances," said Sam, shaking hands. "I'm sorry for your loss."

Barnaby shrugged and scratched his head. "What can you do? You can't live without experiencing loss at some point."

Sam nodded. "I suppose not. You've been working in St. Eves, that's right, isn't it?"

"Yes. My wife and I have been there since September, on a surveying job, but now that's over, we'll be stopping with Dad and Annabel for a while." He gave Sam a wry smile. "You probably already know, but we were staying at The President Hotel. You can check with them, if you like. They can prove we've been there every day since the 15th of September until yesterday evening, when we checked out." His brown eyes darted left and right in his ruddy face. "I've watched enough crime dramas to know that spouses, family members, and close friends are always the first to be considered as suspects in murder cases, until evidence proves otherwise.

Secrets, Lies, and Puppy Dog Eyes

"Speaking of which, I hope you don't mind me saying, but I think you're sniffing at the wrong tree as far as Annabel's concerned. I have no idea how her DNA ended up on Dawn's coat, but if you knew her like I do, you'd know there's no way she could have been involved in what happened to Dawn. Just my opinion, obviously, not trying to tell you how to do your job." Barnaby pulled at his shirt collar. "I'm not used to wearing suits, so I shall be glad when I can get out of this. Well, I'd better get back to the family. Good to meet you, DI Cambridge."

As Sam left the room, he noticed Fern Rudd and Colin Havers whispering together in a corner, and nodded a curt goodbye.

ooooooo

Sam shoved his hands deep into his pockets

"Harvey, can we get a photograph of the coat that Annabel's DNA was found on? I want to see if there's a reaction when I show it to her."

"You think she'll remember it after all these years?" said Harvey.

"If I'd been responsible for someone's death," said Sam, "I'm pretty sure it'd take years before I could even begin to get their image out of my head. Just a thought."

"I'll get on it, boss."

ooooooo

Sherri Bryan

"Thank you for coming in again," said Sam, sliding the photograph across the table.

"What's this?" said Annabel, picking it up, and showing it to Miles.

Sam watched for a reaction, but there was none. Not even a flicker.

"It's the coat Dawn was wearing that had your DNA all over it."

Annabel stared at it. "I don't understand. How could... Oh! Oh!" Her hand flew to her mouth and she burst into tears. "Oh, thank God! I know what happened! *I know what happened*!

"I'd completely forgotten all about this coat, but my sister, Pamela, came over from France—she'd just finished au-pairing for a family there—and she asked me if I wanted it. They'd bought it for her as a thank you present, but she hated purple. She'd always thought it was an unlucky colour after a purple car ran into her at some traffic lights. Anyway, she thought it was unlucky, so she didn't even try the coat on, but *I* did. It was too small for me, though. I remember now that the buttons were gaping all the way down the front.

"Pamela said she was going to see if she could sell it, so she put a card in the village shop window with our parents' phone number on it. I remember her telling me that someone called her an hour after she'd left the shop and said they were interested, so she arranged to meet them in the market square. The woman tried on the coat, loved it, and bought it from Pamela on the spot.

"It must have been Dawn, and that's why my DNA's on it. And the reason why that witness thought it was me is because Pam and I looked really similar in those days. We were both tall, had long blonde hair and similar dress sense, but I was a few pounds heavier. Even from a close distance, I can completely understand how someone might have thought it was me with Dawn. It was just a case of mistaken identity." Annabel breathed a huge sigh. "If you give me a piece of paper, I'll give you my sister's number and you can call her. She'll confirm that everything I've said is true."

She gave Sam the number and he left the room. He'd make the call, but his gut told him that Annabel was telling the truth.

The look of relief on her face when she realised how her DNA had been found at the scene of Dawn's death had told him more than words ever could.

ooooooo

"Her sister backed up everything she said," said Harvey. "And I also went into the village shop to ask the owner, Rob Brennan, for a contact number for his parents. It was a long shot, but they used to run the shop until Rob and his wife, Olivia, took over, so I wondered if they might remember Annabel

Hillier's sister going in to put the card in the window."

"And did they?"

Harvey nodded. "Alec Brennan remembered the woman, but not the coat, and his wife remembered someone asking if they could put a card and a photo in the shop window, but didn't see who it was, because Alec dealt with it. Neither of them knew it was Dawn Hillier who'd taken them out of the window, they just realised some time later that they'd gone. When Dawn died, the fact she was wearing a purple coat wasn't even reported, or it might have rung a bell with them."

"So, Annabel's definitely in the clear." Sam got up from his chair. "Good work, Harvey. Even though this means we've taken a step back from thinking we had Dawn's killer at last, I get as much pleasure from clearing suspects of any wrongdoing as I do from proving it. Come on, let's go and break the good news."

ooooooo

"Did you hear that Annabel had been interviewed by the police?" said Petal, as she and Megan caught up on the recent village gossip.

Megan nodded. "At the last WA meeting, she told everyone what had been going on, and Aunty Sylv reported back.

Apparently, she thought she was going to be locked up at one point."

"It makes you wonder how many innocent people are serving prison sentences, doesn't it?" said Petal. "If she hadn't been able to come up with an explanation about how her DNA ended up on Dawn's coat, I dread to think what would have happened."

The bell above the café door jangled and Sam walked in.

"Morning, DI Cambridge," called Megan from the flower shop.

"Miss Fallon." Sam returned the greeting with a smile.

"No need for the formality," said Megan. "I've been getting on so well with Zoe and Jillian, I feel like one of the family."

Sam grinned. "Two women in my life is quite enough, thank you." He looked over the baked goods display and chose a lemon doughnut and a coffee.

"Are those for eat in or take away?" asked Amisha.

"Actually, I *was* going to take them away but maybe I'll sit down at a table for a change instead of eating on the run." Sam made himself comfortable and took a local newspaper from the rack to read while he had ten minutes alone.

He'd barely read the headline of the front page story when he felt a tap on his shoulder.

"DI Cambridge?"

He turned in his chair to see Edna Longhurst and her sister-in-law, Deborah Kent, on the table behind him.

"Oh, good morning." Sam nodded a greeting. "Nice to see you again." He turned back to his newspaper, and picked up the doughnut Amisha had just delivered to the table.

"We were just talking about old times," said Edna, totally oblivious to the fact that Sam might want to read the paper.

He looked round and smiled. "Yes, it's good to reminisce sometimes."

Deborah opened her handbag and took out a small photo album. "Here, these are my boys. The ones I was telling you about at William's funeral. D'you remember?" She handed the book to Sam and he looked down at two strapping young men dressed in full military uniform. "Handsome lads, weren't they?"

"They certainly were. A credit to you."

"If you start at the beginning, you'll see them when they were kids," said Deborah, getting up from her chair and leaning over Sam's shoulder. "They were always getting into scrapes, but they were good boys." She pointed

Secrets, Lies, and Puppy Dog Eyes

to a photograph of her sons with a group of children. "Here, let me show you. That's my Mark and that's Ralph. And these are my other two, Rosalind and Andrew."

Sam nodded. "There's a definite family resemblance."

"And this one here is William," said Deborah.

"You've got a photo of William?" said Edna. "I didn't realise. Can I see it?"

Sam handed her the book and she peered at the photograph.

"Oh! I remember the day this was taken." Edna blinked her watery eyes. "That was back in the day when everyone used to think he was a girl, because of his hair, do you remember, Deb?"

Deborah chuckled. "He begged and begged you to take him to the barbers, didn't he, but you wouldn't." She turned back to Sam. "I shouldn't laugh, really, but the whole family had got together one weekend for my birthday and all his cousins were teasing him. We were just about to sit down to dinner and William walked into the dining room with all his hair chopped off. He'd taken a pair of scissors from the bathroom cabinet and cut it himself. And he'd made a right mess of the job, too! You were furious, weren't you?"

"Only because I loved his hair," said Edna, "and I wanted him to keep it the way it was. I still don't understand why anyone would want to chop off all those lovely curls. I kept some of them, you know."

"He looked alright once you'd taken him to the barbers to have it tidied up, though, didn't he? In fact, he looked very smart."

"Yes, but he looked too grown up," said Edna. "I just wanted the old Curly back."

Sam's ears pricked up. "Did you say 'Curly'?"

Edna nodded. "That's what his cousins used to call him. Actually, it started off as Curly Shirley, because his hair was so blonde and beautiful—just like Shirley Temple's—but William got so furious about it, they dropped the Shirley and just called him Curly, but he hated that just as much. After his haircut, he told them all that if they ever called him it again, he'd give them a black eye."

"There wasn't much chance of that happening, though," said Deborah, "because we moved away soon after that for my husband's job, and William only ever saw his cousins a few times a year."

"Just to be absolutely sure," said Sam, "William went to the old Bliss Bay School, didn't he?"

"Yes, that's right."

"Mrs. Longhurst, I wonder if you'd mind if I asked you a few questions about

William? Some of them might seem a little strange."

Edna looked puzzled, but shook her head. "I could talk about him all day and all night, so you ask away."

"Did anyone else call him Curly?"

"Not if they wanted to keep their teeth," said Deborah.

"No, just his cousins, as far as I know," said Edna.

"Is there any chance that anyone else might have known his nickname, do you think?"

Edna shrugged. "I don't know, although I suppose it could have slipped out in conversation over the years. We were always getting out the photo albums when visitors called round, so it might have been mentioned then, but I couldn't tell you to whom. It's possible that a few of his friends, their parents, and even some of his teachers might have known, but I couldn't be sure."

Sam nodded. "This may sound like a strange question, but would you happen to know if William had any friends at school who had the nickname, 'Red'?"

Edna frowned. "Not to my knowledge. There were a few kids at the school who had red hair, but I can't remember their names."

Sam felt the excitement ebb from his body. He'd thought he was on the verge of finding out the identity of Dawn Hillier's killer and, possibly, the prime suspect in William's murder, too.

ooooooo

"So, Curly was William Longhurst?" said Harvey.

"Well, we won't know for sure if he's the Curly who wrote the note until we get the results of the DNA tests, but I'd bet all the money in my wallet that he was. It makes sense, doesn't it? He was alive and in good health until the note was found that threatened to reveal Dawn's killer and then, a few days later, he ends up dead." Sam rubbed his hands together. "We're getting closer, Harvey, I can feel it. We're just not getting there fast enough."

Chapter 18

On the day of Zoe's party, Megan arrived at the Cambridge house early to make sure that everything she'd organised arrived on time, and that everything went exactly according to plan.

It had been great to speak with her old suppliers again, some of whom had given her favourable rates when she'd twisted their arms and told them she was just starting out on her own.

She loved the buzz she got when she organised an event, and her stomach was starting to do its usual flip-flops. Hers was nothing compared to Zoe's excitement, though, which had been increasing with every hour that passed and which reached fever pitch when eighteen life-sized red and pink furry unicorns were delivered to the front door.

"Oh my God, Megan, this is going to be SO amazing!" She burst into tears and waved her hands in front of her eyes. "Thank you SO much."

"You're welcome but it's your mum and dad you should be thanking. If it wasn't for them, I wouldn't even be here."

Zoe nodded. "Oh, yeah, I know. I get a bit emotional when they do nice stuff for me, so I haven't thanked them yet, but I will."

She ran off to call her friends for the umpteenth time that day with an update. As it was Saturday, Jillian wasn't working, but Sam was still in Bliss Bay.

"How are things in the village?" said Jillian, as she and Megan took the chance to have a coffee break an hour before the first guest was due to arrive.

"Oh, you know, not bad, but not brilliant. We'll all feel much more at ease once Sam and his team have got things worked out."

Jillian nodded. "I'm sure they will. He's very thorough. And once something gets under his skin, he won't leave it until it's dealt with, however long it takes."

The kitchen door swung open and Zoe appeared in a pink ballet dress with a tutu skirt, red ballet slippers and fluorescent pink tights. Her top lip was painted pink, her bottom lip, red, and her nails were painted in a similar fashion—one red, one pink, and so on.

"Oh wow, I think I need my sunglasses," said Megan.

"D'you like it?" said Zoe, executing a perfect pirouette.

"You look lovely," said Megan. "And I'm very impressed with the moves."

"Years of ballet lessons," said Jillian, as Zoe squealed when her best friends, Suki and Rikki, arrived early and she ran to greet them with more excited squeals as she opened the door and they all admired each other's outfits and chose their masks.

Secrets, Lies, and Puppy Dog Eyes

Jillian picked up her coffee mug and grinned. "Something tells me I'm going to need a paracetamol and a lie down in a dark room by the time the evening's over."

ooooooo

With the party well underway, Megan kept a discreet distance. Her job was done, and she was a guest now, but it was difficult for her to switch off at an event she'd organised. She just wanted to be sure the party was going the way Zoe had planned.

She stuck up her thumb and Zoe danced over, her mask obscuring everything but her eyes. Her pink face weaved in front of Megan's and she shouted above the sound of the music.

"It's awesome! Everyone's having a wicked time!"

Megan nodded, and made her way back to the kitchen, where Jillian had been instructed to remain for the evening, to avoid embarrassing Zoe in front of her friends. As Zoe had said earlier, with a concerned expression on her petite features, "Er, you won't actually come into the living room, will you, Mum?"

"Why?" Jillian had asked, throwing Zoe a suspicious look through narrowed eyes. "What are you going to be doing in there that you're so worried I might see?"

"Nothing, but it's just that you're, like, my mum. I mean, you can say hi and bye, obvs, but if you were to come in and start doing your Mum dance, I swear, I'd die of embarrassment on the spot."

"*What* 'Mum dance'?"

The one you *always* do at weddings and parties when you've had too many glasses of wine. You know the one I mean."

"Well, if *I* can't come in," Jillian had said, "then Megan's going to pop in a couple of times, just to make sure everything's going according to plan. Okay?"

Zoe had thought about it, and nodded her head. "Okay, that's cool."

"How's it all going?" Jillian asked, as Megan sat down at the kitchen table.

"Everything's fine. They're all having a great time, just behaving like eighteen year olds. Well-behaved eighteen year olds, I hasten to add."

"That's good. Thanks for checking. You know, it's all very nice that Sam and I are paying for this shindig, but God forbid that either of us actually show our faces at it," said Jillian, with an incredulous roll of her eyes.

"It's only because you're her mum and dad," said Megan. "If I was her mum, I wouldn't have got my foot through the living room door."

Jillian picked up a mask from the table and pulled the elastic over her head before striking a pose and striding up and down the

Secrets, Lies, and Puppy Dog Eyes

kitchen, a hand on one hip. "D'you think red's my colour? Or would the pink be better for this season's catwalk? What d'you reckon?"

"Very fetching," said Megan.

A squeal interrupted them as Zoe and Suki rushed into the kitchen. "We've run out of marshmallows for the chocolate fountain. Are there any more?"

"Give me a sec to put them into bowls and I'll bring them in," said Megan.

"Okay, thanks." Zoe and Suki ran off, squealing in unison.

Megan made her way into the room with two large bowls of marshmallows, and a fresh supply of wooden skewers. As she turned to leave, the whole room was like a moving sea of pink and red, people swarming towards the chocolate fountain, their faces covered by their masks.

She squeezed through the partygoers and made for the calm of the kitchen, where Jillian was talking on the phone.

"Okay, darling. Look, don't worry if you can't get back for it, because you won't be allowed in the room anyway. Nothing, they're not up to anything, but parents are banned. It's okay, though, because Megan's been keeping an eye on them. Yes, okay, I will. Yeah, see you later. Bye."

"I take it that was Sam?"

Jillian nodded. "He probably won't be back until after the party's over. How did the marshmallows go down?"

"Judging by the speed at which everyone swarmed towards them, I doubt there are any left by now. Actually, it was quite spooky, all those masked faces coming towards me."

"Well, I've seen Zoe's friends and, believe me, some of them are spookier *without* the masks," said Jillian, yawning as she stretched her arms above her head. She leaned on the table and rested her chin in an upturned palm. "Do you have children?"

"Yes, Evie's twenty."

Jillian nodded. "That explains it. You have a way about you that shows you're comfortable around kids this age. Not everyone is, you know." She looked at her watch. "Goodness, it's half-past eleven already! Where's the time gone?" She raised her mug to Megan. "Thanks for staying and sitting out here with me. I dread to think how we would have solved the marshmallow crisis without you, seeing as I'm not allowed to set foot in the living room."

Megan chuckled and touched her mug to Jillian's. "You're forgetting the mask. You could have gone incognito."

ooooooo

Secrets, Lies, and Puppy Dog Eyes

As Megan drove home, with the promise that she'd call back the following day to oversee the collection of all the party equipment, something started to niggle at her. She didn't know what, but it was there, at the back of her mind, niggling away.

As she came to the sign for Bliss Bay, she looked down at the passenger seat, and the party bag Zoe had insisted she take with her. As she pulled onto the drive at Kismet Cottage, she knew that a cup of caramel coffee would be just the thing to go with the slice of the delicious red velvet cake that was in the bag.

She eased off her boots and bent to lift Tabastion into her arms as he ran to meet her. "You've had a long day on your own, haven't you?" He rubbed his face against her chin before jumping out of her arms and slinking off to curl up on the couch.

Megan flicked on the kettle and emptied the party bag onto the kitchen table. She already knew exactly what was in there, because she'd made them up herself: a generous slice of cake, a bag of crystals, a box of sweets, a mini bottle of perfume, a scented candle, a bandana, a friendship bracelet, and two masks—one of each colour—all following the pink and red theme.

Megan took her coffee and cake and went to sit with Tabastion on the couch. She'd been running on adrenaline all day but now the party was over, she was overcome by the need to sleep.

She finished her cake, left everything else on the kitchen table, and went to bed. As she put her cheek to the cool pillow, her last thought before sleep took over was of the niggle that was still in the back of her mind, hanging around like an itch that needed to be scratched.

ooooooo

"What the heck's all this?" said Des, the next day, as he called round with a box of his signature lavender Madeleines after an early start in his kitchen. He peered at the contents of the party bag, still strewn across the kitchen table.

"Oh, it's from the party for Sam's daughter. She insisted I bring a bag home."

"Everything go okay?" said Des, taking a sweet from the box, trying the bandana for size, and pulling one of the masks over his head. "How do I look?"

Megan chuckled. "Pink. And, yes, everything went fine. According to Zoe, some of her friends are going to tell their parents about me, so I might get some more business on the back of the party, which is great. It's not mega money, but I don't need a lot: as long as I've got enough to pay my way, and put a bit by for me and Evie, that's all I want."

Secrets, Lies, and Puppy Dog Eyes

Des nodded and popped another sweet into his mouth through the hole in the mask. "What're you up to today?"

"I'm going back to the Cambridge's place to make sure everything's packed up and collected, but that shouldn't take more than a couple of hours—three hours tops. Why?"

"I thought you might like to come over for lunch. My mate Gerald's given me a barrow full of veg, and I've made a veggie nut roast with them for a change. Thing is, there's enough for the whole village, so if we don't get some help, Sylv and I will be eating it till March." Des admired his reflection in the mirror.

"You seem quite attached to that mask," said Megan. "You can have it if you want."

"Are you sure?"

"Quite sure. I don't need it. Take the other one as well."

"Brilliant," said Des, rubbing his hands together. "Sylvie's started going on at me to wear sunscreen when I'm out in the sun, even at this time of year. She said the rays are weaker, but I should still keep my skin protected. I thought it might be quite funny to put this mask on after I've been out doing the garden for a few hours and tell her I think I've got sunburn because I forgot to put my sunscreen on." He chuckled at his pink-faced reflection. "What d'you think?"

Megan raised a brow. "Well, if you don't give her the shock of her life, she *might* think it's quite amusing. Anyway, I'll be leaving here in about an hour, so I should be back by around one. I can come over then, if that's okay. I've never had a vegetable and nut roast before, so I'm intrigued."

Des took one more look at himself in the mirror before nodding in approval. He took off the mask and picked up the other one from the table. "Okay, love, we'll see you when you're ready."

ooooooo

"Well, I never thought I'd say it but that was surprisingly delicious." Megan mopped the last of the gravy from her plate with a Brussel sprout.

"Yes, I'll definitely be making it again," said Des. "I bet it'd be good in sandwiches, too. And it'd make fabulous stuffing. I might start working on a variation for Christmas lunch. Perhaps I could add a few cranberries and chestnuts."

Megan cleared the table and started on the washing up. "You'll have to give me the recipe so I can make it for Mum and Dad when they get back. And I'll send it to Evie, too. You know how many times she's tried to go vegetarian, although I'm not sure she'll want to be stuck in the kitchen at the moment, because it's coming up to summer in New Zealand. I'm sure the last place she'll want to be is slaving over a hot oven."

"Hmm," said Sylvie, giving Des a sideward glance. "What's happening about you moving out of Kismet Cottage, Megan? You said you were going to look and I keep meaning to ask if you've seen anything in the classifieds."

Megan shook her head. "Not yet, although I haven't really looked seriously. I've settled back in at Kismet so well, I haven't had the inclination. I really must start looking, though, 'cos Mum and Dad'll be back soon."

"Well, they won't mind you being there," said Sylvie. "I know your Mum wouldn't mind if you stayed there permanently."

"I know," said Megan, "but I don't want to take advantage. Now they've both retired, this is their time. They've been so good to me and I know they love to have Lizzie and I around, but they need their own space. Anyway, I'd like to find a place of my own. Close enough that I can still see them often, but where I can shut the door and be on my own at the end of the day."

CHAPTER 19

"Your phone's ringing," called Jack. "It's Petal."

Megan rushed in from outside, almost tripping over Tabastion and Blue on the way. "Hi. No, I was washing the car and then Jack's taking me to Plymouth to buy a new wardrobe. Yes, I know he usually works on Saturdays, but he's making an exception this week because a lot of the guys on the job have come down with a stomach bug, so the workforce is a bit depleted. There was only him and another guy who managed to avoid it, so they decided between them to take the day off. Anyway, why are you calling at twenty-past twelve on a Saturday afternoon? Aren't you working, either? Oh. Really? Where are they? Oh, okay. No, I haven't got a copy here. Are you sure? Okay, thanks. About half-past five? Right, I'll see you then."

"What's up?" said Jack, as he attempted to rescue one of Tabastion's squeaky mouse toys from between Blue's jaws.

"Blossom's helping Petal in the shop today and she saw a couple of flats for rent in the local paper when she was on her lunch break. She remembered Petal saying I was looking for somewhere else to live, so Petal had a look and she thinks they're worth a viewing. I'd take a look myself, but I haven't got the paper."

"Where are they?" said Jack.

"One's on the edge of Bliss Bay, and one's just outside."

"And you're going to see them?"

"Petal said she'd call and make the appointments. She's coming round when she's finished work and we're going to look at them together." Megan chewed on her lip.

"You don't look very excited about it," said Jack.

Megan shrugged. "I suppose that's because I've got used to living here again. I know I should find somewhere else, but thinking about it's a lot less hassle than actually doing it."

"Are you anxious about moving out?" Jack leaned against the wall and crossed his arms.

"You know me, I'm anxious about most things," said Megan, with a half-hearted laugh. "But I'm trying not to be." She let out a small sigh, then nodded, as if to confirm to herself that what she was doing was the right thing. "You know, viewing those places is just what I need. I have no idea what kind of properties are available, because I haven't really looked." She glanced at her watch. "We should have just enough time to get to Plymouth and back, grab a bite to eat and then Petal should be here. D'you want to come along, too?"

Jack raised a shoulder. "Sure, why not."

Sherri Bryan

oooooo

"Are you ready?" Petal called from her car, which she'd stopped outside Kismet Cottage and was tooting the horn from the kerb. "Oh, Jack and Blue are coming, too, Blossom. Let him have the front seat, love, he's got legs like stilts."

As Blossom got out of the car, Megan gasped when she saw her. "Oh my goodness! What on earth's happened to you?"

"My flippin' ear piercings got infected, didn't they, and it's spread to my face," said Blossom sulkily, as she held her cold hands to her scarlet cheeks.

"Feel her forehead," said Petal, swivelling round in her seat. "It's like a radiator. Lionel had to take her to an emergency doctor's appointment yesterday morning because we had a call from the school that she was feeling feverish. The doc cleaned her ears, gave her some antibiotics and some antiseptic cream, and told her to drink plenty of water."

Megan held the back of her hand to Blossom's forehead and winced at her swollen earlobes. "Oh, you poor lamb." She leaned forward and gave her a hug. "Do they hurt?"

Blossom forgot her teenage cool for a moment, and snuggled against Megan's shoulder. "Not any more, but they did yesterday. You should have seen the gunk

Secrets, Lies, and Puppy Dog Eyes

coming out of them. I thought the doctor was going to tell me I'd have to have them amputated. I wish I'd never bothered to have the stupid things pierced."

"They'll be fine once the infection's cleared," said Petal. "Of course, if you hadn't kept fiddling with them, they probably wouldn't have got infected in the first place."

"I wasn't *fiddling* with them," whined Blossom, "I was *turning* them. You're *supposed* to turn them."

"Yes, I know that," replied Petal, "but you're also supposed to do it with clean hands, not during, and straight after, a game of beach volleyball. There must be sand and bits of shell and goodness knows what else in your ears."

"Well, it's not my fault stupid Mrs Deacon decided we should play stupid volleyball on the stupid beach, is it? It was a games lesson," huffed Blossom, "I could hardly not play, could I, just because I'd had my ears pierced?"

"Yes, I know that, love," said Petal, with a sigh, "but it would have been for the best if you'd just left your ears alone for an hour. Anyway, it's done now, so let's keep our fingers crossed that they're back to normal within the next couple of days, and you'll be as right as rain. Alright?"

Blossom nodded and began tapping at her phone.

Sherri Bryan

"Anyway, Megan, here's the paper with the details of those properties." Petal passed a newspaper over her shoulder. "There are no pictures, but they sound okay."

Megan read from the paper. "This well-appointed one bedroom self-contained ground floor flat is situated on the main A38 road between the villages of Bliss Bay and Honeymeade. It is close to all amenities and would appeal to a retired or a professional tenant. This unfurnished property offers a small entrance hall, a modern kitchen with plenty of cupboard space, a lounge/diner, a fully-fitted bathroom with shower, and one bedroom with fitted wardrobes."

"That sounds okay," said Jack, scratching Blue's ever-twitching nose.

"Hmm," said Megan, and shook out the paper to read the next advert. "Situated on the outskirts of the picturesque village of Bliss Bay, this second-floor flat offers two single bedrooms, a partly-fitted galley kitchen, a cosy lounge, a bathroom with original fittings, and a Juliet balcony with far-reaching views across the recreation ground. Please note: this property is in need of some restoration and would be ideal for someone looking for a project."

"Well?" said Petal. "What d'you think?"

Megan caught her friend's eye in the interior mirror. "They sound interesting, but

I'm not sure I'm ready for a full-on renovation project." She passed the paper to Jack.

"Oh, they always say that if there's a bit of painting to be done," said Petal, wafting away Megan's doubts with a flick of her hand. "You wait till you see it. I bet you'll be able to move straight in and work around what needs to be done once you're there. It'll need a good clean, of course, but two bedrooms will suit you better than one, won't it?"

"What do they mean by 'cosy' lounge'?" said Jack. "Is that real estate agent speak for tiny?"

"Well, you can find out for yourself in a minute, because we're here," said Petal.

ooooooo

"Don't worry about the mould on the walls," said the cheery estate agent, running a hand through his heavily-gelled hair. "That'll be easily remedied by a new damp-proof course."

Megan, Petal, Jack and Blossom stood shoulder to shoulder and reached from one side of the cosy lounge to the other.

"But we're on the second floor," said Megan, unable to tear her gaze away from the peeling wallpaper and vast patches of green fur.

"That must be rising damp then, I guess?" said Jack, as Blue sat in his arms with his paws on his shoulders and sniffed the air.

Sherri Bryan

"Rising? More like sprinting," said Blossom, pulling her hair over her ears.

The estate agent's smiled remained fixed on his face. "It's nothing to be concerned about. We can get that fixed before you move in."

"But won't it take a long time to dry out?" said Megan. "Especially with winter on the way."

"Like I said, it's nothing for you to worry about. We'll have you in by Christmas, no problem." The estate agent led the way into the galley kitchen which was so narrow, they had to stand in single-file to look around, unable to pass each other. Under the counter tops were empty spaces which had once housed a selection of kitchen appliances. "The previous tenant ran off with everything when he left," said the agent. "He was in arrears with his rent, so he probably needed the money." He moved a pile of unopened bills on the counter to one side. On each one, the words 'FINAL REMINDER' in big red print were clearly visible through the windows in the envelopes.

"What's to say the debt collectors won't come knocking on the door looking for the guy?" said Jack.

"Good heavens! I hardly think that's likely," said the agent, shuffling awkwardly from foot to foot. He cleared his throat. "So, what do you think? As it's almost Christmas, I can knock £50 off the first month's rent, as a gesture of goodwill." He stood in front of the pile of unpaid bills, a rictus smile frozen on his lips.

"Is it just me, or does something smell *really* bad?" said Blossom. "Like something's gone off under the floorboards."

The agent shot her a glare and took a deep breath. "I can't smell anything."

Petal grabbed Megan's hand. "Thank you, but I think we've seen enough."

ooooooo

After an equally unsuccessful viewing of the one-bedroomed flat that was so small, even Tabastion and Blue might have disregarded it on account of its size, the journey back to Kismet Cottage was a thoughtful one.

"I'm sure something will turn up," said Petal.

"Yeah, it's bound to," seconded Jack.

"Well, it's not like I *have* to move out of mum and dad's place," said Megan. "I can stay there for as long as I like. In fact, Mum will probably handcuff me to the banister when I tell her I'm looking for somewhere else to live."

"You don't want to live there forever, though, do you?" said Blossom, looking up from her phone. "I mean, do you really still want to be living with your mum and dad when you're, like, forty? I mean, that's *ancient* to still be living at home."

Megan looked at Blossom's serious face and laughed. "Thank you. I feel *so* much better about things now."

"Have you decided if you're going to the Hilliers' party on the 16th, by the way?" said Petal, changing the subject.

Megan nodded. "I think so. Jack's coming too, aren't you Jack? I've never been to one before, but Des said usually they're good fun. I have to say, I'm surprised they're having one this year, considering what happened to William, and everything else that's been going on."

"I know," said Petal. "I thought the same, but Olivia popped into the shop to say she'd seen Annabel at the market. She said the family want to carry on with their normal lives as much as they can, for Beatrice's sake. And William always loved their Christmas parties, so Teresa wanted this one to go ahead in his honour."

"That's nice." Megan nodded, thoughtfully.

"They always have a good turnout but I have a feeling a lot more people will come this year than usual," said Petal. "For William. It probably won't make Teresa feel any better, but I hope it makes her realise how many

Secrets, Lies, and Puppy Dog Eyes

people in the village are there to support her, and how much they thought of William."
"Yes, I hope so," said Megan.

Chapter 20

"Do you think this is too much?"

Sylvie appeared in the kitchen sporting a fresh shampoo and set, and wearing a black and silver dress with a pair of rarely-worn wedge-heeled shoes.

"Wow! You look amazing," said Megan. "And, no, it's not too much at all—it's perfect. It probably seems weird because you don't dress up much, so it feels really over the top. It's not, though. Anyway, it's a Christmas party, so you're allowed to be as OTT as you want."

"I'm still not sure about the shoes," said Sylvie. "You know I'm not used to heels, and I don't want to topple over while we're dancing and make a complete idiot of myself."

"Will there be dancing, then?" asked Megan.

"Oh, yes. There's always dancing at the Hilliers' parties, so I want to go well-prepared." Sylvie lifted a foot and studied her shoe. "I know they're not very high, but I think I'd better change them for a lower pair. Have I got time?"

Megan nodded. "It's only quarter-to eight, we've got loads of time."

As Sylvie disappeared, muttering under her breath, Megan pulled a copy of the local paper towards her and flicked through it distractedly. Whatever it was that had been niggling at her had surfaced again recently but, try as she might, she couldn't figure out what it was. She just knew it was irritating her no end. She stopped turning the pages of the paper when she saw the headline on page three.

Still No Clues in Murder of Local Artist

The detective in charge of the investigation into the death of William Longhurst has admitted that although his team are following a number of new leads, they have yet to identify Mr Longhurst's murderer.

Detective Inspector Sam Cambridge said, "Although Mr Longhurst's killer remains at large, I would like to reassure the residents of Bliss Bay that my team and I are doing all we can to bring the person responsible to justice. We are awaiting the results of forensic tests which we are confident will help us to make an arrest in this case."

"Did you see this?" said Megan. "News about William's been relegated to page three."

"Well, they can't keep it on the front page if there's nothing new to say, can they?" Des fed his Christmas cakes with a mixture of cherry juice and fruit tea before re-wrapping them and putting them back in the tin.

"Hmm, I suppose not," said Megan, looking at the close-up picture of the Hillier family arriving at William's funeral, which accompanied the article.

Sherri Bryan

"You know, it's a shame this party isn't one of those masked balls," said Des, as he put the cake tin back in the cupboard and reached up to a hook which held the masks Megan had given him. "Sylvie and I went to one, once, and you'd be surprised how difficult it is to recognise some people when you can hear their voices, but you can't see their faces." He held a mask up to his face and turned to Megan. "You think you know people, but you find out you don't know some as well as you thought"

"You've grown very attached to those masks, haven't you?"

"You know me," said Des. "I love a bit of fun. Here, did you see Blossom when she had that ear infection? Her face was almost as red as this mask, poor thing."

Megan nodded. "I know. She thought she'd have to have her ears ampu—" She stared at Des in his mask, stopped talking and gasped. She looked down at the newspaper. "No. No, it can't be."

"What's wrong?" said Des, hanging the mask back on the hook.

Megan shook her head. "Something's been niggling at me for ages. For the life of me, I couldn't think what it was but looking at you just now in that red mask, thinking about Blossom, and seeing that newspaper have just made me realise what it is. I can hardly believe it, though. It's just too absurd."

"What? What's too absurd?" prompted Des.

Megan shook her head again. "It can't be. It can't possibly be."

"For the love of God, will you tell me what you're talking about?!" said Des. "Come on, spit it out."

"It's going to sound ridiculous," said Megan slowly, scratching her head, "but you know everyone's been thinking that 'Red' is someone with red hair?"

Des nodded.

"Well, what if we've all been looking at it from the wrong angle, and the name 'Red' isn't a reference to red hair at all."

Des gave her a puzzled look. "What else would it refer to, then?"

Megan pushed the newspaper towards him and jabbed at the picture of the Hillier family. "You'll probably think I've lost my marbles, but look at that picture and tell me what you see," she said, reaching for her phone. "What if 'Red' is someone with a red face?"

ooooooo

Colin Havers strode through the dark streets towards the police station.

He'd thought long and hard about what he was about to do. If he was given a choice, he'd prefer not to, but he had to.

Sherri Bryan

He hadn't planned on getting so involved with Fern, nor falling in love with her. He hadn't even been intending to stay in Bliss Bay but now, he didn't want to be anywhere else.

He'd left her at the Hillier house at their pre-Christmas drinks party. When he was finished at the police station, he was hoping to join her back there but whether he'd be able to, or not, would be entirely dependent on what happened within the next few minutes.

He pushed open the door to the police station, the warmth hitting his cold face.

The room hummed with the urgent chatter of the detectives. Squashed around desks which had been crammed into the small space usually used as a waiting room, they barely gave Colin a glance.

"Can I help you?" Fred Denby called from the front desk.

"Yes, I'd like to speak to the detective in charge of the investigation. Or his sidekick if he's not around."

"I've just put an urgent call through to him," said Fred, "so I'm not sure if he's available." He gave Colin a suspicious look. "Can you tell me what it's regarding?"

Colin shook his head. "I'd rather speak to the guys in charge, if you don't mind."

Fred puffed out an indignant breath. "Just a minute. I'll see if one of them can speak to you. It's Colin Havers, isn't it?"

Colin nodded. "That's right."

"Okay, take a seat over there for a moment, will you, Mr Havers?" Fred pushed himself up and walked around to the front of the desk.

At that moment, Harvey appeared on the stairs. "You lot. Briefing upstairs. Quick as you can, please." He looked at Colin. "Fred, we'll fill you in later, seeing as there's someone here."

Every detective got up and followed Harvey up the staircase and into Sam's makeshift office.

"Looks like you'll have to wait a bit longer," said Fred. "Or you can come back later, if you prefer?"

"No, I'll wait, thanks," said Colin. "I'd rather get this over and done with than prolong it."

Fred nodded and walked back to his chair. "Righto. I can't say how long you'll be sitting there, though. Sometimes the briefings go on for ages, sometimes they're over in minutes."

"It's okay, I'll wait."

"Suit yourself," said Fred, and busied himself with a phone call.

Sherri Bryan

Colin took a seat at the bottom of the stairs and absentmindedly played with his phone.

It was a few minutes before he realised he could hear every word of what was being discussed upstairs in the briefing, albeit muffled behind the door.

ooooooo

Sam put down the phone and popped an indigestion tablet from its silver bubble onto his tongue. "Right, everyone. You'll be pleased to know that we've finally got all the DNA results back that we've been waiting for.

"Regarding the textbook, Dawn's handbag and shoes, and the obituaries, no useable DNA was found, unfortunately. Whoever put the textbook behind the lockers must have used gloves to conceal their fingerprints, and the fact that the book had been stuck there for forty years, and sustained water damage, has made it impossible to get a sample from it. Likewise with Dawn's handbag, which had been wiped clean, and her shoes, which were too contaminated to obtain a useable sample from. The guys in the lab were also unable to get anything from the obituaries. Whoever was responsible for those went to great lengths to keep their identity secret.

"However, there *was* some identifying DNA on the note that was found inside the textbook, which came from a portion of a fingerprint." Sam paused. "The only DNA on that note belonged to William Longhurst, which backs up what his mum said about his nickname. William *was* the 'Curly' who wrote the note." He crunched his tablet and burped into his fist.

"What about the other stuff, boss?"

"Much better results. Forensics managed to get a definite match to the DNA on the wool that was found at the scene of Dawn's death, and the saliva on the back of the gold star that was stuck to her forehead.

One of the detectives held his breath, then let it out. "Edmund Hillier?"

Sam shook his head. "No. Well, not exactly."

"What do you mean, 'not exactly'?"

"I mean the DNA contained elements of Edmund's DNA, but it's not an exact match."

"Which means it's someone related to him?"

Sam handed round the results of the DNA test for them all to see. "This, ladies and gentlemen, is the identity of the elusive 'Red' we've been searching for for so long."

He waited for the cheering to die down.

"But that's not all." Sam looked around the room. "We've also got back the DNA results on the piece of driftwood that was found outside William Longhurst's house, and which we were hoping would turn out to be the murder weapon. Sure enough, the test results have confirmed that the blood on it is his, and it was definitely the weapon used to inflict the fatal wound. There's a twist, though. The DNA which was found on the weapon used to kill William is the same as the DNA that was found on the gold star and the piece of wool."

Glen frowned. "You mean Dawn and William were killed by the same person?"

"It looks very much like it," said Sam, getting up from his chair. "Come on, Harvey, we've got a party to get to."

At the bottom of the stairs, Colin Havers got up from his seat and ran from the police station as if his life depended on it.

CHAPTER 21

The Hillier's Christmas party was in full swing.

Music was playing, people were dancing and singing, and the Champagne cocktail was going down a treat.

"Lovely party," said Des, a sausage roll in one hand and Megan's hand in the other as he twirled her round to a Christmas tune.

"Isn't it?" said Sylvie, filling a plate with a selection from the buffet table. "And I like how they always put out a good selection of non-alcoholic drinks. Very considerate. I can't help but feel a bit guilty, though, having a good time under the circumstances."

"I spoke to Annabel when we arrived," said Petal, who was cutting slices from a large ham, "and she said we were to just carry on as normal, because that's what the family want."

"If you're right about you-know-what," whispered Des to Megan, "I have a feeling this party might not last long. As if the family haven't been through enough already. You say DI Cambridge didn't give you any clue as to whether he thought you were on the right track with your theory?"

Megan shook her head. "He just thanked me for letting him know," she whispered back. "Maybe I'm completely wrong. I told you it sounded too absurd to be true, didn't I?"

"Ooh, cut a couple of slices of ham for me, will you, Petal?" called Dora Pickles as she elbowed her way through the partygoers. Her husband, Archie, examined all the food at close quarters, moving quickly along from any plate which looked or smelled like it contained anything 'foreign'.

"Did you know Sandra and Walter are here?" said Sylvie, as Megan spun out of Des's hold and ended up beside her at the buffet table. "I was surprised to see them, seeing as Sandra can't stand the sight of Edmund and she's not keen on Annabel, either. I had a quick chat with her and she said the only reason she decided to come is because the food and drink are free." She nodded to a corner, where Sandra and Walter sat, their plates piled with food, and a glass of sherry each. Walter smiled at guests and made small talk, but Sandra didn't say a word. "Doesn't look like she's found her Christmas spirit yet, by the looks of it," said Sylvie, "but we live in hope."

"And have you seen Laurence and Kelly?" Megan jerked her head in the opposite direction to where Laurence was deep in discussion with a local councillor, his eyes fixed firmly on her ample cleavage, and Kelly was fawning over Edmund, who was charming the mayor and his wife.

Secrets, Lies, and Puppy Dog Eyes

"She won't cause any trouble here, love," said Sylvie. "Don't you worry about her."

"Oh, no, I'm not, I just wasn't expecting to see them. I know everyone kept saying that half the village were going to turn up, but I didn't actually think they would. There are *loads* of people here. Good thing it's a big house. And it's a beautiful house, too."

"You ready for a dance?" said Jack, putting down his glass of Champagne cocktail and rubbing his hands together in anticipation.

Megan raised an eyebrow. "Jack, I've seen you dance. You're about as coordinated as a robot with a glitch on his motherboard. And it's not like there's even a dancefloor. This is just someone's living room, albeit a big one. If your arms and legs flail about like they usually do, you'll probably knock over an antique vase, or kick someone in the shins."

"Oh." Jack looked crestfallen. "But everyone else is dancing."

"Yes, I know, but not everyone else dances like you, do they?" Megan giggled and put down her plate. "Oh, I can't bear those sad eyes. You look like Blue when you do that. Come on, then. Let's have a dance, but please be careful."

Jack grinned and took her hand. "I give you my word," he said, as he began to dance—

jerky movements, totally without rhythm—his arms and legs moving almost independently of his body, as if they had a mind of their own.

Across the room, Annabel and Fern were deep in discussion.

"I can't imagine how relieved you must have been when the police let you go," said Fern.

"I can't describe the feeling," said Annabel, running a finger along the cloth on the canapés table. "It was like living a nightmare. I actually thought I was going to be locked up at one point but then all that business about the coat was resolved and they let me come home."

"We were all so relieved when we heard the news," said Fern. "The family must have been thrilled to have you back, especially after what happened with William." She nodded to Teresa who was staring out of the window, an untouched glass of punch in her hand, and Barnaby keeping her company, an arm around her shoulder. "How's she getting on?"

Annabel shook her head. "Not great. She'd known William almost all her life. They were friends from their schooldays and they'd had an on-again-off-again relationship for years. It's not going to be easy for her to come to terms with his death."

"No, of course not. Poor thing, I really feel for her."

Secrets, Lies, and Puppy Dog Eyes

Annabel nodded. "We'll just have to give her time. What else can we do? We were going to cancel the party, but she insisted we go ahead. She said William would have wanted us to." She looked around the room. "Isn't Colin here?"

"Not yet, but he should be soon," said Fern. "He had something to do—no idea what—but he shouldn't be long."

"How are you two getting along?" said Annabel. "Everything still going okay?"

"Well, a while ago, he was in such a weird mood, I thought he was getting cold feet but everything's okay now. I'm really glad he's decided to stay in Bliss Bay, put it that way, but we're just taking it day by day." Fern's eyes lit up as she saw Colin through the window, running across the road. "He's here. I'll just go and let him in." She put down her drink and rushed to the door. "You made it!" she said, flinging her arms around his neck. "Ooh, you're freezing! Come in out of the cold and have something to eat. And there's some mulled wine, that'll warm you up." She stepped back and frowned. "What's wrong? I can tell by the look on your face that something's wrong. What is it?"

He pushed past her into the living room. "Ah, Colin, glad you could make it," said Edmund, holding out his hand for Colin to shake, but he ignored it, striding over to the sound system and turning the volume down.

"Can I have your attention, please?" he said. "I'm sorry to spoil the party, but I've got something to say, and it can't wait, because the police are going to be here any minute."

Des and Megan exchanged a glance. "Do you think this is anything to do with your call to DI Cambridge?" whispered Des.

Megan shrugged. "No idea. We'll find out in a minute."

Colin turned to Edmund and Annabel. "First of all, I have an apology to make to you both. I came here earlier this year to find you, Edmund, because I wanted to get to know you... to find out the kind of man you really are."

Edmund's eyebrows shot up. "Find me? What on earth for?"

"Because I wanted to find out what sort of man gets involved with another woman just days after his wife dies. You see, to me, that's something only a monster would do, but I had to find that out for myself."

Annabel stepped forward. "Colin, I don't know why you're so interested in something that happened so long ago, but I can see you're very upset," she said in a calm voice. "Why don't we go into the kitchen and we can sit down and talk about this?"

Secrets, Lies, and Puppy Dog Eyes

"No, Annabel. I don't want to go and sit down and talk about this. I want to talk about it here, so that everyone knows what happened." Colin angrily brushed a tear from his cheek.

"Why do you owe us an apology?" said Edmund. "What have you done?"

"It was me who put those obituaries on the noticeboard."

A collective gasp went up.

"No, Colin," said Fern, her hands flying to her mouth.

"It was *you?*" screamed Teresa, her eyes flashing and her face red and contorted with rage. "I hope the police arrest you! Have you any idea what my family has been going through? *Have* you?"

Colin gave her a strange look, then turned to Fern.

"I'm sorry. I never meant to hurt you—or anyone, actually—but I wanted to scare Edmund and Annabel. At times, I felt like I wanted to kill them, but when it came to it, I realised that's not the kind of man I am. I could never have gone through with it."

"Scare us? Kill us? What on earth are you talking about, man?" Edmund glared at Colin and pulled Annabel to him. "I think it's about time you stopped talking in riddles, and just told us what it is you have to say."

Sherri Bryan

Colin took a step towards them. "I'm Dawn's son."

Another gasp went up and Edmund visibly balked. "Her son? That photograph in her purse was you? You *can't* be her son. I was told that her child was adopted."

The scowl left Colin's face. "She had a photograph of me in her purse?"

"*What*? Yes, it was in her handbag," snapped Edmund, "but never mind that. I want to know why you're claiming to be Dawn's son."

"I'm not *claiming* to be her son," said Colin, his voice trembling. "I *am* her son. It was *me* who was adopted. And, for most of my life, I wasn't interested in my birth parents. I didn't want to know anything about them. They'd got rid of me, so they can't have loved me, right?" He looked at Fern, who had tears running down her cheeks.

"But I got curious as I got older, so I tried to find them. I couldn't find my dad, but I found out all about mum. I was so gutted when I found out she was dead, but I knew she'd been married to you, Edmund, so I decided to come to Bliss Bay to see if you could tell me more about her. I didn't just want to turn up on your doorstep out of the blue after all these years, though, so I bided my time. You know, it's amazing what you can find out from some of the villagers if you buy them enough drinks.

Secrets, Lies, and Puppy Dog Eyes

I hung around in the pub with them, asked lots of questions and found out everything I wanted to know. I found out that you'd got together with Annabel while she was organising mum's funeral." Colin looked down and shook his head. "Can you imagine how that made me feel? That you must have had so little respect for mum that she wasn't even in the ground before you started on the next woman?"

"Colin, it wasn't like that," said Edmund, but Colin put up his hand.

"Please, let me finish before the police get here. I have to say it all." He ran a hand through his hair and sighed. "The more I thought about it, the angrier I got. I can't tell you the number of times I've wanted to come to this house and have everything out with you, but I couldn't bring myself to. It's only because I fell in love with Fern that I'm telling you this at all. I couldn't stay in Bliss Bay without coming clean about everything, so that's why I'm here. To tell you *I* wrote those obituaries. I got the idea after I went to the church office to meet Fern for lunch, and she was typing one up.

"I'd already found out everything I needed to know about the family while I was working for Edmund and Annabel. She talked about them all the time, so I knew everyone's name, and who was related to who. Once I decided what I was going to do, I made a point of checking the font Fern used. I don't have the same one on my computer, but I think the one I used is pretty close. He turned to Fern. "And, before you say anything, I didn't get together with you because of that. I knew I wanted to be with you long before I'd decided what I was going to do."

Annabel broke the silence. She stepped forward and put her arms around Colin. "I'm so sorry. You must have been through absolute hell. I know it might not seem like it, but Edmund really did love your mum, you know. That's why he still organises a church service for her every year on the anniversary of her death. I know how it must have looked when we got together so soon after she passed, and I know what a lot of the villagers thought about it, but it was just one of those things. We didn't know we were going to fall in love, but we did. You can't help who you fall in love with, Colin, even if it happens at a time when you know it really shouldn't. I'm so sorry if
that's painful for you to hear, but, believe me, it doesn't mean Edmund loved your Mum any less."

Colin stepped back and looked from her to Edmund. Edmund nodded and slumped into an armchair.

"It's true. Everything she said is true. I loved your mother with every bone in my body, and a part of me will *always* love her. I desperately wanted to have children with her—it had never occurred to me that she wouldn't want the same—but she was adamant that she didn't want any. I had no idea she'd already had a child, although since I found out, it's helped me to understand why she was so reluctant to have one with me. The pain of carrying another baby when the one she wanted so much was out there somewhere, with another family when it should have been with her, must have been unbearable. I'm ashamed to say, I've only recently found out that Dawn had a child, and I'm still coming to terms with it." Edmund shook his head. "She must have desperately wanted to tell me, but I was never very good at listening, or dishing out sympathy, I'm afraid. I'm so sorry."

"Is that why the police are coming, Colin?" said Annabel. "Because they know it was you who put the obituaries on the noticeboard? Because if that's the case, you needn't worry. I'm sure that, under the circumstances, Edmund will agree that we won't press charges, will we, darling."

"No, no, of course we won't. We're just so relieved to know who was doing it."

Colin nodded and put his hands to his face. He was perfectly quiet for a moment. "Thank you," he said, "but that's not why the police are on their way. They have no idea that

Sherri Bryan

I was responsible for the obituaries, although I went to the station to tell them." He heaved out a sigh. "The reason they're on their way, and the real reason I'm here, is because at long last, they know, and I know, who killed my mother."

There was another gasp as everyone stepped forward, not wanting to miss a single word, and two hundred pairs of eyes followed Colin's pointing finger.

"It was you, wasn't it?" he said.

Teresa's face flushed furiously, and Barnaby's hand slipped from her shoulder, his jaw dropping open.

Edmund jumped to his feet and strode to his daughter's side. "Don't be so ridiculous, man! Of course it wasn't her! You can't come in here, throwing accusations around with no proof. I know you must have been under a lot of stress but, really, this is taking things too far. If you don't stop, I'm afraid I'm going to have to ask you to leave."

Colin shook his head. "I'm not wrong. Ask her."

Des nudged Megan in the ribs. "You were right," he whispered.

Teresa's face changed from pink to bright scarlet. "I...I don't have any idea what you're talking about. Anyway, you weren't even around then, so how could you possibly know what happened?"

Secrets, Lies, and Puppy Dog Eyes

"I know, because I've just come from the police station and, while I was there, I overheard them talking. They found DNA on the note from Curly. Curly was William, wasn't it, Teresa? And he knew that you'd killed my mum. That's why he left a note, hoping someone would find it, and the truth would eventually come out."

Colin bowed his head, his voice shaking. "Have you any idea how I've felt since I found the note that almost gave the identity of my mum's killer? I've felt like I've been going crazy these past few weeks. The only thing that had everyone fooled was that we all thought 'Red' was a redhead, but it wasn't, was it? It was William's nickname for you because you blush so much. I'm right, aren't I?

"And, when you heard about the note, you knew it would only be a matter of time before it was tested for DNA and the police might find out that William had written it. You couldn't risk that happening, could you? So you had to stop him from talking when the police went round, asking questions. You've played a good game at being the grieving friend, but the game's up now, Teresa."

Edmund gave a gasp of horror. He clutched Teresa's shoulders and looked into her eyes. "This isn't true, is it? Tell me it's not true. You had nothing to do with Dawn's and William's deaths, did you? *Teresa!*"

Her eyes searched the room, a look of panic on her face. "Of course I didn't. Colin has no idea what happened." She ran a hand through her hair and tried to calm her flustered state. "It's all very well him making these wild allegations, but he has nothing to back them up with." She turned to Colin. "Do you?"

Colin shook his head.

"See, I told you," said Teresa, "he has no proof of anything. Call the police, Dad, and get them to take him away. After all we've been through, the last thing we need is him making things worse."

"Oh no," said Colin, "what I meant was that *I* don't have anything to back up the allegations… but the police do. They found your DNA on a piece of wool near where Mum was found."

"A piece of wool?" said Teresa, looking around the room at her captive audience. "Oh, well, I'm obviously guilty of murder then," she said, sarcastically. "How does that prove I had anything to do with her death?" She rolled her eyes. "This guy's a joke," she said to Edmund and Barnaby.

"It proves you had something to do with it, because the DNA that was found on it is the same as the DNA that was in the saliva on a gold star that was found on Mum's forehead. And the same DNA was found on the weapon that was used to kill William. That's when I knew it had to be you, not Barnaby, because he wasn't here when William was killed."

Teresa's mouth fell open and Barnaby shuffled away from her. "You didn't kill Dawn and William, did you, T?"

"Oh, dear God! Please, please tell me this isn't true," said Edmund, clutching Annabel's hand for support.

Teresa looked around the room again, her eyes darting like a cornered animal, her shoulders suddenly slumping, as if all the fight had been sucked out of her. "Oh, Dad, I'm so sorry. I'm so sorry." She shook her head, tears coursing down her scarlet cheeks. "I didn't mean to kill her, it was an accident."

Edmund fell back into the armchair again and put his head in his hands.

"What happened, Teresa?" said Annabel. "You *must* tell us."

Teresa shuddered and wiped her nose on the back of her hand. "I hated Dawn because I hated that Dad loved her so much. You see, we'd been on our own for so long, just me, Barnaby and him. I didn't want her around, so I thought if I gave her a really hard time, she'd get fed up with the hassle and leave. But she didn't. She just stayed and tried to make me like her, and she never once told anyone how awful I was to her.

"I behaved for all the other teachers, it was just Dawn I gave a hard time when we were on our own. And I never did the homework she set. I had a detention with her on the day she died, because I hadn't given in my homework for two days in a row. When we were alone, I yelled at her that she couldn't give me another detention because I was being considered for netball team captain, and Mrs Baker said she'd only consider girls whose behaviour and performance in other classes was good. I asked Dawn to tell Mrs Baker I'd be a good choice, but she said it was for me to prove that my behaviour and performance records were good if I wanted to be netball captain, not for her to lie about it.

"She told me she thought I had what it took to do really well at school, but I was letting myself down by ignoring the homework she set. She said she didn't think it would take much for me to become one of her gold star students, and that she'd be happy to give me extra tuition at home if that would help.

"I went crazy. Everything I was doing to make her leave was having the opposite effect. On the way out of the classroom, I threw her bag of gold stars on the floor and one stuck to my hand. I don't know why, but I put it in my pocket. Later, William and I were on our way to meet up with some friends before we went to the cinema, and I saw Dawn at the bus stop. I crept up on her, licked the back of the star and stuck it to her forehead. I told her she was such a goody-goody, she deserved it. Then I pushed her.

"I didn't mean for her to fall, I promise, Dad. We tried to see if we could save her, but she was gone. We panicked and ran—anyone would have done the same. I'd touched her handbag, though, so I had to get rid of it. I knew I'd snagged my jumper on a branch, and that I must have left some wool on it, but I didn't think there was any chance the police would ever trace it back to me. That was in the days before DNA testing, remember, and it was just an ordinary black jumper. Loads of people wore them. Dawn was dead, and I thought that was the end of it. How was I to know that William had written that note and it would be found all this time later? When I heard about it, I was petrified that the police would find out what had happened, but I had to keep calm so no one suspected anything."

"And that's why you killed him?" said Annabel. "Because you thought he'd tell the police what you'd done?"

Teresa gave a humourless laugh. "I had to. William couldn't keep a secret to save his life. I knew if they figured out he was Curly, and they'd come to the house to speak to him,

Sherri Bryan

he would have blabbed as soon as he opened the door—you know what he was like. He told me not to worry. He said there was no way forensics would find any DNA after so many years, and that he wouldn't say a word if the police ever spoke to him about it, but I knew he would.

"I didn't want to kill him, I really didn't, but I was so furious when I found out he'd left that note. I went back to our place after he'd been here for dinner. It was the middle of the night, but I knew he'd still be working on the Christmas display. He spent every waking minute on it.

"He was so unconcerned about everything. He just kept telling me not to worry so much, and that no one would ever find out. His attitude made me so mad, I just lashed out. I picked up a piece of wood he was using to texture the paint for his backdrop and... It was like a blind rage. I don't even remember doing it, but I obviously did, because the next thing I knew, the piece of wood was stuck in his neck, and he was dead.

"I panicked. I grabbed the wood, smashed a hole in the glass in the annexe door and left it open to make it look like someone had broken in, threw turps everywhere, and then lit one of William's cigarettes to set the fire. It took hold so quickly, and was blocking the door to the annexe, so I had to leave by the front door. I was in such a rush to get out, though, I tripped over the doorstep and dropped the wood. I couldn't find it in the dark and I couldn't stay to look for it because I knew it wouldn't be long before someone noticed the fire, so I had to leave it there.

"I went back the next day with you, Dad and Polly to look for it. I made the excuse that I wanted to lay a bouquet for William, but all I wanted to do was go back to find the wood I'd dropped. I couldn't get past the police cordon, though, so I couldn't even look for it. I just had to pray no one would find it and realise what it was.

"No one knew that I called William Curly, and that he called me Red. If it hadn't been for the note he wrote, there would have been nothing linking me to Dawn's death, and that's the way it would have stayed. It would have just been another unsolved case that everyone had forgotten about."

The uproar in the room was so loud, the ring on the doorbell almost went unheard. When Annabel eventually went to answer it, she said, "We've been expecting you, DI Cambridge."

Chapter 22

At Kismet Cottage, preparations were underway for the return of Claudia and Nick Fallon from their second-honeymoon-cruise-of-a-lifetime.

"Megan, love, we can't have your mum and dad coming home to a house that looks like it's the middle of February," said Sylvie, as she hung a Christmas wreath on the front door. "We need a little festive spirit about the place."

"Well, I would normally have done it earlier," said Megan. "You know how organised I am. But I've been a bit distracted by things recently."

Sylvie raised an eyebrow. "Hmm, Des seems to have that effect on people. In fact, Des the Distracter's got quite a ring to it. Thank goodness all that business is over and done with."

"You can say that again. I think Bliss Bay's had enough upheaval to last a lifetime," said Megan. "Can you imagine what Dad would have been like if he'd been here? You know how he worries about us all. I reckon he'd have had me and Mum locked in our bedrooms until the case had been solved." She hung baubles and tinsel on the tree and stepped back to admire her handiwork. "I saw Fern yesterday and she was saying how amazing she thinks Annabel and Edmund are for not pressing

Secrets, Lies, and Puppy Dog Eyes

charges against Colin. He just got off with a caution, did you know?"

Sylvie nodded. "I think the past few weeks have shown what Annabel's really made of. She's a really decent person, isn't she? I feel so sorry for everything she and the family are going through. It must be absolutely awful for them, especially Edmund. Annabel popped into the last WA meeting to say she wouldn't be around for a while. She said they're all pulling together and supporting each other, so I hope that'll help them over the next few months. They're not going to be easy, that's for sure. How on earth Teresa got away with what she'd done for so long, I'll never know. And clever you for figuring out that she was 'Red', although it's obvious when you think about it, considering that was her normal face colour most of the time."

Megan shrugged. It was just a fluke. Lots of things had happened that sowed the seed and then they just all came together and pointed at Teresa. I wasn't even sure I was right until the Hilliers' party. It was because of Uncle Des and that face mask that made me realise."

A loud knock on the door signalled Jack and Des's arrival back from the village shop.

"I hope they managed to get a few decorations," said Megan. "Even if we only have a little bit of this and that, it'll brighten the place up, won't it?"

She opened the door to see them each carrying two enormous bags of holly, ivy and mistletoe.

"I hope this is enough," said Des. "You said to get some, but we didn't know how much you wanted."

"For heaven's sake, Des," said Sylvie, rolling her eyes and putting a hand on her hip. "We just wanted a little to drape here and there, not enough to open a garden centre."

"Well, it's too late, we've got it now," said Des, "so the house will just have to look extra Christmassy, won't it?"

"I suppose I could make a couple of centrepieces for the table," said Sylvie, thoughtfully, looking at the mounds of greenery. "We'll have to make sure it's all out of the reach of Tabastion and Blue—we don't want them eating the holly or mistletoe berries."

"By the way, Megan," said Des, "Olivia asked me to tell you that the turkey crisis is over. They're being delivered to the shop on the 23rd."

"That's good," said Megan, trailing the lights around the tree. "She's been worried sick about letting her customers down, so that'll be a weight off her mind." She took a silver star

Secrets, Lies, and Puppy Dog Eyes

from the box of decorations and stood on tiptoe to reach the top of the tree.

"Jack, give Megan a hand, will you?" said Sylvie. "It'll save her putting her back out."

"Be there in a sec," he said, picking Blue up from the rug and striding over to the tree.

"Thank you," said Megan, handing over the star as her phone beeped, and Evie's face popped up on the screen for a Skype call. "Hello, darling, what a lovely surprise! It's so good to see you. How's everything?"

"Fine, Mum, just fine. We're up early today, because a big crowd of us are going hiking. I wanted to let you know I probably won't be around much for a few days, because I'm not sure what the phone signal is going to be like, and I didn't want you to worry if you tried to get hold of me, and couldn't. I'll speak to you when we get back, though, okay?"

"Okay, sweetheart. As long as you're keeping safe, and having a good time, that's the main thing."

"I am, and I am," said Evie, with a grin. "What are you up to?"

"We're just putting up the Christmas decorations before your Nan and Grandad get back later."

"You haven't put them up yet? Mum, it's the 20th of December. They're usually up on the 1st."

"Yes, I know, darling, but there's been a lot going on here."

"Is that Aunty Sylv I can hear in the background?"

"Yes, she's here." Megan turned her phone to face Sylvie.

"Hi, Aunty Sylv."

"Ooh, look, Megan, it's like she's actually there, even though she's on the other side of the world," said Sylvie, whose grasp of technology was extremely limited.

"That's because I *am* actually here," said Evie, laughing. "Oh, hang on, I forgot, you still call the internet That Interweb Thingy don't you? And have you actually made a call on that mobile phone of yours, yet, or are you still only using it to play Minesweeper?" She grinned and Sylvie wagged a finger at her.

"I'll have you know, I've done alright without a mobile phone for the last sixty-six years, so I don't know what all the fuss is about. There's nothing wrong with being incommunicado every once in a while, you know. And, for your information, it's Solitaire, not Minesweeper, you cheeky little bugger." She blew Evie a kiss. "Have a quick chat with Des before you go."

Megan turned the phone round again to see Des, laying mince pies out on a plate. "Just a little treat for the workers, love," he said to

Evie. "You're looking well. How's the weather down under?"

"Hi, Uncle Des, it's a bit of everything, really. Sun, a little rain, but lovely and warm. It's such an amazing country and the locals are the friendliest people I've ever met."

Snuggled in Jack's arms, Blue let out a little bark.

"Is that a dog?" said Evie.

Megan turned the phone back on herself. "It's a Boxer puppy. His name's Blue. He belongs to the friend I told you about. You know, Jack Windsor."

"Oh, you mean, Jelly-Legs?"

Megan laughed. "Yes, that's the one."

"Well," said Evie. "Am I allowed to say hello?"

Megan turned the phone to Jack. "Hey, good to finally meet you after hearing so much about you. This is Blue." He waved the puppy's paw up and down and Blue barked at the screen. "Hopefully, we'll get to meet someday soon."

"Wow! Hi, Jack, yes, I hope so. Oh! He's adorable!"

Megan turned the phone back to face her. "Isn't he the most gorgeous thing you've ever seen? He's got the most enormous feet."

"I couldn't see his feet, Mum, but he looked pretty good from the waist up." Evie's voice rang out loud and clear.

"Actually, I was talking about the dog," said Megan, as she looked up and gave Jack a grin.

"Yeah, okay, whatever you say," said Evie, with a wink.

"No, I really was!" Megan laughed. "Anyway, aren't you supposed to be hiking instead of embarrassing your poor old mum?"

Evie chuckled. "Yeah, I'd better run. If I don't speak to you before, I'll speak to you on Christmas Day, okay? Love you loads and loads. Bye everyone!"

"Love you more, sweetie. Bye!" Megan looked at her watch. "Right, I'm leaving to pick Mum and Dad up from the airport in two hours, so we'd better get a move on."

ooooooo

Around the kitchen table at Kismet Cottage, everyone had tucked into Des's special seabass, a welcome home treat for Claudia and Nick.

"I can't believe everything that's happened," said Claudia, pushing her mahogany curls from her tanned forehead. "Teresa Hillier's always seemed like such a nice woman. I must remember to light a candle for Dawn and William when we go to church." She looked over to where Tabastion and Blue were curled up together on the rug. "And what on earth has happened to Cat while we've been away? He's so placid."

Secrets, Lies, and Puppy Dog Eyes

"What d'you expect," said Des, with a snort. "He's had his whatsits chopped off."

"His name's Tabastion, now, Mum, not Cat."

Claudia shook her head. "I just can't take everything in. I'm not sure if I'm glad I missed all the excitement, or disappointed."

"Well, I'm glad we weren't here," said Nick. "I'm very happy that we were on our cruise, behaving like newlyweds."

Claudia gave her husband a dreamy gaze, and kissed him gently on the lips. "It *was* fabulous, wasn't it, darling?"

"Erm, can we stop with the lovey-dovey stuff, please?" said Megan, trying to erase the image of her parents behaving like newlyweds from her mind.

Claudia laughed and squeezed her hand. "You are funny, love. I feel like I've just been scolded!"

Nick chuckled and turned to Jack, who he and Claudia had insisted stay for dinner. "So is your place all finished now? We heard that you bought the old school while we were away. You probably didn't know, but Claudia and I were very involved in all the town hall meetings to protest against the hypermarket, so we couldn't be happier that the deal never went ahead."

Jack nodded. "I moved in last week, but there's still a bit to do, so I haven't had any visitors round yet. It's going to take a while before I remember I've moved, though. Yesterday was the second time I went back to my Uncle Bill and Aunt Rita's place to find them sitting down to dinner without me. Then I remembered I don't live there any more."

"We'd love to see it sometime, if you don't mind," said Nick. "It's been a long time since we set foot inside that school, and we're thrilled it didn't get knocked down. Good for you for taking it on and keeping all the original features." He raised his glass to Jack.

"D'you know, for the first time this year, I'm actually starting to feel excited about Christmas," said Megan. "It's been so *un*-Christmas like with everything that's happened, I haven't been in the mood at all."

"Well, Lizzie's arriving tomorrow, isn't she?" said Claudia, dropping a little fish into Tabastion's bowl, and then there's the concert on Christmas Eve."

"Hmm, I'm not sure what's happening about that," said Sylvie. "I spoke to Annabel the other day and she said that, as William and Teresa were so involved in organising the decorations and the choir, she's not sure what's going to happen. She's actually been quite involved in it herself, but I think the whole family are giving it a miss this year. She thinks that someone from the choir, who was helping William and Teresa, will take over."

"Poor William. It's so awful," said Claudia, a frown crinkling her forehead. "If only Teresa had confessed to the police what had happened all those years ago—you know, told them it was an accident—it would have been terrible, but at least William would still be alive now, and Teresa wouldn't be in prison."

"It wasn't just Teresa who committed the crime, though, was it?" said Des. "They were *both* responsible for Dawn's death, weren't they? I know William wanted to own up, but didn't because Teresa had threatened him, but he still said nothing after a woman died. That's a decision he chose to make."

Claudia nodded thoughtfully. "I suppose so. What a mess." She stood up to load the dishwasher and Megan stood up to help.

"You go and sit down, Mum, I'll do this."

"It's okay, I could do with standing up and stretching my legs after that dinner." Claudia looked at Megan and pulled her into a sudden hug. "You know how proud I am of you and Lizzie, and that you've both found your way in the world but, as far as I'm concerned, there's no better place to have you both than right here, in my arms."

Megan returned the hug and kissed her mum on the cheek. "I'm so glad you're home!"

ooooooo

"Lizzie!"

"Meggie!

The sisters embraced and chattered loudly at the same time.

"Oh, I'm so happy to see you!" said Megan. "It seems like ages since you were here."

"Where are Mum and Dad?"

"They've gone to the farmer's market. They won't be long. Come on, come and have a coffee and we can have a proper chat."

"How's the village been since all the business with the Hilliers?" said Lizzie. "After you told me what happened, I was checking the news on the internet every day, seeing if there'd been any updates."

Megan shrugged. "I think most people are just getting on with their lives, but it's difficult for the Hilliers, and William's family, of course. Colin—the guy I told you about—has moved in with Fern, now, and I think he's trying to move on. Jack knows him better than I do, and he said he seems to be doing okay."

"That's good," said Lizzie, as Tabastion wandered in and rubbed himself up against her legs. "He's not such a good guard-cat now, is he, since he had the chop?"

"Damn," said Megan. "I've just remembered I meant to get some milk earlier. I'm going to run down to the shop. I won't be a sec."

Secrets, Lies, and Puppy Dog Eyes

As he often did, Tabastion followed her out of the door and down the road, waiting outside the shop until Megan came out, when he followed her back home again.

As she made her way back up the road, she became aware of the low purr of a car engine and her heart sank when she saw her ex-husband, Laurence, in his red sports car, driving towards her, waving her down. Her first thought was of Evie.

"What's wrong? Is Evie okay?"

Laurence shrugged and scratched his head through his thick blond hair. "I guess so. She was when I spoke to her yesterday."

Megan heaved a sigh of relief. "What do you want?"

"I just wanted to let you know that Kelly was very upset after the incident in the bank." He grinned, as he rolled along beside her. "As much as I love the thought of my ex and my wife brawling about me, I thought you should know that her branch manager told me she was very unsettled by it."

Megan shook her head in disbelief. "Well, I don't believe that for a second, but I'm not even going to get into a conversation about it with you, apart from to say that I wouldn't brawl over you if you were the last man on earth. And if it wasn't for Evie, I'd quite happily never see or speak to you again."

"Oh, come on, Megan. You've been back in Bliss Bay since July. That's plenty long enough for you to have decided what you think about us. If you still have feelings for me, why don't you just admit it? I won't tell Kelly."

She stopped walking and glared at him. "Are you out of your mind? There is no 'us', and I can assure you, I don't have *any* feelings for you. I'm surprised you haven't had to trade that car in for one that's big enough for you *and* your massive ego. Go away, Laurence, and, unless it's about Evie, please don't bother speaking to me again. And stop kerb-crawling around the neighbourhood. It makes you look even sleazier than you really are."

Laurence ignored her. "Look, why don't we go for a little Christmas drink? Just to celebrate the season? We can just slip over to The Duck and—"

A low yowl which grew louder stopped him mid-sentence. He looked around, a look of fear on his face, his eyes coming to rest on Tabastion who had appeared at Megan's feet, his tail low and twitching, his ears up, and his gaze firmly fixed on the driver of the red sports car.

Having come off worst during an encounter with Tabastion in the past, Laurence had no desire to repeat the experience. Unfortunately for him, Tabastion had other ideas, and with a blood-curdling screech, he launched himself at Laurence's arm, which was resting on the car window frame.

"Aarrrggghh!" yelled Laurence, as the tabby swung from his shirtsleeve by his claws. He shook his arm, but Tabastion held on. "Megan! Get him off! Get him *off* me!"

She waited a while before detaching the cat from her ex-husband's arm, upon which, Laurence wound up the window, mouthing swear words at Megan as he drove off.

"Bye! Merry Christmas!" she called after him, chuckling, before bending down and making a big fuss of Tabastion. "Good boy, Tab." She called out to her sister as she opened the front door. "Liz, you know you were just saying that you didn't think Tabastion had it in him to be a guard cat any more?"

Chapter 23

Sandra Grayling knocked on the door of the small house, conspicuous among those around it due to the lack of Christmas decorations and lights.

"Is Colin here?" she asked Fern, when she opened the door, a look of surprise on her face.

"Yes, but I don't think he's really up to having visitors. As you can imagine, the past few days have been very stressful and they've taken their toll on him."

"I can appreciate that," said Sandra, "but I really would like to speak to him. I think what I have to tell him might make him feel just a little bit better."

Fern eyed Sandra with suspicion. She'd never had much to do with her, for the simple reason that anyone who came into contact with Sandra Grayling seemed to come off worst, and she had no intention of putting Colin through any more than he'd already been through.

"*Please*, Fern." Sandra's voice was almost pleading, which was most uncharacteristic. Sandra Grayling didn't do pleading.

Fern relented. "Come in, and I'll go and ask him if he wants to see you, but if he doesn't, you'll have to leave. I don't want any arguments about it. Okay?"

Secrets, Lies, and Puppy Dog Eyes

"Very well," said Sandra, stepping into the house. "If he doesn't want to speak to me, I'll leave, but will you please tell him that what I have to say concerns his mother."

"Now, listen, Sandra," said Fern, her eyes blazing. "Ultimately, it's *because* of what happened to his mother that he's in the mess he's in. I don't want him upset any more."

Sandra nodded. "I understand, but I very much doubt that what I have to say will upset him. As I said, if anything, I believe it will help to ease his pain."

Fern stared at her, then nodded. "Wait here."

Minutes passed before Colin appeared in the doorway. "Fern says you've got something to tell me about mum? I'm warning you, I'm not in the most hospitable of moods, so can you just tell me whatever it is you have to say, and then go?"

"Do you mind if I sit down?"

"Whatever," said Colin, and slumped into a chair.

Sandra smoothed her skirt over her knees and self-consciously touched her hand to the ever-present hair grip that held her fringe in place across her forehead. "Your mother desperately wanted to keep you, but her parents made her give you up. They wanted Dawn to have a career and the prospect of her having a child didn't fit in with their plans at all. I have no idea who your father was. All I know is that it was someone she loved very much."

She shuffled in the chair. "Anyway, back when you were born, it wasn't like it is now. There was a stigma that went along with being an unmarried mother and your mum's parents didn't want her to suffer because of it. It's ironic that, ultimately, their decision to separate the two of you caused her more suffering than they could have ever imagined. I was honoured that your mum chose to confide in me, Colin, because I know she didn't tell anyone else in Bliss Bay. The only thing I didn't know was if her child was a boy or a girl, because she didn't say, and I didn't ask. All I know is that she loved you with everything she had, and I hope knowing that will bring you some comfort."

She looked at Colin for the first time since she'd begun to speak, to see that his eyes were full of tears. She reached into her handbag and took two photographs from it, before passing them to him. One was of Dawn on the clifftop outside The Roundhouse, laughing as the wind whipped her hair into the air.

"She often used to come round to the house," said Sandra. "As you can see, that was a particularly windy day, but she was determined to have her picture taken. She was laughing because the wind had just blown her hat off. That was such a happy day, and I like to think this picture captured her spirit exactly—her *true* sprit—which was carefree and fun-loving."

She pointed to the other picture. "This was taken during our lunch break one day at the school. When it was sunny, she used to take a big blanket outside and sit with her lunch by the clock tower, just enjoying the fresh air and watching the world go by. She loved the school. All she ever wanted was to help people and be happy, and for everyone else to be happy. After she lost you, though, she struggled to find her happiness sometimes. She was only a slip of a girl, but she was strong. And brave, and good, and all the things anyone would want in a mother."

Sandra wasn't expecting Colin to fly across the room and fling his arms around her neck.

"You'll never know how much you coming here to tell me that means to me. Thank you, Sandra. Thank you so much."

ooooooo

"Oh my gosh! It's absolutely stunning."

It had been so long since Megan had been to a Christmas concert in Bliss Bay, she'd forgotten how beautiful everything looked. Thousands of tiny white lights illuminated a giant fir tree, and hundreds of candles lent their glow to the entire market square.

"I told you it was gorgeous," said Lizzie, holding hands with her boyfriend, Shaun, who had arrived earlier that day. "It's much better since the square's been remodelled."

"It's lovely, isn't it?" said Petal, who was with her husband, Lionel and her daughter Daisy.

"Where's Blossom?" said Claudia, wrapping her scarf around her neck once more to keep away the chill.

"She's in the choir, believe it or not. I have no idea what they're singing, though, because it's all been very hush-hush. I didn't even know she *liked* singing."

"Has she given you a taster of what's on the programme for this evening?" said Claudia.

"Huh, you must be joking. I asked her to give me a sneak preview the other day and she looked at me like I'd just landed from Mars. You know what an awkward teenager she can be sometimes." Petal dug her hands into her pockets and watched her breath form a cloud in front of her face.

"Jack! Jack!" Megan waved and called out as Jack made his way through the crowd. "I'm glad you made it."

He nodded. "Me too. I've left Uncle Bill and Aunt Rita on the other side of the square with Des and Sylvie. Can you see them?

Secrets, Lies, and Puppy Dog Eyes

They're at the front, sitting on the benches. I think they're planning on a harmonica duel later on."

Megan chuckled. "Christmas wouldn't be Christmas without one!"

"Look!" Petal squealed and nudged Megan in the ribs. "There's Blossom, look!"

The choir filed onto the makeshift stage at the edge of the market square, and the lights that were trained on them suddenly all went off. Then a spotlight came on, shining on Blossom, who began to sing a solo of Silent Night, her voice pure and clear, unfaltering as she sung the first verse acapella.

A fat tear fell onto Megan's cheek as she watched Petal, Lionel and Daisy all bawling their eyes out.

"Please join in for the second verse, everyone," said Blossom, and the entire choir began to sing, accompanied by the school orchestra.

A deep voice rang out, over everyone else's, pitch perfect and as smooth as silk.

Megan turned and looked up at Jack, who was singing his heart out.

"How can someone who has no rhythm sing like that?" she said when the carol had finished. "You sing like an angel."

He shrugged. "Dunno. Guess my brain doesn't communicate with my legs the same way it does with my mouth."

Sherri Bryan

The concert was joyous. After the events of the past few weeks, it set the tone for the festive season perfectly.

"We're going to the midnight service later," said Megan, holding on to Jack's arm as they made their way out of the square. "D'you fancy coming along?"

He shook his head. "Sorry, no can do. I've got a date tonight."

Megan let go of his arm and forced a smile. "Oh. Right. Okay. Well, have fun."

He nodded and gave her a dimpled grin. "I will. And you have a great night. Merry Christmas, everyone." He dropped a kiss on her cheek, and then he was gone.

As everyone chatted with everyone else, Lizzie and Shaun appeared at Megan's side. "Have you got a thing for him?"

"What? Don't be ridiculous, of course I haven't," said Megan. "I'm just surprised he's got a date. I don't know *why* I'm surprised, mind you: he's adorable and kind and fabulous." She smiled at her sister. "In a best friend kind of way, obviously." She linked an arm through Lizzie's, and the other through Shaun's. "Come on, let's go home and have some egg nog. Mum and Dad will be chatting to everyone for ages."

ooooooo

"Are you almost ready?" said Megan, as she dabbed perfume behind her ears. "It's twenty-five to twelve."

"Almost," said Nick, "but the church is only a hundred steps away, so we don't need to rush."

"Yes, I know, but you know how busy it gets on Christmas Eve. It'd be nice to get a seat, rather than have to stand all the way through the service."

"I just have to change my scarf," said Claudia. "This one's all scratchy."

"And I need my ear muffs," said Lizzie, scrabbling in her vast handbag.

Already wearing her hat, coat, scarf and gloves, Megan waited impatiently for her family. A bang on the door signalled the arrival of Des and Sylvie.

"Open up, it's freezing out here!"

Megan opened the door to see her uncle and aunt on the doorstep.

"You're still here, then?" said Des, peering over her shoulder.

"Obviously," said Megan.

"Are we too late?" said Sylvie, to Claudia.

"No, you're not." Claudia raised her eyebrows at her sister.

Megan looked over to where Lizzie and her dad were standing, mumbling about something together.

Sherri Bryan

"It's almost twenty-to twelve," said Megan. "All the good seats are going, while we're just standing here." She drummed her gloved fingers against the banister.

"Oh, hang on, I must just run upstairs and get my gloves," said Nick.

"Dad, there are a pair here." Megan held up a pair of gloves that were on the coat stand.

"Oh. Er, no. I don't want those ones," said Nick, running up the staircase.

Megan noticed that he caught Claudia's eye on the way up and winked. Her parents had been behaving very strangely since they'd got back from their cruise.

Two minutes later, Nick ran down the stairs. "Okay, I think I'm ready now."

"Right, said Megan. "Is everyone else ready? And who on earth can that be?" she said, in response to a sharp rat-tat-tat on the door. She opened it to see Jack standing on the doorstep. "Oh, hi. I thought you had a date?"

He nodded and grinned. "Yeah, I did. I had to go and collect your Christmas present."

"Present? What present?"

He stepped aside, and the person Megan wanted to see more than anyone else in the world took his place on the doormat.

"Merry Christmas, Mum."

ooooooo

The church was so full when they got there, it was standing room only, but Megan couldn't have cared less. She clung to Evie's arm, as if she couldn't quite believe she was there, and sang every carol at the top of her voice, with a grin on her face that wasn't leaving any time soon.

Back at Kismet Cottage after church, for hot chocolate and a mince pie before bed, Megan hugged her mum and dad, then smothered Evie's face with more kisses.

"So, you paid for Evie to change her flight, so she could come back for Christmas?"

Claudia nodded. "We Skyped each other last month, and Evie said she was having a fabulous time, but she felt homesick when she thought about Christmas. Your dad and I talked about it afterwards, and we called Lizzie to ask her opinion, and then we Skyped Evie again to tell her we'd pay for her to change her flight if she really wanted to come home. She said no, but we said it would be our Christmas present to her. We didn't force you to come back, did we, sweetheart?"

Evie shook her head. "Not a bit. I really wanted to come home, but there was no way I could have afforded the flight. I told Nan and Grandad I couldn't let them pay for it, but they were very insistent. It's a bit lame, I know, to go halfway across the world and come home mid-way through the trip because you miss your family, but I don't regret it at all. I'll be staying until the seventh of January."

"But how did Jack pick you up from the airport?"

"Because Nan and Grandad called Uncle Des and Aunty Sylvie to tell them what was going on, and they asked him if he could help out. He was sworn to secrecy, though."

"So when you saw him when you called the other day, that wasn't the first time you'd spoken to him?"

"No, but I had to pretend it was. Sorry, Mum, but we couldn't spoil the surprise. I hadn't seen him before, though, so it helped me know who to look out for at the airport."

For the first time since she'd set eyes on Evie, Megan realised Jack was nowhere to be seen. "Where is he?"

"He went home after he dropped me off. He's staying with his aunt and uncle, isn't he?"

Megan nodded and stood up from the table. "I'll be back in a bit."

ooooooo

Jack's aunt and uncle's house was in darkness when she arrived, but she knew Jack's bedroom was at the front of the house. Trouble was, she wasn't sure which one. She picked up a small stone and threw it at the smallest upstairs window. She was about to do it again when she heard a bark. A light went on and a curtain moved, and Jack's face appeared at the window.

Secrets, Lies, and Puppy Dog Eyes

"Megan? Is everything okay?" he said, as he opened the window and poked his head out.

"I'm sorry to come round so late," she whispered, "but will you come down for a minute, please?"

A minute later, he opened the door, Blue in his arms. "What's up?"

Megan stepped forward and kissed him on the cheek before pulling him towards her in a huge hug.

"I had to come and say thank you after I found out what you'd done. You've no idea how happy I am to see Evie, and I wanted you to know how much I appreciate you helping to get her here."

Jack gave her a little bow. "Well, it was a joint effort, but my pleasure."

Megan smiled and stroked Blue who mouthed her hand with his needle-sharp teeth. She walked down the path and blew a kiss before she got back in the car. "Merry Christmas, Jack."

Chapter 24

"I feel like it's been ages since we had a good old catch-up," said Petal, as she and Megan sat around the fire in Bliss Bay's oldest pub, The Duck Inn, having met up for a post-Christmas lunch in Petal's lunch break.

"I know. So much has happened over the past few weeks, it's been a bit frantic," said Megan. "It's all passed by in a bit of a blur."

"It was lovely to see Evie. Isn't it great that she and Daisy get on so well?" said Petal. "Daisy said they had a real laugh together when Evie helped out in the charity shop yesterday. I think they're going to miss each other when she goes back to New Zealand."

"Oh, don't!" said Megan. "I can't even bear to think about it. Can we talk about something else?"

"Okay, you big softie," said Petal, with a grin, and changed the subject. "I saw Fern this morning." She pulled the sleeves of her jumper over her hands and leaned closer to the fire. "She said she and Colin have both had such a stressful time recently, but she's convinced that them both being adopted is one of the reasons they get on so well. Since she found out about Colin's background, they've talked and talked about stuff that they've never talked about with anyone else. Apparently, it's been good for them both. Colin met her parents for the first time on Christmas Day, and she's

Secrets, Lies, and Puppy Dog Eyes

going to meet his family in the New Year. And did you know that she and Colin went to The Roundhouse to spend Boxing Day with Sandra and Walter? *Sandra and Walter*! Can you believe it?!"

"I know, it's amazing, isn't it? Mum said Sandra mentioned it when she and Aunty Sylv saw her in the village shop the other day. I was sure they must have misheard, but they were adamant that's what she said."

Petal nodded. "Fern said that when Colin found out how his mum died, it completely knocked the stuffing out of him, but Sandra went round on Christmas Eve and had a long chat with him about her, and it did him the world of good. Apparently, she gave him some photos of Dawn, and told him that if he ever wants to know more about her, to just pop round to see her. Fern said talking about Dawn seemed to do as much good for Sandra as it did for Colin: it was like a therapy session for them both."

"I'm glad," said Megan. "After she saw her, Mum said it was like having the old Sandra back, before she went through all that loss. She talked a little about Colin and said she was so glad she'd been able to share her memories with him."

Petal nodded. "I can imagine. Oh, and Fern said Walter told her that he and Sandra are thinking of opening up The Roundhouse as an artists' retreat. After she and Colin visited, and were completely blown away by the view, Walter said someone else had told them recently that it was a seascape crying out to be painted.

"He said he and Sandra had been talking since then about what a great place the house would be for people to go to paint. All that peace and quiet, and natural light and space would make it an ideal artist's studio. I don't know if they're thinking of doing it as a business, or what, but Fern said they're really excited about it. Walter said they could do with a bit of life around the place, and it was about time they welcomed people in to share the house with them. He said it'll be a real tonic for them both."

"And Sandra's okay with it?"

"It was her idea, apparently," said Petal. "I almost fell over when Fern told me."

Megan smiled. "That's good. And I never thought I'd say it, but I actually had quite a pleasant conversation with her the other day when she passed by the house. I was pulling up the weeds in the front garden and she stopped to say hello. I must have looked really gormless, because I just stood there with my mouth hanging open, I was so surprised. I mean, she's always been such a cantankerous old mare, hasn't she? *And*, Tab didn't even let out so much as a hiss while she was there. He

Secrets, Lies, and Puppy Dog Eyes

just looked her up and down and carried on washing his paws.

"I reckon she must be giving off a different vibe these days because you know what a good judge of character Tab is. He's got a sixth sense about people. I know he's had the chop, and the vet said it might calm him down, but that only seems to have been the case with animals, not people. I remember Mum telling me that Sandra thought cats were evil freaks of nature—she even got a swipe of Tab's paw once—but she gave him a little stroke behind the ears while we were chatting, and he just sat on the wall and let her do it. She was a bit hesitant but, considering she used to freak out if she even *saw* a cat, it's a pretty big step. Seems like she's spreading the love, and every*one* and every*thing's* getting a piece of it."

"It's about time she had something to smile about," said Petal. "I'm glad things are working out for her. "By the way, I meant to tell you that Fern said one of the pictures Sandra gave Colin is of Dawn sitting outside the old school in front of the clock tower. Apparently, it was her favourite place to sit when the sun was shining. It's a coincidence, isn't it, that Colin ended up working on the exact spot where his mum used to sit all those years ago.

"Yeah, it is, isn't it?" said Megan, thoughtfully. "Isn't it funny how things work out?"

"Have you seen Jack recently, by the way? Three days till New Year and they've finished work on his place just in time. Have you seen it yet? Lionel and I are going round tomorrow after work for a nosey."

"I'm going to see it after I leave here," said Megan. "I've been dying to see it, but Jack's been really secretive. He said I couldn't see it until it was done."

"I suppose I'd better get back to work," said Petal, stretching her arms above her head and yawning. "And we'd better get the bill."

"If I don't see you before, I'll see you at Jack's party," said Megan, taking her purse from her bag.

As she walked back across the green to the cottage, she made a mental note to tell Jack what she'd just learned about Dawn Hillier.

ooooooo

"Okay, you can open your eyes now."

Jack took his hands away from Megan's face and she blinked in the sunshine. Outside, the Old School House on the hill looked exactly the same, but cleaner, and brighter, the clock and bell tower still dominating the building, as they had for decades.

Secrets, Lies, and Puppy Dog Eyes

A gravel drive had taken the place of the old cracked tarmac and the new lawn was neatly cut, with borders filled with plants supplied by Petal and Lionel's flower shop. The old Willow tree looked better than it had for years, following Jack's call to an Arborist who had taken a look at it and worked her magic.

An outside seating area was covered by an awning, under which sat simple furniture and an array of colourful plants in pots.

Gone were the rusty school gates and railings. In their place, a smart, wooden fence defined the border of Jack's land.

The old Arts and Crafts block—now renamed Bay View—still stood independently from the main building, but had been transformed into a two-bedroomed, self-contained apartment, with wide reaching views across the bay, ready to take the overspill of Jack's visiting family and friends.

Classrooms had been turned into four bedrooms, all with bathrooms, natural wood furniture and floors, and decorated with rugs, and bright curtains at the windows.

The old dining hall had been transformed into a huge kitchen, with natural stone floors, new units and modern appliances, and a solid wood table in the middle of the room, big enough to seat twelve.

The former assembly hall was now an enormous living room with a large open fire, bookcases waiting to be filled, and steps leading up to a more formal dining area

The bay could be seen from every room in the house, but the best view had been saved for the clock tower. Unused and unloved for decades, the clock had been repaired and restored to its former glory, and housed in a glass case to form a feature window in the tower which had been transformed into Jack's den, accessed via a mahogany staircase. The crowning glory was the bell at the top of the tower, which had been polished until it gleamed.

"I think that must be about the millionth time you've said 'wow' said Jack, as he showed Megan around his new home.

"Yeah, that's because I can't think of a better word to describe everything you've done. I think it might just be the most beautiful place I've ever seen."

"Well, if it wasn't for the team of guys, who were awesome, there's no way we would have been finished in time for New Year. They worked all hours, in all weather."

"Are they all coming to your New Year's Eve party?"

"You betcha," said Jack. "You'll be coming, won't you?"

"Am I invited?"

"Do you even need to ask? Of course you're invited, and your whole family, too. I'll mention it to them. I've already told Lionel and Rob, so Petal and her gang and Olivia will be there, too. I've been spreading the word around, so I reckon a lot of the villagers will be here, if only to have a nosey around the place."

Megan nodded. "Okay, it's a date. I'll look forward to it."

They sat on the steps outside the school door, and Megan told Jack what she'd learned about Dawn.

"Wow, it must have been a weird feeling for Colin to know his mom had taught at the school he was coming to work at," said Jack. "Poor guy."

"It might not have had a negative effect on him," said Megan. "If anything, it might have made him feel a bit closer to her."

Jack threw the rope toy for Blue, who scurried off along the grass to bring it back. "I dunno." He shrugged. "If I'd come back to Bliss Bay, looking to find out about my mom, I think I'd feel sad to know I was working in the same place she used to come to every day."

"You should ask Colin to show you the photo Sandra gave him," said Megan. "It must have been taken right there." She pointed out of the window to the clock tower. "I think it's a lovely memory for him to have." She looked at Blue, who was sitting patiently at Jack's feet, waiting for him to throw his toy again, but Jack was distracted by his thoughts.

Sherri Bryan

"What's on your mind?"
Jack threw the toy again, and turned to face her, running a hand across his jaw. "Okay, you need to tell me if this is a good idea, or a bad one…"

Chapter 25

It seemed like the whole village had turned out for Jack's New Year's Eve party.

The Old School House met with everyone's approval, even the few who'd have misgivings when they'd heard the news that Jack was planning on turning it into his home.

"I wouldn't believe the transformation unless I'd seen it with my own eyes," said the surveyor who'd recommended Jack get rid of the Willow tree. "It really is amazing. And that tree looks like it's had a new lease of life."

Sylvie and Claudia approached and each grabbed an arm.

"You've done a fabulous job, love," said Sylvie

"You should be proud of yourself," said Claudia. "We protested for so long to stop that hypermarket being built here, you can't even begin to imagine how happy we are that you took it on, and that you've treated our beautiful old school with such respect. It's gorgeous, Jack."

"Well, there's no way I can take all the credit. There's a whole team of guys who worked their guts out to make this happen. And *I'm* proud of *them*."

Megan appeared with Evie, having given her a tour of the house. "O.M.G. I've just had to put my eyes back in their sockets. This place is fabulous."

Sherri Bryan

"I'm glad you like it, but if I get any more praise, my head's going to be too big to get through my front door tonight, so why don't we have a dance instead?" Jack grinned. "This is a party, after all."

"Uh-oh," said Megan. "Stand well clear, Evie, or you're likely to get injured."

The party went on until just before midnight, when Jack turned off the music and turned on the radio so they could ring in the new year to the chimes of Big Ben.

At the first chime of the bell, cries of 'Happy New Year' filled the air, and silent fireworks lit up the sky. In the scrum of partygoers finding people to hug, kiss, and shake hands with, Megan and Jack found themselves face to face in the crowd. As they both leaned forward to kiss each other on the cheek, their noses banged and their lips brushed together instead.

Megan jumped back as if there was static between them, but Jack stood his ground. "Sorry about that," he said. "I was aiming for your cheek."

"Yeah, I was aiming for yours."

They held each other's gaze for a while, then Megan put her arms around him and planted a kiss on his cheek. "That's better. Happy New Year. I'm so glad you're back in the village."

"Likewise," said Jack.

"And I love that you've had silent fireworks," said Megan.

"Well, I didn't want Blue and Tab getting scared. They're cuddling upstairs on the bed and I'd have hated to disturb them. Anyways, I hate the noise of fireworks. I much prefer to see them without the noise."

Megan smiled. "You're such a sweetheart."

Jack returned her smile and cocked his head. "Why, thank you, Ma'am."

"When are you going to make your announcement?" asked Megan.

He looked around the room. "I reckon now's as good a time as any." Running upstairs, he came back down with a stack of envelopes. He stood on the bottom of the staircase and called for quiet. "If I could just have your attention for a minute, please, and then we can get the party started again." The noise died down and he began to speak again. "So, a lot of you have told me how much you love the place, and have congratulated me on what's been done with the old school."

A cheer went up.

"The thing is," he continued, "if it hadn't been for the guys who worked on this with me, I'd still be stripping decades-old paint from the walls and wondering what the heck to do next. So, with that in mind, I'd like to say an enormous thank you to every single one of the team and give each of them a bonus, as a token of my appreciation. I couldn't have done this without you."

When he'd handed out the last envelope, another cheer went up as he was swamped by his entire workforce, who proceeded to lift him onto their shoulders as they sang, 'For He's a Jolly Good Fellow'.

ooooooo

The party went on into the early hours, when people started to drift off.

"Jack, are you going to speak to him before he leaves?" said Megan.

"I dunno." Jack rubbed at the frown at his brow. "I'm starting to think it wasn't a very good idea, after all."

"Don't be daft. It was a *brilliant* idea. And what are you going to do if you don't tell him? Get rid of it? You *have* to tell him. Look, they're coming over now." She jabbed Jack on the arm. "Go on, tell him!"

Colin walked towards Jack, Fern falling back as she stopped to chat with Megan.

"We're going to make a move, but it's been a great party. And thanks for the bonus. That's really going to help me and Fern out."

Jack nodded and shook Colin's hand, trying to ignore the messages Megan was giving him with her eyes.

"Look, Jack," said Colin, with a slight frown, "I feel like we got to know each other

Secrets, Lies, and Puppy Dog Eyes

pretty well while I was working for you. Is that fair to say?"

Jack nodded. "Yeah, I reckon so."

"And I got the impression you're a pretty straightforward guy. You're easy-going, down to earth, and you say what you mean. Am I right, so far?"

"That's about right."

"Then why do I feel like you've been walking on hot coals all evening?" said Colin. "Every time I've spoken to you, it's like you've been on edge, and you're holding something back. You've been fine with the other guys, it seems like it's just me." He scratched his chin and looked at the floor. "Maybe I'm just paranoid after everything that's happened, but I can't help but feel that you've got something to tell me." He tipped his beer bottle to his lips for the last drop. "Call it gut instinct, but that's what I feel. And if that's the case, I'd appreciate it if you just told me what it is. Have I done something wrong? Was it something on the house that I messed up?"

Jack and Megan exchanged glances and Jack heaved a huge sigh. "Oh Jeez Louise, what a relief! You're spot on about everything, Col. Well, apart from you messing up on the job, because you didn't. You're right. I *have* been on edge, and I *have* been holding back about something." He ran his hands through his hair. "In fact, I've been worrying that *I've* messed up."

Colin's eyebrows dipped in a frown. "Messed up what?"

Megan squeezed Jack's hand. "Don't worry about it. Have a little faith." She turned to Colin and Fern. "I don't know how on earth Jack managed to arrange this at such short notice, but he was so determined to do it, he made it happen. Now it's time for the big reveal, though, he's doubting himself. Before you find out what it is, you should know that what he's done has come from a good place, and his thoughts behind it were sincere."

"Well, if I was confused before, I'm completely befuddled now!" said Fern.

Jack took Colin's empty beer bottle from his hand. "Come on, let's get this over with. Get your coats on."

"Our coats?"

"Yep, we're going outside."

They followed Jack across the path on the lawn towards the clock tower.

"This is a surprise," said Colin.

"I like surprises," said Fern. "I hope it's a good one."

"Yeah, I hope so, too," mumbled Jack, "or I'm going to look like a complete klutz."

"I love how these lights are sunk into the ground," said Fern.

"Colin did those," said Jack.

"Really? I *love* them!" said Fern. "They give just enough light to see everything without being in your face. Perhaps we could get some for our place, Colin?"

They came to a stop by the clock tower and Fern stopped chattering.

Colin looked around warily. "Why have we stopped here?"

Fern gasped. "Oh! This is *exactly* the spot in the photo Sandra gave you! Your mum must have been sitting just about there." She pointed to where a sheet covered something on the lawn.

Colin nodded, blinking quickly. "Yeah, it's nice to think she had some happy times right here."

"Well, in that case," said Jack, "I hope you'll understand why I thought this might be a good idea although, I don't mind telling you, I'm feeling a little nervous about it now." He pulled at the sheet to reveal a wooden bench bearing a bronze plaque.

Colin frowned, then stepped forward and peered at the engraved dedication.

Dawn's Bench
In loving memory of Dawn Hillier, who loved to sit here, and who was so loved
by many. 1952–1977

He blinked again, and sat down, Fern beside him, tears plopping onto her cheeks.

Megan squeezed Jack's arm. "I think you're in the clear," she whispered. "Come on, let's leave them for a while."

They turned to walk back to the house, but Colin called out. "Wait!" He stumbled towards Jack, his arm outstretched. "Thank you," he said, his voice faltering. "I don't know how to thank you. That was an amazing thing to do."

"No problem," said Jack. "But what's with the handshake? Let's hug this out, buddy." He opened his arms and pulled Colin into them. "You're welcome to come and sit here any time. It'd be nice if it was used by the person who loved her most of all."

Colin stood back and nodded. "I did. Even though I didn't know her, I loved her. And I know now that she loved me, because she carried my photograph with her everywhere. I hope she's at peace."

"She will be," said Fern. "Now she knows you're happy, she will be."

Secrets, Lies, and Puppy Dog Eyes

CHAPTER 26

Ever since the revelations at the Hillier's Christmas party had become the topic of conversation throughout the village, Fern Rudd had become the subject of some unwanted attention from the local press, who had taken to following her and shouting questions in the street.

"Do you think Colin will eventually find peace now his secret's finally out?"

"As the girlfriend of the man who was responsible for terrorising the Hillier family, can you tell us your side of the story?"

"What's Colin Havers *really* like? Can you give us the inside scoop?"

The more polite reporters had left Fern alone once they realised she had no intention of talking to them, but the more persistent ones would follow her from her house to wherever she was going, even all the way to work. This wasn't so bad on the days she was working alone but on the days she was working with Julie, things became very difficult.

Not that Julie was opposed to members of the press pushing their way into the church office. She was quite happy for a bit of press attention, but only if it was focused on her. Unfortunately for Julie, it wasn't. The reporters were only interested in what Fern had to say and jealous Julie didn't like that one little bit.

Sherri Bryan

It got to the point when, after the third time a reporter stopped by the church office to speak to Fern, Julie couldn't take any more.

"The trouble with you is that you've let all the press attention go to your head," she snapped, as she watched Fern manhandle a reporter out of the door with threats to call the police if he didn't stay out. "You're nothing special, you know, but you've got far too big for your boots and you need taking down a peg or two."

"I don't ask them to follow me," said Fern, "but they won't leave me alone. The sooner all this dies down, the better. I'm sorry, Julie, I know it's causing a bit of disruption, but they'll get fed up and move onto someone else soon."

Julie looked out of the window at the pair of reporters on the pavement. As she filed her nails, she made a decision to take matters into her own hands and stop the disruption once and for all.

ooooooo

"Well, thank you for letting me know, Julie. I had no idea things had got so bad. With Christmas approaching, I was a little too preoccupied with the festive arrangements to notice what had been going on with the daily running of things. My fault, of course, but you and Fern run everything so smoothly, I rarely have to get involved." Patrick Beale showed

Secrets, Lies, and Puppy Dog Eyes

Julie from his office, a deep frown between his brows.

"However, if you tell me that Fern's encouraging the press to interfere with work, then that's not acceptable. And I had no idea she'd been such a disruptive influence for so long—you shouldn't have covered up for her like you have. How you've managed to do your own work, as well as all the things Fern misses, is nothing short of a miracle, Julie. Now, you go home and don't worry about it any more. I know you didn't want to, but you shouldn't feel guilty about coming to speak to me. Rest assured, I'll give the matter some thought tonight, and I'll deal with it tomorrow. You and Fern are both in tomorrow, aren't you? I might like to speak to you together."

"Yes, Patrick," said Julie, fluttering her eyelashes innocently. "I'm sorry to have bothered you with this, but I just couldn't let it go on."

"Don't worry. You've done the right thing by coming to speak to me. This is a new year, so maybe we really should think about starting afresh in certain areas."

As Julie made her way out of the office, a wide smile replaced the look of concern she'd been wearing for Patrick's benefit. If everything went her way, Fern Rudd would be out of a job this time tomorrow and Julie would be recommending her cousin as a replacement.

oooooo

Megan started another circuit of the village green, picking up her pace.

She was quite aware that she'd never have the body of a twenty-year old again, but having put on more than a few pounds over Christmas, her jeans were starting to feel uncomfortable around the waist. Determined not to buy a pair in the next size up, she'd vowed to exercise her way back into them.

"Megan! Meggie, darling, wait for me!"

Megan turned to see her mum jogging towards her in harem pants and one of her husband's sweatshirts.

"Hello, sweetheart," said Claudia, giving Megan a hug. "I heard you slip out, so I thought I'd join you. I've really over-indulged the last couple of weeks, and on top of the cruise, I think I must have put on at least a stone and a half. Even these baggy pants are starting to feel snug."

"I know what you mean," said Megan, swinging her arms as she walked. "I saw myself in a mirror in the village shop yesterday and it took a couple of seconds to realise that the woman who looked a lot like me, but was much rounder than I remembered, actually *was* me."

"Morning, you two."

Secrets, Lies, and Puppy Dog Eyes

Megan and Claudia turned to see Evie behind them.

"Hello love," said Megan, slipping her arm through her daughter's and dropping a kiss on her cheek. "Did I wake you?"

Evie shook her head and yawned. "No, I've been dozing for about an hour, so I heard you both go out. I thought I might as well get up and walk with you. I'll be leaving again in a few days, so I want to make the most of the time I've got left."

Megan felt her heart sink. "Oh, please don't talk about it yet, love."

"Sorry." Evie reached into her pocket for her phone. "I think this'll make a good selfie: three generations at the start of a new year, all with new plans, hopes and dreams. Say cheese!"

"I'll have one of them for my album, please, Evie," said Claudia.

Evie nodded. "I'll print you a copy later. And one for you, Mum." Her phone rang. "I'd better take this—it's Val from New Zealand. I'll catch up with you later."

Megan and Claudia walked on, chatting away until they approached the church. "Look. Isn't that Fern?" said Claudia. She waved a hand in the air. "Morning, Fern!"

Fern barely raised her head as she waved back.

"Is she crying?" said Megan.

They walked over to the church office, where Fern was fumbling with a large bunch of keys.

"Are you alright?" said Claudia, frowning when she saw her tearstained face. "What on earth's the matter?"

"Oh, it's nothing." Fern wiped her eyes. "I'm just being silly." She smiled, then her face crumpled and she began to cry again. "I'm sorry, I wasn't expecting to see anyone this early. I was going to go into the office and make myself look presentable before anyone else arrived."

As the mother of two daughters, and a grandmother to a twenty year old, Claudia's shoulder had become accustomed to the odd tear over the years. She pulled Fern into a hug and spoke comfortingly in her ear. "Come on, love, let the tears out. It's not good to keep them in."

Fern clung to her and sobbed, then stepped back and blew her nose. "Thank you, you're really kind. I can't tell Colin because I know he'll want to fight my battles for me, and that'll only make things worse."

"Would you like to tell us?" said Claudia. "You know, a problem shared, and all that."

Fern nodded, and they followed her into the church office. "It's Julie. Most of the time, I can deal with her, but she can be so spiteful

Secrets, Lies, and Puppy Dog Eyes

and nasty for no reason, and after everything that's happened over the past few weeks, I suppose I'm feeling a bit vulnerable. I feel ridiculous. Look at me. I'm a grown woman and here I am, boo-hooing like a baby. I don't know what's wrong with me."

"There's nothing wrong with *you*, Fern, it's Julie that has the problem," said Megan, crossly, pulling two tissues from the box on Fern's desk and handing them to her. "I only told Mum recently that Kelly's the same with me. The whole group from school still hang around together, and they're just nasty bullies, but it must be worse for you, having to work with Julie. At least I can avoid Kelly most of the time. But I know what you mean. You feel that you should be able to cope with things because you're a certain age, or you're a mum, or you're supposed to set an example, but things still get to you, doesn't matter how old you are."

Fern nodded. "Thank you. That makes me feel slightly less of a blubbering idiot." She managed a smile. "I think Julie's complained to Patrick about the reporters who've been following me to work. They come into the office sometimes and they caused a bit of a row between us yesterday. I don't want them here any more than she does, but I can't stop them following me. *And* I had a call from Patrick last night. He said he wanted to see me about something today. He didn't sound very happy, so I'm sure Julie must have complained about it. I mean, it's not like the disturbances ever stop me from doing what I'm supposed to do, because I always stay late if I'm falling behind with something, but they must disturb Julie, too, so I guess she's had enough of it."

Claudia looked at Fern and gave her another hug. "I'm sorry, love. It must be horrible for you. Can we do anything to help?"

Fern shook her head. "There's nothing you can do. I'm sure it'll all blow over in a few days." She looked at the clock on the wall. "I'd better get on. Thank you for listening. It's helped a lot."

As Claudia and Megan walked out into the fresh air again, they exchanged a glance.

"For heaven's sake! Of all the places you'd wouldn't expect to find a bully, it's here," said Claudia, irritably, gesturing to the church behind her. "Bullies have no place in our society, and not in our village."

"Tell me about it," said Megan.

Claudia looked at her watch. "Come on, we're taking a detour."

"Where are we going?"

"To see Patrick Beale."

ooooooo

Claudia stood up and shook Patrick's hand. "Sorry to have to be the bearer of bad news, and so early in the day, but I thought you should know what's been going on, and I wanted to catch you before you got to the church."

Patrick shook his head. "I'm ashamed to say, you're not the first person to have spoken to me about Julie's attitude, and I've been very remiss in not having dealt with it. Des and I had a conversation not so long ago, so it a very poor show on my part that I've missed what's been going on under my own nose. I was so busy with church business, I took my eye off the ball. Even if parishioners don't take the time to keep me informed, I should be instinctively aware of situations like this, but I missed it completely. Thank you, Claudia. I appreciate you coming in to see me. I'll have to give some thought as to the best way to tackle this, but tackle it I shall, you mark my words."

"I don't like to get anyone in trouble," said Claudia, "but when things get to this stage, I think strong action needs to be taken. And you're the only one who can take it."

Patrick nodded. "Oh, I will. Rest assured, I will."

oooooo

"Why do you think he wants to see us both?" said Fern, as she and Julie sat in the office, waiting for Patrick.

"How should I know?" said Julie, blowing a bubble that popped all over her jammy red lips.

"Ah, Fern, Julie, thanks for staying after hours," said Patrick, sticking his head around the door. "Could you both come into my office, please? I won't keep you long."

They trailed in behind him, Julie pushing Fern away from the comfy leather chair with the armrests and a reclining back so she could swipe it for herself. As there was nowhere else to sit apart from Patrick's chair behind his desk, Fern perched on the edge of a hard plastic chair with a crack along the edge.

"Now, Fern, I understand from Julie that since the business with Colin... How is he coping now, by the way?"

Fern looked surprised. "Oh, he's coming to terms with everything now, thank you. He's a lot better than he was."

Patrick smiled. "Good, good. So... it's been brought to my attention that the press have been pursuing you, is that right? Following you and lying in wait for you every morning when you arrive at work?"

Fern looked at her lap. "Yes. I'm sorry. I've told them to leave me alone, but they're very persistent."

"And I understand that they've been coming into the church office, causing quite a disturbance while you and Julie have been trying to work? Is that right?"

Fern hung her head. "Yes. I've done my best to keep them out but, apart from locking the door so *no one* can get in, it's a bit difficult."

"And what have you done to help Fern while all this has been going on, Julie?"

Julie looked up, the smile vanishing from her lips in an instant. "Huh?"

"I wondered what you had done to help Fern when she so obviously needed help?"

"I, er, well, I've helped her to get rid of the reporters from the office loads of times," said Julie, sending Fern a glare that dared her to contradict what she'd said.

"Ah, I see," said Patrick. "I only ask, because I took the liberty of calling a couple of local newspapers this morning and had a long chat with the editors. They told me that their reporters had been trying their best get a story from Fern, but they hadn't been able to, because she won't talk to them. However, they also told me that *you'd* offered to give them a story, as Fern's colleague, and that you'd turned quite nasty when your offer was refused."

As Julie shifted uncomfortably in the chair, her mouth opened, but no words came out. This wasn't going the way she'd planned at all.

"You mind your leg on that broken chair, Fern," said Patrick. "I should have thrown it out ages ago, but I've been so distracted, it completely slipped my mind.

Perhaps you could make a note to dispose of it and order a new one in the morning?" He smiled, before turning back to Julie.

"Now, Julie. What you said, or didn't say to the press, is of no concern to me. What does concern me, however, is your failure to offer support to a colleague who so badly needed it. You know the importance I place on a happy working environment but if we're unable to show compassion, sympathy, empathy and kindness to one another, I don't know how we're going to achieve it."

"I hope that's not a reference to me, Patrick," said Julie, pursing her lips, "because if you ask Fern, she'll tell you that I'm *always* supportive and kind. Aren't I Fern? *Fern!*"

Fern looked at her, then looked away.

Patrick nodded. "I see. You can go now, Fern, thank you for staying. I'll see you in the morning."

Julie picked up her bag and coat and stood up to leave. "Not you, Julie. I'd like to talk to you for a while longer, if you don't mind. I won't take much of your time."

Ten minutes later, and with a face like thunder, Julie stormed from the office, Patrick Beale's words ringing in her ears.

"...your attitude has been noticed by parishioners."

"...your behaviour does not represent our values"

"...I will not tolerate bullying."

"...I suggest you go home this evening, and give some serious thought as to whether the church is a place at which you would like to continue to work."

At that point, Julie had sworn at Patrick and resigned on the spot. "And if you think I'm working my notice after being humiliated like this, you've got another think coming! Let Little Miss Perfect run the office on her own."

As she marched across the village green, she glanced over to Kismet Cottage, where a silver tabby cat sat on the wall, catching the last of the autumn day's sunshine. She had no proof, but she was sure that Megan Fallon's uncle Des had carried out his promise to speak to Patrick, and had put in a *bad* word for her after he'd put in a *good* word for Fern.

At least I'm not the only one who's not happy about Megan Fallon being back in the village, she thought.

With a grim expression on her face, and a huge chip on her shoulder, Julie set off in search of comfort from her friends.

Chapter 27

"Did you hear that Julie Cobb's on the warpath because she's out of a job?" said Petal, as she flicked through a catalogue of the latest floral design ideas.

"What? Why?" Megan looked up from the mug of caramel coffee she was sipping as she leaned against the counter in the flower shop.

"She resigned. Apparently, Patrick suggested she might want to reconsider her future at the church because there had been some complaints about her attitude. About bloody time, too. She's a horrible woman."

"And she's on the warpath because people complained about her?" said Megan, thinking back to the conversation her mum had had with Patrick.

Petal raised her eyes from the catalogue. "Just so you know, rumour is she seems to think your Uncle Des had something to do with it. Not that she'd take it out on him, of course, but you're the closest thing to him and considering your history with that gang of lowlifes, I thought I should let you know.

"Not that they'd do anything physical—they're not that stupid—but take that stunt Kelly pulled in the bank, for example. It was all around the village for a couple of days that you're some kind of husband-stealer. That's the kind of thing I'm talking about, and with

Secrets, Lies, and Puppy Dog Eyes

you trying to get your new business off the ground, I wouldn't be surprised if they spread a few malicious rumours to put off any potential customers. They're so spiteful."

Megan sighed. "It's Kelly who stirs things up. If ever the Guinness Book of Records was looking for The Holder of the Longest Grudge, they wouldn't need to look much further than her."

"Daisy's got the day off, Mum, so we're going into town now. I'll see you later, okay?"

They were so engrossed in their conversation—Megan with her back to the room and Petal with her eyes on the catalogue—that neither of them had noticed Evie standing behind Megan.

"Oh, right," she said, giving Petal a guilty look as the realisation dawned that Evie must have heard some, if not all, of their conversation about her stepmother. "Okay, love, I didn't see you there. I thought you were still chatting to Amisha."

"Obviously," said Evie, with a grin at Megan's horrified expression. "Look, Mum, you don't need to censor anything you want to say about Kelly around me. I already know what a total bitch she is, but she's married to Dad, so I just be as pleasant as I can, but have as little to do with her as possible. I don't want to play happy families with her, but I don't want to rock the boat, either."

Sherri Bryan

    She slid an arm around Megan's shoulder. "It's obvious she's furious that you've come back to Bliss Bay, but she's just going to have to get over it, isn't she? I overheard her talking to one of her friends the other day—someone called Julie—and when she realised I'd heard, she looked like she was going to cry. *And* I heard about what happened in the bank." Evie tossed her hair over her shoulder and rolled her eyes.

    "How did you find out?" Megan asked, with a fretful look. She always went out of her way to keep any animosity she had for Kelly far away from Evie.

    "Duh? Because people talk. Someone told someone who told someone who told Daisy, who told me. She was so mad when she heard, she wanted to go and bang on Kelly's door and scratch her eyes out. Not as much as I did but considering she's not family, she's totally got your back. You're really lucky, Mum, you've got such a great support network here. Daisy, Petal and Blossom would all stick up for you, and you know that Nan and Grandad, and Aunty Sylv and Uncle Des would stand in front of a train for you.

    "And, d'you know why? Because you're fab. You're a good person, and you're an even better Mum." She rested her head on Megan's shoulder. "I know she must get to you sometimes, but don't give Kelly the pleasure of seeing that she winds you up. I can assure you, if she wasn't my stepmother, I'd be the first in line to punch her on the nose. I'm pretty sure she wouldn't have pulled that bank stunt if she'd known I was coming home—she never says a word against you when I'm around. She's so mean, I honestly don't know what Dad sees in her."

"Bedroom tricks, your Aunty Sylv thinks," said Megan.

"Eeewww! Mum! Right, this conversation is *definitely* over," said Evie, pulling a face and dropping a kiss on Megan's cheek. "I want to say goodbye to a few people before I leave tomorrow, so I'd better get on with it. I'll see you later."

ooooooo

After an emotional goodbye at the airport, accompanied by all her family and friends, Evie boarded a plane to take her on the next leg of her travels.

"I'll be back before you know it," she told Megan, as they wiped away each other's tears. "And don't let those witches get you down," she whispered. "You're a strong, amazing woman, and you've got an awesome support system."

"Go on, go and get on the plane before I buy a ticket and come with you," said Megan, taking her daughter's face in her hands and smiling through her tears. "You wouldn't like your mum hanging around, cramping your style, would you?"

Evie grinned and moved over to Laurence who told her not to do anything he wouldn't do.

Megan rolled her eyes. *That guy is such an idiot.*

"Bye, Kelly," said Evie, with a nod to her stepmother. "No need for us to kiss, or hug, or anything."

Megan turned to hide her smile. Evie always knew the perfect thing to say for every occasion. She waved until her daughter was out of sight, then turned with Petal and Claudia, each holding a hand.

"I know how you feel, love," said Claudia. "Remember what I told you? There's nothing better than seeing the children you brought up spreading their wings, but there's no better place to have them than in your arms." She squeezed Megan's hand. "Come on, your dad and Des are going back to the house to get dinner started, so how about we leave them to get on with it and go to The Duck for a drink?"

ooooooo

"You feeling better?" said Petal, as she put a glass of wine down in front of Megan.

"Much," she replied. "I love to think of her going off to have a brilliant time, but it's the saying goodbye that I hate. Thanks for that, I'm just nipping to the ladies'."

It wasn't until she was washing her hands that Megan became aware of someone else in the room. There were only two cubicles. Had someone just come out of the other one? She turned, but no one was there, and both cubicle doors were open.

She looked back in the mirror and almost jumped out of her skin. Standing behind her, stepping out of a dimly-lit corner, were Kelly and Julie.

Megan gulped, but ignored them. She did a quick round of anti-anxiety deep breathing exercises as she made a meal of washing her hands, before turning round to face them.

"What do you want?"

Kelly came right up to her face. "Now that Evie's left, there's no need for us to play nicey-nicey any more. Because of you and that stupid old duffer of an uncle of yours, Julie doesn't have a job any more, and she's not very happy about it, are you Julie?"

Julie's thin lips almost disappeared in a grimace. "No, I'm bloody well not." She took a step closer. "It's not going to be a very Happy New Year for me, is it? I've had to take a job back at the petrol station and go home every night stinking of diesel, all because of you and your uncle."

"I warned you to watch your back, Megan," said Kelly. "But you didn't listen, did you?"

Suddenly, Megan felt a calm rush through her and Evie's words rang in her ears. *You're a strong, amazing woman, and you've got an awesome support system.*

She summoned every ounce of courage and smiled. "Actually, Julie, you lost your job because you're a nasty piece of work. It had nothing to do with me, or my Uncle Des. You did it all on your own." She pushed her way between Kelly and Julie, who were so stunned, they didn't even try to stop her. "'Scuse me. I'd love to stop and chat but, actually, I really don't want to."

"Where d'you think you're going?" said Kelly. "We haven't finished talking yet."

"Oh, haven't you?" Megan tilted her head. "Well, I have. Ta-ta."

As she walked back to the table, she felt as though her heart would pound out of her chest. She was sure her legs were going to collapse under her, but she kept walking until she fell into her chair with a bump.

"You alright, love?" said Claudia.

"Yes, Mum. I'm fine."

Petal caught her eye as she noticed Kelly and Julie walk out of the ladies' room, whispering and wearing matching scowls. Kelly shot a threatening glare in Megan's direction and mouthed the words, *I'm watching you.*

"Everything okay?" said Petal, with a frown, her green eyes flashing.

Megan took a big glug of her wine. "It is now."

"Ooh, look, Jack's just walked in," said Sylvie, waving a hand in the air. "Jack, we're here!" she bellowed.

"Hey!" He waved back and came and sat next to Megan. "I went to your place and your dad told me you were here. Did Evie get away okay?"

Megan nodded. "Thanks for taking us out for dinner the other day. She really enjoyed it. We both did, actually. She grew quite fond of you while she was here."

Jack smiled. "Well, likewise. She's a great kid. She obviously takes after her dad." He winked and Megan punched him playfully on the arm. "Sorry I couldn't get to the airport, but Lionel, Rob and I have been playing golf. I haven't played for ages."

"Good game?"

Jack raised an eyebrow. "Let's just say I don't think I'll be playing again any time soon."

"Ah, right. Well, in that case, do you want a beer?"

Sherri Bryan

"No, I've got to get back. I've left the guys at my place, being terrorised by Blue. I just wanted to run something by you."

"Oh? What's that, then?"

Jack dropped his voice. "This is going to sound really weird, but let me finish and then just let the idea sit a while before you make a decision, okay?"

Megan turned to face him. "You've really got my attention now. What is it?"

"Well, I was driving back from golf and I suddenly thought, why don't *you* come and live in my apartment? I don't know why I didn't think of it before. It'll mean you can stay in Bliss Bay. It has two bedrooms, so you can have people over to stay if you want to, it's all ready for someone to move in, and the rent's reasonable. I actually thought about not charging you rent at all, but I'd rather keep things above board, you know? And I'll be a really good landlord." Jack grinned. "I'd cover the council tax, but you'd pay for the utilities.

"You can come over to the house to hang out sometimes, if you want to, or just stay in the apartment if you prefer. We never have to see each other if you'd rather not, although it'd be nice to get together from time to time. No strings, obviously." He took a deep breath. "Wow, I think I said all that in one take. Anyways, what d'you think?"

Secrets, Lies, and Puppy Dog Eyes

Megan stared at him, and became aware that everyone was pretending not to listen. "Erm, well, you've taken me by surprise. A *nice* surprise, but it was the last thing I was expecting you to say. I thought you were keeping the apartment for when your family and friends come over and there's not enough room in the house for everyone?"

"Yeah, I was, but that was before I thought it might suit you better."

Megan chewed her lip. "Can I think about it?"

Jack nodded. "Take all the time you need. It's just an offer, from one friend to another, so there's no pressure. Let me know when you've decided. And I won't be offended if the answer's no." He grinned and his dimples made an appearance. "Anyways, gotta run. See y'around. Bye, everyone."

No one said a word until the pub door had closed behind him.

"Did Jack Windsor just ask you to move in with him?" asked Claudia, her eyebrows raised halfway up her forehead.

"No, he asked me if I wanted to be his tenant in the purpose-built apartment which is totally separate from the house. That's a completely different proposition altogether from what you're thinking," said Megan.

"But you'll be in the same grounds," said Petal.

"Yeah, just metres away from each other," said Daisy.

"You'd be so close, you could even end up kissing without meaning to," said Blossom without looking up from her phone, and curling up in a fit of giggles.

Megan gave them all a sarcastic smile. "*If* I accepted his offer, then yes, I'd be in the same grounds, and yes, we'd be living very close together, but we wouldn't end up snogging, thank you very much, Blossom. We're adults, not hormone-fuelled teenagers, so I think we'd manage to keep our hands off each other."

"Well," said Sylvie. "Are you going to take him up on the offer? He's a good catch, y'know. You could do a lot worse than snapping him up before someone else gets their grubby paws on him."

Megan rolled her eyes. "How many times do I have to tell you before it sinks in, Aunty Sylv? I don't *want* to snap anyone up! As long as I've got my friends and family, I'm quite happy without romance in my life, thank you very much."

"Good for you," said Daisy. "We don't need men to define us, do we, Megan?" She did a double victory sign from across the table.

"You haven't answered my question," said Sylvie. "Are you going to take him up on the offer?"

Megan shrugged. I don't know. I'll have to think about it."

"It'd be lovely to have you close by, love," said Claudia.

"Jack and Megan sitting in a tree," sang Blossom, "K-I-S-S-I-N-G," before dissolving into a fit of giggles again.

Megan joined in the laughter, and relaxed as the conversation flowed. She put Jack's offer to the back of her mind.

There'd be plenty of time to think about it later.

ooooooo

The next morning, Megan jumped out of her old bed at her old room at her parents' home. She looked around and realised how much she loved her room, just down the hall from her mum and dad's, and next door to Lizzie's when she was around.

She thought of all the celebrations they'd had there. Birthdays, Christmases, christenings, and anniversaries. And she thought of all the good times.

She remembered her dad teaching her to ride a bike down the path in the garden. And putting her first tooth under her pillow and shrieking with delight when she saw the coin the tooth fairy left. She recalled writing letters to Santa and pegging up Christmas stockings above the fireplace, and tap-dancing to Uncle Des's harmonica on the kitchen tiles. She remembered being carried upstairs to bed when she fell asleep on her dad's lap and, best of all, she remembered the first time she'd brought Evie to the house, and the look of absolute joy on her parents' faces.

She remembered all those things and felt the love that seemed to seep out of the walls of the house that had been her home for so many years.

She brushed her teeth and pulled on her tracksuit bottoms and trainers, before gathering her hair in a messy ponytail.

She had to do this right away, before she changed her mind. It was for the best, she knew it.

She grabbed her keys and her phone and started up her old Mini. Vinnie the Mini wasn't partial to the cold mornings, but he'd never let her down yet. With a screech and a bang, the old car started and she let the engine warm up before setting off for The Old School House. It was early—maybe too early for Jack to be awake—but she remembered him saying that Blue had been waking him up early to be let out.

She rang the bell and waited.

She heard a little bark and the sound of Blue's tiny nails on the wooden floor.

She heard Jack say, "Hold on, I'll be there in a minute." His voice was gruff;

Secrets, Lies, and Puppy Dog Eyes

probably his pre-the-first-coffee-of-the-day voice.

The door opened, and he stood, looking at her, as Blue escaped and bounded onto the lawn to do his business.

"Hey. If I'd known the late night and early morning calls were going to be a regular thing, I wouldn't have taken so long to answer the door, but I wasn't expecting anyone at..." he glanced at his watch, "quarter-to six. Is everything okay?"

Megan nodded.

"You want to come in?" said Jack. "It's pretty cold out there."

She shook her head. "No, it's okay. I've come to give you my answer."

"Oh, right. Are you sure you don't want to come in?"

"No, thanks. I've been up, most of the night, thinking. Y'see, I never thought I'd ever want to leave Kismet Cottage, but when I got married, I did. And then, I never thought I'd want to leave Bliss Bay, but when everything went downhill with Laurence, I did. And I never—not in a million years—ever thought I'd come back here again to live, but I did. And I've realised that I absolutely *love* living back in the village, at Kismet Cottage, where me and my family have had such great times."

"Oh," said Jack. "Okay, well, no worries. I appreciate you coming all the way over here so early to tell me." He grinned. "No hard feelings, I just wanted to give you first refusal."

Megan shook her head. "Oh, no, you don't understand. I haven't explained it properly. What I meant was that most of my life in Bliss Bay has been at Kismet Cottage, and I've loved every minute of it. Ninety-nine percent of the memories I have of living there are happy. But now that I'm back, I need to make my own memories, in my own place. Apart from during my short-lived marriage, I haven't lived anywhere else but at Kismet Cottage while I've been in Bliss Bay, but I need to live somewhere else. Without the strings, of course." She smiled. "I need my independence."

She took a deep breath and looked at her old friend, laughing at the bemused expression on his face.

"Yes, Jack. The answer is yes."

The End

Secrets, Lies, and Puppy Dog Eyes

BOOK THREE PREVIEW

Details of my other books can be found on page 383 but, to give you a preview of what's to come, here's the first chapter of the next book in the series.

Malice, Remorse and a Rocking Horse

Chapter 1

Jerry Braithwaite walked back to his cell with a cocky swagger. His fellow inmates whooped and called out his name, and he acknowledged their enthusiasm with an exaggerated grin.

"Better luck next time, eh?" said the guard when they reached his cell.

As the door shut behind him, Jerry's jaw—aching from the fake smile to disguise his disappointment—sagged as he slumped onto the bed and put his head in his hands.

"Sorry it didn't go the way you'd hoped." The guard threw a sympathetic nod in Jerry's direction before locking the cell door, and leaving him alone with his thoughts.

Since the day of his arrest, he'd protested his innocence, but nobody had wanted to listen. He'd decided early on that the best way to deal with his jail term without going mad was to keep his head down, keep out of trouble, and keep busy. His behaviour couldn't have been better.

He flung himself back on his bed and fixed his eyes on the bottom of the top bunk. It had been a long day but, as tired as he was, he knew sleep would be a long time coming tonight.

What had gone wrong? He was the model prisoner. Even the prison guards couldn't believe he wasn't a free man by now. Everyone had expected his request for parole to be approved. For his right to freedom to be granted.

But that day wasn't today.

ooooooo

Outside the prison gates, a mass of Jerry's fans grew increasingly restless.

A skinny, peroxide-blonde in a leather jumpsuit, and wearing a ring through her nose, held up her hand to the crowd. "Ssshhh! There's some news about Jerry's parole hearing." The crowd fell silent as she held her phone to her ear.

"And news just breaking," she called out, repeating the newcaster's report. "In the last few minutes, Jerry Braithwaite, lead singer of the band, Rocking Horse, has been denied early release by a parole board for the third time during his twenty-year sentence."

The crowd hissed and booed and the leather-suited fan hushed them again, pressing her phone close to her ear. "Bliss Bay-born Mr Braithwaite, who also has a home in Oxeter, was jailed fifteen years ago after being convicted of the murder of Zara Brett. We'll bring you more news as we have it."

She shoved her phone back into her pocket and addressed the crowd. "We have to let him know we'll never forget him, and we'll be waiting for him when he finally gets out!" Looking up at the dreary sky, she began to sing Jerry's most well known song, 'Little Dove'. "Through the darkness, you brought me light."

The crowd picked up the chorus, swaying along with the words.

"You never failed me.

You brought me peace, hope and love,

Little dove, little dove."

As the song ended and the crowd roared Jerry's name over and over, a fan watching from a distance pulled up the hood of a dark jacket and left.

ooooooo

In the café across the street around a table of coffees and teas gone cold, the conversation was all about Jerry Braithwaite.

"I was sure he'd get parole this time, weren't you?"

"I can't believe they didn't let him out. He's served enough time."

"Don't be ridiculous! He killed that woman. He'll *never* serve enough time in my opinion. He should have been given life."

"But he didn't do it intentionally—it was an accident. He's innocent!"

"You would say that, wouldn't you? You're a die-hard fan."

"They probably didn't release him because they think he's still a danger to society."

"Don't talk such rubbish! He never *was* a danger to society! If he says he didn't kill that woman, then he didn't kill her."

"Well, he's bound to say he didn't do it, isn't he?"

The lively discussions went on, back and forth, until everyone left for home. Everyone except the solitary, hooded stranger sitting at a small table in the corner, engrossed in the first edition of the evening newspaper left by a previous customer.

** STOP PRESS**
ROCK SINGER DENIED PAROLE FOR A THIRD TIME

Jerry Braithwaite was arrested fifteen years ago, after the body of thirty-year old Zara Brett was found in his bathroom at The Princess Hotel in Oxeter, following an after-concert party to which a number of fans had been invited.

Secrets, Lies, and Puppy Dog Eyes

A post-mortem established the cause of Miss Brett's death to be strangulation, refuting Braithwaite's insistence that the woman must have fallen asleep in the bath and drowned. He has always denied any involvement in her death but, as there was no one else in the room apart from him and Miss Brett, he was arrested on suspicion of her murder the following morning.

At the time, reaction to his twenty-year sentence was mixed. Some thought it was too lenient, but many others considered it too harsh for the crime, a popular theory being that the judge was making an example of the flamboyant singer.

Though Braithwaite maintained his innocence, and his legions of loyal fans protested at his arrest, it took a jury less than three hours to return a guilty verdict.

Following the unsuccessful hearing, Mr Braithwaite has a maximum of five more years to serve behind bars. Whether he applies for parole again remains to be seen.

The stranger read the article twice before paying the bill and leaving the café. Once home, behind a desk in a concealed room, a single, unshaded light bulb hung from the beams in the ceiling, swinging gently from its cable and casting shadows across the walls.

Sherri Bryan

Reaching out a shaky hand for the framed picture of Jerry that sat on the edge of the desk, the stranger held it close, and said,
"You should have got parole. You should have got it. You've more than paid for what happened. I thought I'd done enough to avenge you, but I was wrong. I'm sorry I let you down but it won't happen again... I promise."

ooooooo

Christopher Duncan straightened up from digging the flowerbeds in his back garden and wiped the perspiration from his forehead with a muddy gardening glove.

"Want a cup of tea?" his wife, Stella, called from the kitchen window.

"Of *course* I want a cup of tea!" he snapped, from behind the crimson flowers of the vast rhododendron on the edge of the lawn. He leaned on a garden fork and surveyed his morning's work.

The previous residents of the cottage—an elderly couple who hadn't touched the garden in years—had left plenty for him to do. He'd tidied the beds and borders, but was putting off tackling the bindweed-infested lawn until Stella could help. It was a two-person job, but it could wait until she'd finished preparing the inside walls of the house for decorating; a job he was thankful not to be doing. He turned up the volume on the

Secrets, Lies, and Puppy Dog Eyes

radio and chuckled to himself, wondering how long Stella would wait until suggesting he turn it down.

Stella was keen to make a good impression in Crocus Dell, the quiet village to which she and Christopher had recently moved. That meant—according to her self-imposed rules—no loud music, no talking too loudly outdoors, and absolutely no power or garden tools until she'd forewarned the neighbours of the noise as a courtesy. As far as Stella was concerned, it just wouldn't do to fall out with the neighbours before they'd even met most of them. The exception was the couple next door. Helena and Lucas Perry had brought round a fruit cake and a flask of tea when they'd seen the removal van, with a promise to call round again in a few days with a bottle of bubbly to properly welcome them to the neighbourhood.

Christopher had scowled at the gift. He didn't see the need for people to live in each other's pockets just because they happened to be neighbours, and had been on the verge of telling Helena and Lucas just that when Stella have given him one of her looks. He usually ignored them but decided, on that occasion, perhaps it was better to say nothing.

He let out a sigh of contentment as he closed his eyes and lifted his face to the sun's warmth. The move had been a long time coming and it felt good to relax at last. He looked forward to his retirement; he planned to golf and fish as often as possible. Only the previous week, when he'd joined the local golf club, he'd got chatting with some of the other members who'd invited him to join them on a group trip to Ireland. "Excellent for golf and fishing," they'd said. Not that Stella enjoyed golf or fishing, but that wasn't his problem. She'd have to find some other way to occupy her time.

There was only one thing keeping him from complete happiness.

Jerry Braithwaite.

The man had followed him around for years, like chewing gum stuck to his shoe. If someone wasn't talking about him on TV, they were writing about him in the newspapers.

It had been bad enough being Jury Foreman at his murder trial fifteen years ago. He'd tried hard to forget the stress it had caused, but each time a parole hearing came up and he saw Jerry's face plastered all over the news, it brought back terrible memories of the trial and its aftermath.

After the verdict, Christopher had thought that would be the end of it; case closed. He'd begun to get on with his life but just when everything had finally got back to normal, anonymous hate mail had started dropping through his letterbox. Cards bearing menacing pictures of funeral wreaths started arriving with alarming regularity at his home, the sender venting their displeasure at the way the trial had ended.

*It was **you** who delivered the guilty verdict.*

You as good as put Jerry behind bars yourself.

You deserve to be punished.

Individually cut letters from newspapers and magazines had been stuck onto the cards to form every word, each message ending with the words, *For Jerry*.

The fact that someone had found out his name and address made Christopher feel nauseous. The court had never referred to any of the jury members by their names, only by numbers.

Ten cards had arrived over the space of the next ten weeks. They all bore the same message, but each one had felt a little more intimidating than the last. He'd reported them to the police and handed them over as evidence but, in his opinion, the police hadn't treated the matter seriously enough. They'd given him a lame reassurance that if they got any leads, they'd investigate and let him know.

He'd hoped they'd give him some protection, or even station a car outside the house, but they hadn't. They said whoever had sent the letters was simply trying to make him uneasy, and offered to send a patrol car to drive past the house a couple of times after dark. But nothing else.

As Christopher had explained to the police many times, as Jury Foreman, he was just doing a job. It was nothing personal. It wasn't *his* fault Jerry Braithwaite had been sentenced to a lengthy prison term.

However, he'd never told them he'd had no trouble in finding Jerry guilty. He hadn't even needed to deliberate with the other jurors to be sure of his guilt. As soon as he'd laid eyes on Jerry, he'd made up his mind that the scruffy rock singer had killed that poor girl. *Disgusting reprobate.* Christopher had done all he could to make sure the maximum sentence was handed down.

When the hate mail stopped as suddenly as it had started, Christopher and Stella had managed to put the stress behind them and get on with their lives.

Now, they had their dream cottage in a quiet village, with primrose-coloured wooden shutters on the windows, a country garden, mature fruit trees, and the vegetable patch he'd always wanted.

He shuddered and put all thoughts of Jerry Braithwaite from his mind. All that was fifteen years behind him. He had only to look forward now.

Secrets, Lies, and Puppy Dog Eyes

Stella walked towards him with a mug of tea in each hand. "Here we are."

"About time." Christopher took his tea from her and cupped his gloved hands around the mug.

"Don't you think you should turn down the volume on the radio?" said Stella, a frown line running all the way down her forehead to her nose.

"Why?" Christopher hid his inner smile and blew on his tea.

"You know very well why," said Stella, turning the volume knob to the left before stretching out on the lawn. "That's better. And thank goodness those workmen have stopped their infernal drilling and gone for a break. The constant sound of that hammer drill pounding on the pavement outside the house is enough to drive you mad. I shall be glad when they pack up their things and leave."

Christopher ignored her and nodded to the rhododendron. "We'll have to add moving that to our to-do list. I've no idea how were going to do it, though; it's so huge, the roots must go for miles."

"Well, don't look at me," said Stella, swatting away a wasp with her hand. "You know I've never been blessed with green fingers. Didn't Lucas say he'd be happy to give us a hand if we needed any help with the garden?"

"You mean that idiot from next door?" Christopher shook his head. "You know how I feel about people we barely know nosing around in our business."

"For heaven's sake, we'd only be asking him for a little help moving a bush," said Stella tightly, a nervous tic causing her nose to twitch. "It's not as though we're going to give him our bank statements to look through."

Christopher glared at her. "Well, *you* ask him, then," he huffed. "And don't get too friendly. I don't want him thinking he can pop round here every five minutes. You know what some people are like. You give them an inch and they practically move in."

"I'll do that, then." Stella's shoulders dropped visibly as she relaxed. "We'll only need him to help with a few bits out here. I don't think we'll have to do much with the front garden at all, do you? I love the magnolia tree, and the honeysuckle has such a glorious scent, it'd be a crime to cut it down. I'm quite happy for both of them to stay where they are." She cocked her head. "Was that the doorbell?" She started to push herself up to her feet.

"I'll go." Christopher put down his mug and took off his gardening gloves. "In any case, I want to check what you've done inside so I know how long I'll need to set aside to re-do it properly."

Secrets, Lies, and Puppy Dog Eyes

Stella bit back a retort, lay on the grass, and closed her eyes. Several minutes later—according to her watch—she woke up. Looking around, she saw that Christopher's mug of tea was still on the edge of the raised flowerbed. *It must have been the neighbours at the door. They're probably chatting.* She got up and dusted herself off, hoping that Christopher hadn't been too offhand. He could be quite rude if he wasn't in the mood for socialising. She, on the other hand, was very much looking forward to making new friends. Picking up the mug of cold tea, she made her way back to the house.

"Who is it, Christopher?" she called, putting the mugs in the sink. She frowned as she caught sight of her messy decorating clothes in the mirror and smoothed them down as best she could. She hated greeting guests when she wasn't looking her best. Pushing up the ends of her hair with her palms, she fixed a smile on her face and made her way through the kitchen and the dining room to the front door

Strange, I can't hear any voices. They must be in the front garden. Stella stepped into the small hallway and stopped dead in her tracks.

Christopher was lying in a heap on the doorstep.

Sherri Bryan

    She let out a scream and rushed to him, her hands flying to her mouth when she saw the message written on one of his hands which simply said, *For Jerry.*

Secrets, Lies, and Puppy Dog Eyes

JOIN MY READERS' GROUP

If you'd like to receive an email notification of my new releases, please join my Readers' Group at https://sherribryan.com.

OTHER BOOKS BY SHERRI BRYAN

The Charlotte Denver Cozy Mystery Series
Tapas, Carrot Cake and a Corpse - Book 1
Fudge Cake, Felony and a Funeral - Book 2
Spare Ribs, Secrets and a Scandal - Book 3
Pumpkins, Peril and a Paella - Book 4
Hamburgers, Homicide and a Honeymoon - Book 5
Crab Cakes, Killers and a Kaftan - Book 6
Mince Pies, Mistletoe and Murder - Book 7
Doughnuts, Diamonds and Dead Men - Book 8
Bread, Dead and Wed - Book 9

The Bliss Bay Village Mystery Series
Bodies, Baddies and a Crabby Tabby - Book - 1
Secrets, Lies and Puppy Dog Eyes - Book 2
Malice, Remorse and a Rocking Horse - Book 3
Dormice, Schemers and Misdemeanours - Book 4

Sherri Bryan

ACKNOWLEDGEMENTS

Thank you for buying my book. I can't tell you how much I appreciate your support.

Also, a massive thank you to Alan, whose help and guidance with the cover production of this book helped to lower my anxiety levels.

Thanks, too, to my reading team, Jenny, Dominique, Dylan and Helen—you're all brilliant.

And thank you to my editor, Francis, who has the patience of a saint.

Hugs and gratitude to you all.

Secrets, Lies, and Puppy Dog Eyes

A Message from Sherri

Thank you for buying my book. I hope you enjoyed it.

Whether you're the chatty type, who reads my books and gets in touch to let me know you enjoyed them, the silent type who doesn't, or the type who reads, reviews and spreads the word, I want to say that I appreciate each and every person who takes an interest in my work. I can't thank you enough.

If you'd like to get in touch, even just to say hello, please do. You can contact me by email at sherri@sherribryan.com, on my Facebook page at https://www.facebook.com/sherribryanauthor/ or on Twitter at @sbryanwrites.

If I take a while to answer, please bear with me. I get quite a few messages, and I don't have an assistant, so all the replies come from me.

Thanks again for your support—it's very much appreciated.

With my best wishes,
Sherri.

Sherri Bryan

ALL RIGHTS RESERVED

No part of this publication may be reproduced, distributed, or transmitted in any form, or by any means, including photocopying, recording, or other electronic or mechanical methods, without the prior written permission of the copyright owner, and publisher, of this piece of work, except in the case of brief quotations embodied in critical reviews.

This is a work of fiction. All names, characters, businesses, organizations, places, events and incidents are either the products of the author's imagination, or are actual places used in an entirely fictitious manner.

Any other resemblance to organizations, actual events or actual persons, living or dead, is purely coincidental.

Published by Sherri Bryan - Copyright © 2019

Secrets, Lies, and Puppy Dog Eyes

Printed in Great Britain
by Amazon